TRAPPED AND TESTED

TRAPPED AND TESTED

A DEELO MYER CAT RESCUE MYSTERY

SHARON MARCHISELLO

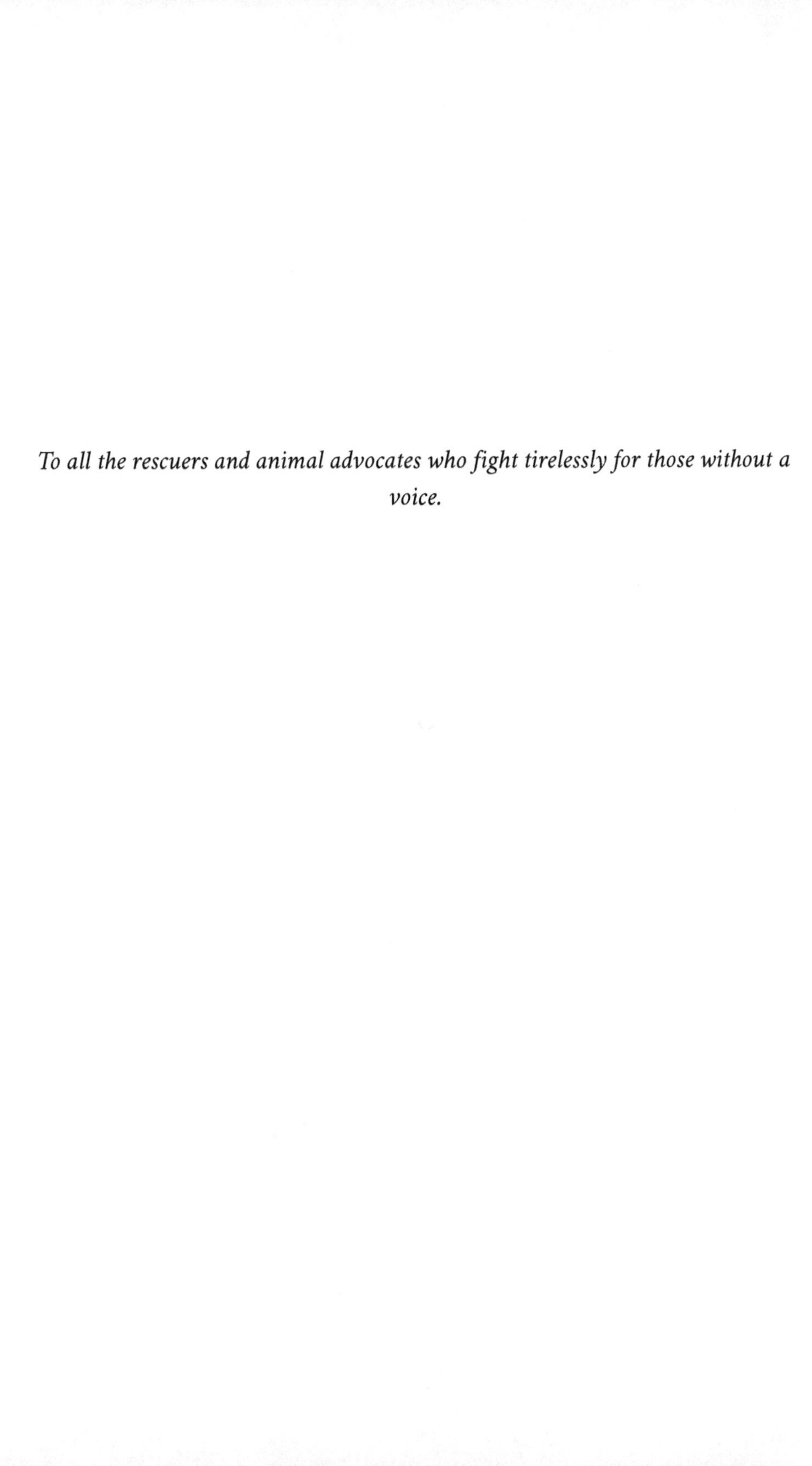

To all the rescuers and animal advocates who fight tirelessly for those without a voice.

Praise for Trapped and Tested

"Sharon Marchisello will cat-a-pult DeeLo Myer into your heart forever with *Trapped and Tested*. The small town girl with the big heart balances family life with an insatiable curiosity and need to help family, friends, and stray cats. DeeLo navigates the twists and turns of dangerous drugs, hidden family secrets, and a romance on the rocks, to solve the mystery of who killed the executive while solidifying herself as a sleuth to be reckoned with."—Cathy Tully, *USA Today* bestselling author of the ChiroCozy Mystery Series

"There is so much happening in this well-written mystery with subplots that keep you guessing through to the end. Short, snappy chapters and realistic dialogue make for a fun, easy read. With the right mix of real-life situations and a murder to solve, *Trapped and Tested* will inform, as well as entertain, the reader."—Ivanka Fear, author of the Jake and Mallory thrillers and the Blue Water mysteries

"*Trapped and Tested,* a cozy mystery that purrs with heart and intrigue, is a delightful addition to the genre that cleverly weaves animal advocacy, politics, and small-town drama into an engrossing page-turner. Set in the sleepy Southern suburb of Pecan Point, Georgia, this novel follows DeeLo Myer as she navigates community service, feral cat rescue work, and—inevitably—murder. DeeLo's determination to protect Pecan County's feral cats while solving murders makes her a protagonist worth rooting for."—Frank Spinelli, author of *Precious Friends: Murder in Sag Harbor*

Chapter One

My niece, Demi, was the type to jump into a pond without looking first, ignoring vital considerations like depth, water temperature, or the presence of snakes. Sometimes, she dragged me with her. Tonight, she'd talked me into playing wingman at a face-to-face meeting with a stranger who claimed to be her brother.

Leonardo's, her selected meeting site, was one of Pecan Point's most popular upscale restaurants, where everyone went to see and be seen. I'd lived in this sleepy southern suburb of Atlanta for over a year now, and the restaurant already held many memories for me—some good, and some not-so-good. I had a feeling I was about to make another not-so-good one.

Perched on a small hill overlooking the Pecan Creek Nature Reserve, the limestone edifice with its terra cotta roof and wide terrazzo veranda evoked a Tuscan villa. The restaurant specialized in my favorite northern Italian cuisine. If Demi was dragging me out to meet a stalker, at least I'd get a good meal.

Since the weather was pleasant, we'd chosen a table in the corner of the patio with a view of the entrance as well as the greenbelt. Demi started on her second glass of red wine while I nursed an iced tea. I was the designated driver.

Order pad poised, the server stood at our table. "Have you ladies decided?"

I closed my menu, glanced at my watch, and then at Demi. "How long do you want to wait?"

My niece took a sip of wine and smacked her menu shut. "Caesar salad with chicken. Hold the anchovies."

"A regular Caesar salad for me." I smiled. "And you can put her anchovies on mine."

"Got it." The server's mouth puckered as she wrote, and I suspected she shared Demi's dislike of anchovies.

After the server left, I asked Demi, "Do you think that guy is still coming? Uh…Kwintone?" I wasn't comfortable referring to him as her brother. How trustworthy were those ancestry DNA sites, anyway? Her *alleged* brother. *Kwintone.* It seemed strange for Demi to have a brother who was not related to me. And whose name didn't start with D, like everyone else in our family.

"Yes, *Aunt Delores.*" She drawled my given name, instead of *DeeLo*, the nickname I preferred. When we were children, I loved insisting that she address me as "Aunt," even though she was a year older. Now she only did it when she was annoyed with me.

Despite being related, Demi and I looked nothing alike. My blond hair, blue eyes, and petite frame reflected my Germanic/Anglo-Saxon heritage. While Demi shared half that ancestry, her towering height, darker skin, and resemblance to the pop star Beyoncé favored the other branch of her family tree. Whatever it was. For years, we'd speculated whether her father might be Black, Hispanic, or Polynesian.

Demi used to pretend she was heir to an obscure African kingdom. When I was six and she was seven, she went through a phase where she'd boss me around, make me bow down to her, and address her as Princess Demi. I didn't put up with it for long and soon called her "Princess Demon."

"Oh, no," I huffed, my gaze landing on the pompous, fortyish woman with big auburn hair who had just strolled onto the terrace like a contestant in a beauty pageant. She flashed the plastic smile she'd worn ever since announcing her candidacy for the Pecan County Board of Commissioners. "Not her again."

Demi turned. "Isn't that Victoria Barton?"

I nodded. My boyfriend's ex-wife was the last person I wanted to see tonight—or any other time. "She turns up everywhere I go. And even though she and Barry dissolved their business partnership when they divorced, she still drops into the office every couple of weeks, acting like she owns the place."

"Who's that silver fox she's with?" Glancing at the couple out of the corner of her eye, Demi fumbled with the stem of her wine glass.

"Commissioner Roy Don Whitehead. The reason she dumped Barry. I'm sure Roy Don's feeding her inside information for her campaign."

"Weren't you working with that commissioner on the pet thing… or whatever it was? About the feral cats."

"Yes. The ordinance change, to make Trap-Neuter-Vaccinate-Return legal in Pecan County." Updating the county animal ordinance to sanction twenty-first-century policies was still my goal. Trapping free-roaming cats, getting them fixed and vaccinated, and then returning them to their outdoor homes (TNVR) had proven to be an effective and humane way to control overpopulation. But the way the county's animal ordinance was currently written, TNVR could be construed as illegal. "Roy Don agreed with my edits, but then he tried to tack on a lot of controversial initiatives that had nothing to do with TNVR and would never pass."

"Oh, yeah. I remember now." Demi's eyes began to gloss over, as they usually did whenever I talked about TNVR.

I took a sip of tea. "Well, I'm looking forward to this election and picking up the project again with the new commissioner, who I hope won't be Victoria."

The couple approached our table. Roy Don broke out in a grin when he spotted me. "Well, hey there, little lady."

"Commissioner," I acknowledged, stiffening at his usual sexist greeting. Trying to keep my tone civil, I added, "Victoria."

"Good to see you, DeeLo." Less sincere words had never been spoken, but she was in public and running for office. She'd never addressed me by name before she threw her hat into the ring. It was always just, "Hey, there," or "Surfer girl," her pejorative reference to my California roots.

Victoria's politician-fake smile never wavered, as if it had been painted on her Botoxed face. "And who might this be?" She didn't realize Demi didn't live in Pecan County.

"Demi Myer." My niece extended her finely manicured hand. "Pleasure."

Traitor.

"Likewise." Victoria returned the handshake like the politician she had become. She knew better than to try to shake mine. Even if she ran unopposed, I'd rather write in my cat's name than cast a vote for Barry's ex-wife.

As Victoria stepped away, a dark-haired man in his mid-forties, wearing an expensive-looking suit, approached her. "Ms. Barton?" He held out a hand for her to shake. "Aiden Green from Neuroscience Laboratories." He lowered his voice. "Got your email. Can we go talk somewhere private? I think we can help each other."

Roy Don and Victoria led him to a table across the patio, far away from us. I wondered what kind of crooked pay-to-play-influencer deal they were cooking up.

"She doesn't seem that bad." Watching Victoria leave, Demi sipped her wine.

I harrumphed and checked my watch again. "Victoria's groveling for votes, so she has to be nice to people. Even me, if anyone is watching."

Demi's phone vibrated on the table. She held up her hand, read the text, and then let out an exasperated sigh.

"Was that Kwintone?" I took my eyes off Victoria and focused on my niece.

She frowned. "Those racist Pecan Point cops stopped him."

"What for?" I flashed back to my own experience of being stopped by the police not long after I'd moved to Georgia. It had nothing to do with race.

"Speeding. A few blocks from here." From her accusatory look, one would think it was my fault. Demi must have forgotten she was the one who chose the meeting location.

Police Point was a nickname some long-term residents had given our town. The local cops tended to stop younger motorists and those with out-of-county license plates. "That's too bad. Is he still coming?"

"I don't know yet." She studied her phone. "Looks like he started to write something and got interrupted."

The server brought our salads, mine loaded with extra anchovies. I gave her a thumbs up.

Demi curled her lip. "I don't see how you can eat those stinky things. You must be part cat."

"I'll take that as a compliment." Smiling, I dug in. "It's not Caesar salad without anchovies." I lifted one with my fork and held it in the air, licking my lips. "Mmm… delicious."

She averted her eyes and concentrated on her own salad.

Booming bass and the deafening vroom of a V-8 engine unencumbered by a muffler stopped all conversation in the restaurant. Heads turned toward the entrance.

Something told me Kwintone had arrived.

Chapter Two

Heads pivoted as the tall, well-built young man swaggered into Leonardo's like it was his private villa. Bleached, twisted ringlets fell onto his shoulders, reminiscent of those hunks on the covers of the romance novels my older sister, Desiree, used to read. He wore a purplish-gray three-piece suit *sans* tie with the top buttons of his shirt left undone. The outfit would have once been considered a size too small, like a grown man trying to stuff himself into his high school prom tux, but now seemed to be the latest fashion.

My niece rose from her chair and waved enthusiastically at the newcomer. Flashing a dimpled grin, he beelined to our table and sat down next to Demi.

"You made it," said Demi, as the two searched each other's faces, probably hunting for a family resemblance. Their skin was the same shade of dark bronze. His nose was slightly wider than Demi's, his lips a bit fuller, but the two had the same mesmerizing hazel eyes. From his clean-shaven, baby face, I pegged him in his mid-twenties, a few years younger than Demi.

I took another forkful of salad, feeling invisible. I wanted to learn more about Demi's mysterious father and how much this "brother" knew about him. Supposedly, he had told Demi he had a lead on their father's identity.

Kwintone wiped his brow with the back of his hand. "That racist cop gave me the third degree."

Maybe he just stopped you because you were speeding. I held my tongue for Demi's sake.

Demi threw him a sympathetic eye roll. "You have to be careful in these hick towns."

I bristled, offended by her characterization of Pecan Point, the town where I'd settled last year after my divorce and move to Georgia from California. I'd chosen Pecan Point because Barry lived and worked here, and he offered me a job. Also, the memory care facility he'd helped us find for my mother was here. Demi certainly didn't mind popping in unannounced and inviting herself to stay at my place several times a month.

Before Kwintone could disparage my town, I introduced myself. "I'm DeeLo Myer, Demi's aunt."

Kwintone's reply was a quirky smile, with one eyebrow and one side of his mouth raised. He had a gap between his two front teeth like Demi used to have before she got braces in middle school. "Pleased to meet you, ma'am."

Having grown up in California, I was still getting used to Southern honorifics. But being addressed as "ma'am" made me feel old. "Just DeeLo, please. I'm younger than Demi."

He smiled again, exposing a dimple in his cheek just like Demi's. "DeeLo, it is then."

I cleared my throat. "So, Kwintone, where did you grow up?"

The server came over and brought Kwintone a menu. "Can I get you something to drink, sir?"

He declined the menu. "Black coffee, please, ma'am." Just when I thought he'd dodged my question, he answered. "I've lived all over the place. My mother was in the Army." That probably explained the "ma'am" thing.

"Did you grow up with a single mom, too?" Demi couldn't take her eyes off this newfound brother of hers. Although technically, Demi had grown up with a single mom, she'd been mostly raised by my parents. Desiree was only sixteen and still living at home when Demi was born. As Desiree grew older, many of her career and lifestyle choices were not compatible with parenting, so Demi continued to live with us.

Kwintone nodded, lowering his long lashes, clearly a guy who knew how to play the sympathy card.

"Demi said you found a lead on your father." I gestured toward my niece. "Yours and Demi's. I know she's been wondering about him all her life. Her mom refuses to talk about him."

Demi smiled eagerly.

"Yeah, I have a few leads." Kwintone pulled a wadded-up piece of paper out of his shirt pocket and unfolded it. "This is such a bummer."

"Did that cop give you a ticket?" Demi peered over his shoulder.

Kwintone handed it to her. I took another bite of my salad.

Demi examined the citation. "Ouch. Your insurance will go up. Unless..." She turned to me. "Maybe they'll let you do community service to get it off your record."

I held my breath. Was she going to tell him? This relative stranger?

"DeeLo got a DUI last year, and she did community service with the Pecan Point Humane Society."

Yes, Demi was blabbing my embarrassing history. I was glad no one was sitting at the table next to us because she was speaking in her outside voice.

"Her boyfriend is a lawyer, and he arranged it. She works in his office, and she still volunteers with the humane society, so she has *connections*. DeeLo?" Demi looked at me expectantly. "You'll help Kwintone get out of this, won't you?"

He grinned. "I'd be most grateful, DeeLo."

I set down my fork. "It's not up to me. It depends on your record and how fast you were driving. The judge—"

"But you'll talk to Barry, won't you?" insisted Demi.

Kwintone put his hands together in a praying gesture.

"Barry's not a criminal attorney. He does wills, trusts, and wealth management." My niece was trying to make her purported brother's speeding ticket my problem.

"But Barry helped you get out of your DUI, didn't he?"

Kwintone's eyebrows shot up.

I winced every time Demi said, "DUI." There was a big difference between Barry advising his girlfriend and intervening with the criminal justice system for a total stranger. "I didn't 'get out of it.' The judge determined community service was an appropriate sentence in my case."

"And the same should work for Kwintone. After all, speeding isn't nearly as bad as a DUI." Demi patted her newfound brother's arm. "DeeLo will help you."

I glowered at my niece. What was she getting me into?

Chapter Three

When I told Barry about Demi's brother's dilemma, he recommended that Kwintone talk to the judge before the court date and propose community service as a solution. Apparently, Kwintone took the advice because the next thing I knew, he'd signed up for the Trap-Neuter-Vaccinate-Return program at the Pecan Point Humane Society.

I assumed Catherine Foster, the senior TNVR guru, would train and supervise him as she did with me. Catherine liked cats a whole lot more than people, and she had no qualms admitting it. She'd wipe the cocky grin off Kwintone's face and make him realize community service with us was no free pass.

But she assigned him to me.

"I'm putting you in charge of the criminals, DeeLo," she'd said. "You can relate." *Criminals* was Catherine's politically incorrect terminology for volunteers who joined our organization to fulfill court-ordered community service. That was how I got my start with the group.

On my first night with Kwintone, we were scheduled to trap feral cats in the woods behind the new Oakwood Studios soundstage. Employees had been feeding them, and the property manager said the felines could stay if we got them all fixed and vaccinated so they wouldn't reproduce exponentially.

I asked Kwintone to meet me in the Oakwood Studios parking lot at nine p.m. and arrived a few minutes early to scope out the surroundings. A waxing gibbous moon lit the vast asphalt lot, empty except for two dark-colored sedans and a large, unhitched storage trailer. The eerie silence was pierced by the occasional hoot of an owl from a nearby stand of trees. I shivered. Even though I was getting used to trapping cats at night in deserted areas, there was still a creepiness about the vulnerability, the exposure to unknown dangers. However, the felines were most active after dark; nighttime was my best chance to capture them.

Nine p.m. came, and no Kwintone. I was hardly surprised given his late arrival at our restaurant meeting.

I checked my phone every few minutes in case he got lost or decided to cancel. I'd hoped to take advantage of the young man's muscles to carry my humane traps. The long, rectangular wire cages were unwieldy even without a cat inside.

At nine-thirty, I gave up waiting for Kwintone. After locating a level, somewhat protected spot, I set my first trap and placed a plastic bowl of pungent sardines on the trip plate. As Catherine had shown me, I tied a hot-pink ribbon to the gravity door that would tell me from a distance if an animal had entered.

Still no Kwintone. I set the next trap. His tardiness meant he missed the hands-on training. I wondered if that was his plan. Let me do all the work.

Just as I walked away from the last of my four traps, a clunk sounded from the second one I'd set. A glance over my shoulder confirmed the ribbon was down. I grabbed a large towel from my car to cover the cage, calming the cat inside its prison.

A muffler-free vroom pierced the air, loud enough to scare away any cat within miles of my traps. Hip-hop music blared through the open windows.

I waited until Kwintone had killed the engine and shut off the music before I picked up the trap with the captive cat. No use upsetting the animal even more.

My niece's professed half-brother appeared from a fire-red Mustang and sauntered toward me, a big smile across his face, flipping his mane like a dark-skinned Fabio. His attire suggested he was going clubbing instead of trapping feral cats. He'd even doused himself with an earthy cologne, which was sure to attract mosquitoes.

"I thought we said nine." I pointed to my wristwatch.

"Sorry. Had to work late." The sorry-not-sorry grin he flashed suggested he was used to charming his way out of unpleasant obligations.

"Guess you didn't have time to change clothes."

"Is that a problem?" He looked down at his polished shoes.

"Only for you. Sometimes the fields get muddy."

His eyes swept the area. "What are we doing here, anyway?"

"Did you read the information I sent you about Trap-Neuter-Vaccinate-Return?"

He bit his lip. "Uh…haven't had time."

Of course not. Kwintone struck me as one of those "the dog ate my homework" students who could flutter those long lashes and persuade a teacher to make an exception.

"I've already set the traps." I gestured toward the one at my feet. "And I've caught one cat so far." I couldn't resist adding, "You know I won't be able to sign off on your community service hours unless you do your share of the work."

He grinned again, his dimple showing, and then…was that a wink? "You're cute when you're mad; you know that?"

I huffed. "Help me carry this to the car. And keep the cage level so you don't jostle the cat."

"You got it." Kwintone bent down, lifted the towel, and peered into the trap. "Hey, there, pussy cat."

The gray tabby hissed and lunged against the bars of the cage. Kwintone jumped back. "Whoa. Not very friendly, are we?"

"Careful," I warned. "If you keep the cat covered, it will stay calmer." I eyed him. "You know, feral cats aren't like the house pets you might be used to. Most of these cats are born outdoors and avoid humans. If we don't tame the kittens before they're three months old, it's unlikely they'll ever become socialized."

With a disinterested shrug, Kwintone picked up the trap by the handle, swung it a bit roughly into place, then steadied it against his leg. "Where're we going?" He flinched at the caged cat. "Hey, don't scratch me."

I led him toward my Lexus SUV and raised the hatch. He set the trap on the tarp I'd spread to protect my carpeting. "Careful," I admonished again.

He let me take over after that.

I closed the hatch. "While we wait to catch more cats, I'll explain how to set the traps since you missed the demonstration. Next time, I'll expect you to do it yourself."

"What are we doing with these cats after we catch them?"

I glanced at his Mustang. I would have loved to assign him the trip to the spay and neuter clinic in the morning, but his vehicle wasn't big enough. Besides, I didn't trust him enough yet to care for the cats overnight and get them there in time for surgery. "We take them to a clinic in College Park called the LifeSaver—"

Before I could expound on the TNVR process, a Beyoncé ringtone interrupted me. Kwintone held up his hand and answered his cellphone.

I'd forgotten to tell him to mute it. Not that he would have listened.

He turned his back to me and walked across the parking lot, taking his conversation out of earshot. Holding the phone against his ear with one hand, he waved the other around to emphasize whatever point he was making to his caller.

Another trap door clanked. Kwintone had drifted about fifty yards away, still on the phone, so, fuming, I covered and moved the cat myself.

I'd caught a third cat by the time Kwintone hung up and returned to my side. "It's about time," I remarked as I shut the hatch to my car again.

"Listen, Princess." He put on a condescending smile he must have thought I'd find endearing. "Something has come up, and I gotta go." He nodded toward the remaining trap I'd set. "Looks like you've got things under control anyway."

That's not the point.

His hand dove into his hip pocket, and he retrieved a crumpled sheet of paper. From his shirt pocket, he pulled out a gold Cross pen and smoothed the paper over his palm. "Do you mind?"

"Do I mind what?" I stared at the timesheet. Did he really think I'd sign it?

He glanced at his phone. "It's been almost an hour, maybe more with travel time from downtown Atlanta. Shall we round—?"

The expression on my face made it clear that I wasn't letting him get away with doing nothing tonight.

"Okay then." He put away the pen and paper. "You have a nice night."

With that, he headed back to his Mustang and revved the engine.

* * *

It took me another hour to capture the last cat and clean up my work area. The felines were quiet as I started my car and headed out of the parking lot.

I turned onto a wooded access street toward the main road. When I rounded the corner, I passed Kwintone's red Mustang parked on the shoulder. The windows were down, and there was no one inside.

Chapter Four

I slowed beside the stationary Mustang. Should I stop? Maybe Kwintone ran out of gas or had a mechanical breakdown. I parked in front of his car.

Key fob and cellphone in hand, I stepped out of my SUV and walked toward the Mustang.

I peered inside the open window. His phone lay on the passenger seat. "Kwintone!" I called, scanning the surrounding area.

Why would he leave his vehicle unlocked? And not take his phone? Most kids his age considered their phones another appendage. "Kwintone!" I yelled again, my voice more fearful.

I leaned against his car. If he'd just gone to relieve himself, he should be back soon. I could hang around a few minutes to ensure he was okay.

Five minutes passed with no one in sight. Several large oak trees stood just off the road, but there had been no sign of movement near them. I called out his name a few more times, but got no response. My stomach churned.

What if he were in trouble? Should I call 9-1-1? They'd tell me it was too early to report a missing person.

What if he was up to no good? My calling the cops would throw a wrench in his plans and perhaps put me in danger.

I called Demi.

My niece usually lets my calls go to voicemail unless she wants something, but she answered on the first ring. "DeeLo, what's up?"

"Have you heard from your… brother?"

Music and chatter in the background must have drowned out my words.

"What? Speak up; I can barely hear you."

"Kwintone." I raised my voice. "Have you talked to him tonight?"

"Yeah, he's supposed to meet me here at Sam's Bar for a drink. Want to join us?"

"I take it he's not there yet?"

More background noise. It sounded like Demi put her hand over the phone to speak to someone. "I'm sorry, what did you say?"

"Kwintone isn't there yet?" I glanced around me, feeling exposed.

"Not yet."

"I just finished trapping. He got a phone call and left a while ago, but now I'm standing by his car parked beside the road behind the Oakwood Studios soundstage, and he's nowhere in sight."

"What?" Music blared.

"I'll text you." I hung up and punched in a quick message with the location.

Demi called back right away. The background noise was more distant; maybe she'd stepped outside the bar. "He's missing? What do you think happened?"

"I think I should call 9-1-1."

"Don't do that."

"Why not?"

She covered up the phone again for a muffled conversation with someone. In a moment, she was back on the line. "I'll be right there."

Before I could argue, she'd disconnected the call. I surveyed my surroundings. An open field separated the woods from the parking lot. The closest building, a massive Oakwood Studios soundstage, lay at least a hundred yards away, and its few windows were completely dark.

As I stared at the blocky, gray concrete structure, a symphony of insects broke the silence. An outdoor floodlight flashed on, and a shadow streaked across the wall. My breath caught. Someone must be over there—a person or an animal large enough to set off the motion detector.

"Kwintone!" My spine tingled.

There was no answer; he might be too far away to hear me. The light extinguished.

I cupped my hands over my mouth to make my voice travel farther. "Kwintone!" Still no response.

Shivering, I got back in my car, locked the doors, and grabbed my canister of pepper spray from the glovebox. I'd never had to use it and wasn't sure I remembered how, but it made me feel safer.

While I waited for Demi, I composed a text to Barry. He'd know what to do.

Barry had been dubious about my involvement with Demi's supposed brother. My niece wasn't his favorite person, and he believed most things she touched turned into disaster. Probably a fair assessment. Furthermore, he wasn't thrilled about my continuing TNVR activities for the local humane society after completing my court-ordered community service. He couldn't understand why I'd willingly wander around deserted locations at night. After all, while doing my community service, I'd found a dead body and been shot at by a crazed police officer. My finger hovered over the arrow that would send my message but didn't press it.

Most likely, Barry would tell me to report the abandoned vehicle and go home.

But Demi was already on her way.

* * *

The sound of an approaching car startled me. I looked up from my phone, relieved as Demi's MINI Cooper rolled up beside me. She veered to the side of the road and parked in front of my Lexus.

We emerged simultaneously from our vehicles and hurried toward Kwintone's abandoned Mustang. I brought my pepper spray.

Demi pulled open the driver's door.

"He left his phone." I pointed at the obvious.

"Right, Sherlock." Even in the dark, I could sense her eye roll.

"Doesn't that seem odd?"

"Definitely." Demi picked up her brother's phone.

"Isn't that password-protected?"

She gave me a knowing nod. "I watched him unlock it the last time we met for drinks."

"You little sneak."

Ignoring me, she scrolled through his call log. "Two missed calls from me. Hmm…this one is not labeled as a contact."

"He got a call shortly before he deserted me. At nine forty-seven."

"Nine forty-seven?"

I shrugged. "I was logging his community service time."

She gazed at the phone and nodded. "This must be it."

Before I could suggest it, Demi hit redial. She cupped the phone to her ear and waited.

"Put it on speaker."

She did. Nothing but ringing, and then the call disconnected. She twisted her mouth in puzzlement. "Not even voicemail."

"What do you want to do?"

She pocketed the phone. "Let's look for him. He could be hurt or something."

I hoped she wouldn't suggest we split up. Like an ominous warning, the cricket concert surged to a crescendo. "Why don't we head toward that studio building? I saw a light flash on a little while ago."

"Let's do it." Demi took off toward the imposing structure, and I struggled to keep up with her long strides over the flat terrain.

As we neared the multi-story soundstage, blinding floodlights illuminated the surrounding area. Shielding my eyes from the glare, I scanned the pavement for signs of Kwintone or his mystery caller. The cars I'd noticed previously were gone. Which way to go?

Demi and I squinted at each other and shrugged. She took her brother's phone from her pocket and hit the redial icon again.

The faint ringtone of an old-fashioned landline. Not from the phone she held, but from the large oak tree just outside the circle of light.

Wide-eyed, we headed toward the sound.

Chapter Five

My heart pounded. What was Demi getting me into? Were we about to walk into a clandestine drug deal? Or worse?

The lights flicked off a moment after we passed out of the monitored orbit. The ringing continued as we approached the oak.

Slowing our pace, we turned on our cellphone flashlights and rounded the tree. My foot bumped against something. A root? I aimed my light down at… a leg. I gasped.

Demi screamed.

"I'm calling 9-1-1." My fingers shook as I hit the emergency number. A body lay sprawled on the ground, a dark spot expanding from his left side and across his chest. Blood?

"H… help…me," rasped a faint voice from the man at our feet.

"What happened?" My niece knelt beside him. "Who are you?"

I studied the man's face. It wasn't Kwintone, as we'd expected, but there was something familiar about him. Where had I seen him before?

"What's your emergency?" came a southern twang in my ear.

"A man… something awful happened…" Heart throbbing, I strived to steady my voice. "This is DeeLo Myer, and I'm behind the big Oakwood Studios soundstage. Studio One, I think it is. Quick, send an ambulance!"

"Slow down, ma'am. What happened?"

"I don't know. We were looking for my niece's brother and found a man who's been hurt. He's lying on the ground, bleeding."

"Okay, ma'am. Where did you say you are?"

"The backlot of Oakwood Studios, at the end of Oakwood Lane."

"And your name again?"

"DeeLo Myer."

"Okay, DeeLo, an ambulance is on its way. What can you tell me about the injured person?"

I stared at the man on the ground. "Male in his forties, maybe early fifties. Most likely Caucasian. Medium build, dark hair."

"Is he breathing?"

"Barely." I could hardly breathe myself. "Demi's trying to talk to him. He asked for help. Please, hurry!"

"You said he's bleeding. Are you putting pressure on the wound?"

Demi had managed to remove the man's jacket and was pressing it against his side, which appeared to be the source of the injury.

"My niece is."

"Do you have anything available to cover the victim? To prevent him from going into shock?"

"I have a blanket in my car."

"Is your car nearby?"

"About fifty yards."

"You said someone is with you and the victim, correct?"

"My niece, Demi Myer. She's pressing on his wound."

"Then go get the blanket."

I put my hand over the phone and screeched to Demi, "I'm going to my car for a minute to find a blanket."

She threw me a distressed look, but before she could reply, I was off, phone to my ear. "I'm headed to my car now. Where's the ambulance?"

"Ma'am, it's on the way. How did the victim get hurt?"

I scanned the field surrounding the parking lot. In the moonlight, the trees morphed into menacing shapes. An attacker could be lurking anywhere. "I don't know." Where was Kwintone? Should I mention him?

I reached my SUV and lifted the hatch. One of the cats I'd caught earlier let out a plaintive wail, which got the others howling. I felt like joining them. "Shh…" I yanked a blanket from underneath a trap and grabbed a clean towel, too.

"Beg your pardon?" said the emergency operator.

"I found something to cover him."

"Good."

As I closed the hatch, I did a double-take. Something was wrong with this scene, and I'd been so absorbed with my call that I hadn't noticed. But now, it hit me. Kwintone's Mustang was gone.

Chapter Six

Demi was still bent over the injured man when I returned. She pressed the towel I handed her against his wound and helped me spread the blanket over him. It smelled slightly of dead fish and cat urine, but the victim was in no position to complain.

"Kwintone's car is gone," I murmured to my niece as we tucked the blanket around the man's shoulders.

Demi wrinkled her nose. "You need to wash this thing."

"I will. Tomorrow. Did you hear what I said?"

Her expression was hard to read in the dark. "Kwintone's gone?"

"Gone." I wondered why we hadn't heard that loud engine start up, but perhaps it happened when we were on the far side of the parking lot following the ringtone.

"Do you think someone stole his car?" Demi looked up.

"Or maybe he hightailed it out of here when the situation got out of control." I indicated the moaning man.

Demi shook her head. "Kwintone would have seen my car and tried to find me. We were supposed to meet."

Before we could speculate further about Kwintone's whereabouts or trustworthiness, an ambulance skidded into the parking lot, siren wailing, followed by a Pecan Point police car. Flashing red and blue lights washed the area like a strobe, illuminating the trees into hovering giants. Memories of my past brush with another trauma scene surfaced, but I blinked them away.

As the siren stopped, paramedics jumped from the ambulance and rushed to the bleeding man. "Step aside, ladies," said a burly EMT with bulging pectorals and sharp elbows.

Demi and I moved out of his way.

"Oh, my God." Eyes still on the patient, my niece bit her fingernails. "I hope they can save him."

The EMTs went to work on the victim. The man emitted another moan, then mumbled something unintelligible. At least he was still alive, and maybe our efforts had played a part.

A uniformed officer strolled up. "Ladies, what can you tell us about this situation?"

We exchanged glances; the panic on Demi's face mirrored my emotions.

"Nothing much, sir," Demi piped up. "We found him like this."

I nodded in support.

"And what were you doing out here?" He gestured around the darkened lot. "Are you employees of Oakwood Studios?"

"No." I swallowed. "But I have permission from Zach Kirkpatrick, the studio's property manager, to be on the lot. I'm a volunteer for the Pecan Point Humane Society, and I came here to TNR some free-roaming cats."

"TNR?" The officer scrunched his face as if I'd said I arrived in a flying saucer.

Demi rolled her eyes as I explained Trap-Neuter-Vaccinate-Return and how the program had been proven to be the most effective, most humane method of controlling the overpopulation of community cats.

The officer, who hadn't written a word, waited for me to take a breath, then asked, "So, where are the cats you trapped?"

"In my car. I'm parked over on the road if you want to see them." I pointed in the direction of our vehicles.

"And I was helping her," Demi added, flashing him a bright smile, her straight, white teeth glowing in the dark.

I stared at my niece. *Why does she feel the need to embellish the story?*

The officer nodded. He'd lost interest in the cats. "Either of you know the victim?"

"Never seen him before in my life," replied Demi, a little too forcefully.

I squinted, still trying to figure out where I'd seen him before. "I don't know who he is."

The officer jotted something down. "How did you happen to find him?"

I opened my mouth to tell the officer about Kwintone—his abandoned car, his phone, how he, and now his car, had vanished from the scene.

Demi spoke first. "I was chasing after a cat and…" Making a horrified face, she motioned toward the figure the EMTs were placing on the gurney.

"Demi, that isn't…" Not only was she lying, her story was implausible. *Chasing after a cat? That's not how TNVR works.*

However, the officer, who knew nothing about TNVR and probably hadn't absorbed half of what I'd told him, seemed to buy her tale, not even picking up on my contradiction. "What happened to the cat?"

Demi shrugged. "Got away. Then we found this poor man and called for help."

The officer thanked us, verified our IDs, and recorded our contact information. He then turned his attention to his colleague, who had been searching the scene.

"We're taking off now," Demi called. "Unless you need us for anything else." Nudging me to follow, she started toward our vehicles.

None of the officers or EMTs voiced an objection.

"Why didn't you tell them about Kwintone?" I demanded once we were out of earshot. "Someone might have stolen his car. He could be in trouble."

"We don't need to involve the police." My niece cast a backward glance over her shoulder. *"We'll* find Kwintone."

How did she think we'd do that? And did I really want to know?

Chapter Seven

Demi spent the night at my house. As she settled onto my couch with a glass of red wine, I silently replayed my time with Kwintone, this stranger she'd thrust into my life. Why didn't she want to involve the police in his disappearance? I knew better than to lie to them, yet watching Demi do it without intervening made me complicit. Barry would be furious if he found out.

"You still have Kwintone's phone, don't you?"

Nodding, she pulled his cell from her purse, balancing the wine in her other hand. "Wish I knew how to get hold of him."

"Send him an email? He must have another way of accessing his messages." The wine glass leaned precariously as she focused on the device.

"Already did. He hasn't responded."

"Social media?"

"I follow him on Instagram, but he hasn't posted anything since last Wednesday when we went out for Mexican food and posed with the mariachi guys."

"Can you find out the name of the person he called?" I eased the wine glass out of her hand and set it on the coffee table.

She typed in her brother's password. "The number isn't a regular contact."

I put on my sleuthing hat, trying to remember the steps the protagonist followed in the most recent cozy mystery I'd read. "Can we look at his texts? Voicemails? Emails? See if we can figure out why they were meeting."

Demi thumbed through Kwintone's texts. She smiled. "Here's the last one from me."

"Not helpful," I said, trying to keep her from getting distracted. "Listen, did it ever cross your mind that your 'brother' could be in trouble? That telling the police the whole truth might have helped him?"

Demi's face twitched. She didn't want to admit I was right. She never did.

"What does Kwintone do for a living, anyway?"

She stroked the stem of her glass as if it were the most fascinating object in the room. Her eyes flitted everywhere but my face.

"I know you've talked a lot since the night we met him at Leonardo's. Gone out together a few times." Kwintone was like her new BFF. She'd spoken incessantly about him for the past few weeks, and I'd tuned her out. I should have paid more attention. "Are you any closer to meeting your father?"

My cat, Manny, wandered over to the couch and hopped onto my lap. The animal was the only ally I could count on. I rubbed his head to show my appreciation.

"Kwintone's working on it." Demi took another sip of wine and then answered my question about her brother's occupation. "He's in sales."

I caressed Manny's silky fur. "What does he sell? Does he work for a company?"

"Some software start-up. He talks a lot about it, but…" She yawned and patted her open mouth. "Boring."

"He showed up for his community service in a suit. Said he'd come from work." I watched my niece's face for a reaction.

"Yeah, I think he had a business dinner with a client."

"What about the guy in the Oakwood Studios parking lot? Did Kwintone tell you about that meeting?"

"Not really." She shifted her eyes away.

"What does that mean, Demi?"

She set down her almost empty glass. "Kwintone said his community service assignment was a blessing in disguise because he'd found a way to make some money on the side."

I knitted my brows together. "Make money from trapping cats? How?"

Demi shrugged. "We were supposed to get together for a drink afterward. I figured he'd tell me more then."

"Are you afraid Kwintone might have hurt that guy?" Raising my head from petting Manny, I caught her flinching.

She splayed her hand against her chest. "Of course not. My brother wouldn't hurt anyone."

Kwintone's phone rang.

Scrambling for it, Demi knocked over her wine glass, and drops of red liquid splattered onto my beige carpet like spots of blood.

Chapter Eight

I grabbed a handful of paper towels, a bottle of white vinegar, and some carpet cleaner, desperate to soak up Demi's wine spill before it permanently stained the carpet.

Demi stared at Kwintone's ringing phone. The caller ID showed an Atlanta area code and no name. After another ring, she answered and put it on speaker. "Hello?"

There was a long pause punctuated by heavy breathing.

"Hello," Demi said again. "Kwintone?"

"Wrong number," muttered a gruff male voice. Then the line went dead.

Demi and I exchanged baffled expressions. Was it really a wrong number, or was the caller confused when a woman answered?

I leaned closer to the screen. "Is that number in his call log?"

She scrolled through his history. "Yes. Yesterday. And again, two days earlier." She hit redial.

Still on speaker, the phone rang incessantly until a message came on that the subscriber was not available, and the mailbox was full.

I set down my cleaning products. "Text him."

"What should I say?"

"Tell him to call back."

Demi spoke as she typed, "Call me back, and I'll explain."

We stared at the silent phone, willing it to ring again, but there was no response.

I sighed, deflated after my adrenaline boost. "What now? Does Kwintone have any other phone numbers? A landline, maybe?"

Demi snorted. "Does anyone still have a landline?"

"Well, if he lives with a parent or grandparent, maybe."

"I'm pretty sure he lives alone."

I examined my carpet. The spot was still wet, so it was premature to declare victory over the stain. "Do you know where Kwintone lives?"

"He has a place downtown. I've never been there, though." She pulled out her hot pink iPhone and scrolled. "Sh—. I don't have his address in my contacts. I thought he gave it to me. No landline either. This is the only number."

I wasn't crazy about driving to downtown Atlanta this late at night, searching for Kwintone's apartment, so I was relieved Demi didn't have his address. "Let's see what we can find out about the injured man. If he's awake, maybe he can tell us what happened to Kwintone."

"Will the hospital give us any information?"

"Worth a try." I googled our local hospital and called the number, placing my phone on speaker. When the operator answered, I described the victim brought in that evening.

She paused. "Are you a relative?"

"Yes," hissed Demi.

I shook my head, certain we wouldn't get away with that claim. The operator would probably ask me to identify him. We didn't even know his name. "Uh, no. But I'm the one who found him and called the ambulance. Just wanted to see how he's doing." *Following up like a good Samaritan.*

"I'm sorry, but I can't release any information about our patients."

The fact that she'd referred to him as a patient was a good sign. It implied he was in the hospital and not the morgue. Or maybe it didn't mean anything, and she wouldn't have told me if he didn't make it.

"Thanks anyway."

Before Demi and I could discuss our next steps, my phone rang. I glimpsed the screen and winced. Barry. No doubt, he was worried about me. I took the phone off speaker and answered my boyfriend's call.

"DeeLo, are you home? How'd it go tonight?" Barry's baritone breathed some normalcy into my frenzied life.

"Uh…I caught four cats I'll have to take to the clinic in the morning." I didn't need to add that I might be late to work.

"Good for you." Barry waited; he must know there was more.

"Uh, Demi's here."

I detected the groan he tried to suppress. "Did Demi's brother show up to help you?"

I couldn't lie to Barry, and besides, I could use his advice. I recapped my evening, continuing to talk despite his gasps and exclamations of "DeeLo—" every time I admitted to questionable judgment.

"And you still don't know where Kwintone is?"

"We have his phone, so it does no good to call or text him."

Barry was silent for a moment. "What's your next move?"

I'd expected him to tell me what I should do. But his tone was distant, not fully engaged. "We're still trying to figure out what happened to Kwintone. We don't know the name of the person he was meeting. Or whether there's any connection to the injured man we found. What do you suggest?"

"Go to the police."

"We already spoke to the police."

"You know what I mean. You didn't tell them Kwintone was missing. Or that he'd even been there." Barry's voice grew softer. "He could be the perpetrator, but he could also be a victim. What if he's still lying out there, injured too? What if someone stole his car? They have a big head start now."

"We weren't sure—"

"Why is Demi hesitant to tell the police about her missing brother?"

I glanced at my niece, who stared into space, her eyelids heavy from the wine. "I don't know. Maybe she's not sure he's really missing. Maybe Kwintone never saw us or the wounded guy, and he just got in his car and drove home."

Barry made a sound between a grunt and a snicker. "Do you believe any of that?"

"Not really."

"As usual, I'm afraid Demi will drag you into her bad choices."

Before I could protest, his doorbell chimed, and he excused himself.

It was close to midnight. Who would be coming to Barry's apartment at this hour?

Victoria's lilting voice rang in the background. My blood boiled. What was his ex-wife doing there?

Barry returned to the line and, before I could make a snarky comment, he mumbled, "I'll call you back."

I stared at the phone, listening to silence, trying not to think about what was happening between Barry and Victoria.

Chapter Nine

Demi had nodded off while I talked to Barry; her head lolled forward into what had to be an uncomfortable position. I coaxed her off the couch and into my guest room. Manny followed and curled up on top of the folded quilt at the foot of her bed.

I couldn't sleep yet. My reporter friend, Jill Hernandez, was a night owl, and I doubted I'd wake her if I texted.

She phoned me right back. "I'm at the hospital, DeeLo. What's—?" A page over the intercom drowned out the last part of her sentence.

Jackpot. "Are you covering the story about the injured man found at Oakwood Studios this evening?"

"Why?" She lowered her voice. "How do you know about that?"

"I almost tripped over him. I was trapping cats near there."

"What?" She slipped into journalist mode. "Let me get this down. What happened?"

I avoided telling her about Demi's alleged brother and that he was missing; therefore, I couldn't mention the ringing phone that led us to the victim. Jill was a friend, but she was also the press. There was no such thing as a secret if a story was at stake.

"The man was lying by a tree, and I stumbled right into his leg."

"Wow…that was… Was he conscious?'

"Barely, but he muttered, 'Help me.'"

"So, what did you do?"

"Called 9-1-1, of course."

She paused as if consulting her notes. "Tell me again how you found him.

Was he near your traps?" Did Jill think asking the question in a slightly different manner would produce a different response? Did she correctly suspect there was more to my story?

"Jill, stop being the tricky reporter. It's my turn. What's the guy's name? I didn't have time to search for an ID."

Papers shuffled. "According to his driver's license, he's Aiden Lee Green, age forty-eight next week, lives in Pecan County, brown eyes, five-foot-ten, 175 pounds, needs corrective lenses. And he's an organ donor."

Aiden Green... Why does that name sound familiar? "Do the police know what happened to him? The scene was chaotic, and the paramedics rushed him away without saying much."

"My contacts here say it looks like a stabbing."

All that blood. Maybe that's why he lost consciousness. Did Kwintone carry a knife? I hoped Demi's alleged brother had not hurt this man. "Is Aiden awake yet? Any idea what he was doing in the studio parking lot after hours?"

"Last I heard, he was still unconscious. Intensive care. But I've done some background research about him for my story."

"And? Does he work at Oakwood Studios?" As we spoke, I typed his name into my Google search bar and got multiple Aiden Lee Greens with LinkedIn profiles.

"No. He's the CEO of Neuroscience Laboratories."

Neuroscience Laboratories. Aiden Green was the man who came up to Victoria at Leonardo's the night Demi and I met Kwintone for the first time.

"What's Neuroscience Laboratories?" I asked, trying to decipher if one of the profiles I'd displayed mentioned that company.

"It's a research facility. They perform neurological tests on animals."

I shuddered. I'd signed dozens of online petitions to university and government leaders protesting the use of animals in scientific research. Most of those experiments had become obsolete. In many cases, there were more effective ways of testing products that did not involve harming animals. "Is that still allowed?"

"Unfortunately. Even though most of their research could be conducted without animal subjects, some companies find it cheaper and easier to keep using animals."

I felt my concern for Aiden Lee Green's welfare slip down a notch. Yes, he was a human being and didn't deserve to be attacked, but from what I'd read, some of those tests performed on animals were clearly abusive, every bit as painful as a stab wound. "Where is Neuroscience Laboratories located? I haven't heard of them."

"Just off Loop Road, on the outskirts of Pecan Point. Hold on." It sounded like Jill cupped her phone, and a male voice asked her something I couldn't make out. "Go talk to that nurse over there," came her muffled reply.

"Sorry about that." Her voice was clear again. "Neuro Labs hasn't been in the news much lately, but two years ago, huge protests from a radical animal rights group almost shut them down."

My sympathies were on the side of the protesters. "What happened? Why weren't the activists successful?"

"Someone pushed it too far, and there was property damage. Broken windows, a small fire. I think a security guard got hurt, too, which lost them some public sympathy. The FBI was even involved. They cracked down on the group and locked up the ringleaders."

I made a note to research this protest, find out who the ringleaders were. Possible motive… "But didn't the protests call attention to what the company was doing? Enrage the more reasonable, law-abiding citizens?"

"At first. But then the fervor died down. Neuro Labs announced they'd received a grant to upgrade their testing methods so they'd no longer have to use animals."

"And the public bought it?

"They told a good story. I even covered it."

"And now?"

"They're keeping a low profile. But I've been following them, and I suspect they're back to using animals—if indeed, they ever stopped." Jill took a breath, but her voice still shook. "Mostly cats."

My stomach heaved. I thought about Manny, my sweet pet. And Mittens, Octomom, Big Mack…and all the other ferals I'd trapped over this past year.

"Jill…do you think Aiden Green might have been attacked because of his connection to Neuroscience Laboratories?"

After a pause, she replied, "It's a possibility."

Would the police automatically include cat advocates in their suspect pool? Someone like me, who had been at the scene?

Chapter Ten

emi was scheduled to work an early flight and had left by the time I rose to chauffeur the cats to the clinic. She'd taken Kwintone's phone with her. I wished we'd thought to check his search history; I'd remind my niece to do it when she had a chance.

The receptionist at the LifeSaver smiled at me as I entered, lugging one of my traps. I wasn't sure if being recognized as a regular was a badge of honor, but it expedited processing. "Good morning, DeeLo. Who do we have today?"

"Four ferals. This one, and three more in the car." Like the seasoned trapper I was becoming, I handed her the paperwork I'd filled out in advance.

"I'll get one of the interns to help you bring them in. Bill to the Pecan Point Humane Society or Oakwood Studios?" She raised her eyes to peer over the rim of her glasses.

I cocked my head. "They're from Oakwood Studios, but—"

"Great." She made a notation on the page. "Zach Kirkpatrick called yesterday and opened a two-thousand-dollar line of credit for the studio. He said you might be bringing some cats in. We'll go ahead and charge that account."

Wonders never cease! I'd expected to have her bill the PPHS, and if we were lucky, I'd convince Zach to make a donation to cover the cost, but that was taken care of now. In spades.

* * *

I wasn't sure how best to approach Barry at the office. I was dying to ask him why Victoria had come to his door at midnight—and how long she'd stayed—but hesitated to play the jealous girlfriend. I decided to keep my mouth shut until I could say something civil.

Barry was standing at the coffee pot when I walked in. As usual, his blue button-down Oxford was tucked neatly at his trim waist, and his wavy brown hair lay in place, projecting the image of a confident young lawyer. Sexy, but in a nerdy way. He looked up through thick, black-framed glasses. At least his eyes weren't bloodshot; maybe Victoria hadn't kept him up all night. "Good morning, DeeLo. Would you like a cup?"

It was hard to maintain my scowl while he was fixing me a coffee with just the right amount of half and half. Especially since I hadn't had my morning dose of caffeine yet. Our fingers grazed as he handed me my cup. His were warm from the coffee, while mine were cold from the chilly fall morning.

"Did you know the Rotary Club is hosting a 'Meet the Candidates' forum this evening?" Barry stirred sugar into his coffee. "Victoria asked if we could pass out flyers for her."

Victoria. "Oh, is that why she dropped by at midnight?" My words came out sharper than intended. And was it just a coincidence that she was out and about the same night one of her campaign donors got stabbed? Maybe their meeting hadn't gone so well…

Barry set down the spoon. "Vicky and I have had our differences, but she really is the best candidate."

Lord, help us. "I'd like to hear what the other contenders have to say before I commit to campaigning for her." I headed for my cubicle with my steaming coffee. No way would I pass out literature touting the virtues of Barry's ex-wife. Not tonight, not ever.

"That's certainly your prerogative," he called after me. "It's good to keep an open mind."

* * *

My four tomcats were among the first surgeries of the day, and they were all alert when I picked them up that afternoon. Rather than house them overnight in my garage as I often did, waiting for the anesthesia to wear off, I decided it would be safe to return them to their outdoor home.

Back to the scene of the crime. Literally.

There were a few cars in the vast Oakwood Studios lot, but they were close to the mammoth building, and I didn't see anyone around. Perfect conditions for releasing feral cats. No use calling attention to my TNVR activity in case someone had actually read the Pecan County animal ordinance and strictly interpreted its provisions.

I parked in the far corner, near the woods where I had trapped them the night before. One by one, I hauled the cages from my vehicle to the edge of the lot and positioned them facing the trees. Carefully, I lifted a trap door, and the first cat shot out, disappearing in a blur of grey fur that quickly blended in with the surroundings.

The second one hastily joined him. The third hesitated as if the door to freedom might be a trick. Then he, too, took the gamble and dashed off into the forest.

I'd just released the last cat and started to gather my traps when the wind whipped up dry leaves and sent something white fluttering past me. It stopped when it lodged against the curb. I bent down to inspect the item: a business card.

On the front was a logo of intertwining loops of blue, gray, and black, a QR code taking up a quarter of the card's real estate, and the company name in a bold sans-serif font: Digital Design, Inc. Underneath: Kwintone Johnson, Sales Manager. And an address.

I pulled out my phone, snapped a quick picture of the card, and texted it to Demi.

"What do we have here?" A familiar voice drowned out the rustling breeze in the trees.

I jerked around to face Pecan Point Police Detective Paul Ross, his emerald eyes sparkling in the sunlight, picking up the green flecks in his tweed jacket.

"Oh, nothing. Just some trash." If Demi didn't want the police searching for her missing brother, she certainly wouldn't want them to suspect he'd been near the scene of the crime. I crumpled the card and slipped my fist behind my back.

The detective held out his hand. "Let me see. It might be relevant to the case I'm working on."

Reluctantly, I relinquished the wadded-up card, glad I'd captured a picture of it.

He studied the card, and his face made an indecipherable twitch. "You know about the stabbing that happened here last night." It wasn't a question. Detective Ross must have read the report and seen my statement. I wondered when he'd invite me into the station to elaborate.

I nodded. "Did you find the weapon?"

His head jerked up. "Not yet."

"Is that what you're searching for?" I gestured around the parking lot and pointed to a nearby oak. "We found the guy right over there."

The detective's expression warned that the investigation was none of my business.

I tried a different tactic. "How's the victim doing?"

"Still unconscious, last I heard. In ICU and intubated, so interviewing him is not an option right now." Detective Ross gazed at Kwintone's business card again. "Does this name mean anything to you?"

Something about the way he eyed me said he'd know I was lying if I denied it. "My niece recently matched with Kwintone Johnson on one of those ancestry DNA sites. She's trying to find her father."

The detective raised his eyebrows. I realized Demi's search for her father had nothing to do with his investigation, and he probably wondered why I brought it up.

"Kwintone might be her brother. He was helping me trap here last night." *Supposed to be helping.*

"Oh, I remember that unusual name now. He got a speeding ticket on Loop Road a few weeks ago. Community service?"

I nodded. "But he left before Demi and I found the stabbing victim."

Detective Ross narrowed his gaze at me. "Why did he leave early?"

I swallowed. "He got a phone call. Said he had to go."

"Do you think he was meeting with someone from Oakwood Studios?"

"I don't know. He didn't tell me."

"Do you know anybody who works at Oakwood Studios?"

I cleared my throat. "I've been in contact with Zach Kirkpatrick, the property manager, about TNVR for the cats. But I've never met him in person."

"What about Eddie Fenton?"

I shook my head. "Never heard of him."

The detective glanced at his phone, perhaps consulting notes. "Have you spoken to this Kwintone since he left your trapping site?"

I kicked at a pebble, sending it clicking across the asphalt. "We haven't been able to reach him."

Detective Ross glanced at Kwintone's business card. "Is this the number you use to contact him?"

I leaned over to study the card and nodded.

I could feel the detective's eyes on me, trying to read between the lines of what I'd disclosed. I guess, in a roundabout way, I'd reported Kwintone missing. Demi would have a fit.

Chapter Eleven

etective Ross helped me carry the empty traps to my car. "So, you're still volunteering with the Pecan Point Humane Society?" We had met when I was doing my community service; I'd trapped and fixed some feral cats his wife was feeding.

"There's always more work to do, and the PPHS doesn't have enough volunteers." I raised my SUV's hatch so he could slide the trap inside. "And after the election, I'll approach the Board of Commissioners again to change the animal ordinance."

"I remember you spent a lot of time on those updates last year."

"Yeah, such a letdown when they didn't put my proposal on the agenda."

My phone pinged. I glanced at the text from Demi but did not read it.

The detective had seen it, though. "Important? Do you need to respond?"

I put my phone in my pocket. "It can wait."

We headed back to the clearing to pick up the other two traps. "How's Lisa?" I asked. "Did she ever find another job?" Connors Insurance, his wife's last place of employment, had closed.

"It took a while, but yes. She's working at a place called Neuroscience Laboratories. But right now, she's—"

"Neuroscience Laboratories?" I halted my steps. "The facility that conducts tests on animals?"

"I knew they did scientific research, but…" He frowned. "Are you saying you value animal lives above humans? Some of those tests are necessary to find cures for debilitating diseases. Don't you have a mother who's suffering from Alzheimer's?"

"Yes, but—"

"And my son. He's been—" The detective stopped and shook his head.

My mouth dropped. "What about your son?"

"Never mind. Forget I said anything. Lisa's… no." A flash of something that looked like pain crossed his face, then vanished. "My point is that there are plenty of perfectly good reasons to do those tests on animals. There are policies in place to keep them ethical and humane."

I wasn't in the mood for a philosophical discussion about the morality of animal testing. There was no way to win an argument against someone who believed humans to be the most valuable species and that other "lesser" beings should be expected to sacrifice their lives to make ours better. "I'm not saying the tests don't have benefits. But I've read that, in some cases, there are new methods that are more effective and don't involve harming animals. Subjects who don't have a say in what happens to them."

The detective sighed, obviously not wanting a debate either. "Lisa's just a receptionist. She's not involved in the lab or with the animals."

"Well, she must know the…" I flashed back to my conversation with Jill last night. How much of the story had she published? "The guy who got stabbed. He's the Neuro Labs CEO."

Detective Ross cocked his head. "How do you know that?"

"Uh. It was on the news. Wasn't it?"

He shrugged. "Maybe."

We finished loading the traps into my car. The cats were long gone, back in their element but no longer able to breed. And fortunately, not in a laboratory. I turned to face Detective Ross as I closed the hatch. "Thanks for your help. Guess I'll see you around."

"You're welcome. And, DeeLo, you'll tell me if you hear from Kwintone?"

"Of course." I pasted on an agreeable smile. *Doesn't he want to interview me? He's usually much more thorough with his investigations.*

* * *

The Pecan Point Rotary Club embraced the mission of keeping the citizens informed and involved in their community. Whenever there was an election, the club hosted a public forum to help voters compare the options. Tonight, the program was all about the open position on the Pecan County Board of Commissioners.

When I arrived at the community center, I scouted around for Barry. The spacious, modern building had high ceilings, crystal chandeliers, and walls of tall windows looking onto a small lake. Already, at least eighty people had gathered. My eyes swept the crowd and then stopped.

There was my boyfriend, at home in the extra folding chair behind his ex-wife's information table, chatting animatedly with a potential voter.

Each candidate had set up a display in the lobby, where they passed out literature and introduced themselves to constituents before the program. Victoria's spot was the flashiest, flanked on one side by a life-size cardboard cutout of her, dressed to the nines, with a smile as artificial as the two-dimensional photographic image. A large glass bowl filled with assorted mini-chocolate bars lured voters with a sweet tooth like feral cats to a feeding station.

I pivoted. So much for suggesting that Barry and I find seats together in the auditorium.

In addition to Victoria, two other candidates were competing for the open position, but neither had put much effort into campaigning apart from throwing a hat into the ring. Without making eye contact with Barry, I wandered toward the other tables.

Down the hall from Victoria stood an unattended opponent's station. It had no tablecloth, no brochures, only a hand-printed tent card that read, "Dr. Steven Smythe." As I examined the name on the card, a harried middle-aged woman rushed up, clutching a bag smelling of greasy French fries. Breathless, she plopped into the chair behind the table and threw me a lopsided smile. "Hello, ma'am. I hope my husband can count on your vote in November."

I cast my eyes around the room. *Where is he?* "What can you tell me about him? Why is he running for the Board of Commissioners?"

"Oh… you know." Eyes roving, looking everywhere but at me, the woman fiddled with her fast-food bag. "This county needs more good Christian men like him."

I smiled sweetly. "How's that?"

Before she could answer, a heavy-set, balding man, also breathing heavily, face flushed and beaded with perspiration, nudged her aside and took the spot behind the table. He plunked down a stack of printed postcards with a headshot of him, with more hair and smaller jowls, that must have been taken a decade earlier. Another photo showed him with an adoring wife at his side, surrounded by two adult children, a toothless grandchild, and a Golden Retriever.

I inspected a postcard. His list of qualifications included: resident of Pecan Point for twenty years, married to Pamela for forty years, father of three, grandfather of seven, and deacon at First Baptist Church.

While I read the campaign card, the couple gossiped about someone I assumed was a family member. Then, still not making eye contact with me, the rosy-faced doctor glanced at his watch. "What time should we head in there?"

I cleared my throat. "Dr. Smythe?"

He blinked, then extended a puffy hand. "Hello there, young lady, I'd sure appreciate your vote."

"How do you feel about…" But he'd already turned away, and I abandoned my question.

"Got to go find my place on stage." Dr. Smythe patted his wife's shoulder and excused himself.

People moved toward the auditorium, so I followed. Instead of hunting for Barry in the audience, I headed to Jill. She sat in the front row, laptop open, her long black hair hanging down her back.

"Saving this for anyone?" I asked as I slid into the empty seat beside her.

She moved her sweater out of my way. "It's yours."

"What's the scoop on the candidates?" I peered at her computer screen.

"I know you hate to hear this." She cut her eyes at me. "But Victoria Barton is the clear frontrunner. The other two bozos haven't even given the newspaper a statement or arranged an interview. Free publicity, and they can't manage to take advantage."

I scowled.

"To be fair, one candidate just entered the race, so maybe he'll get his act together soon. I'm going to reach out again and offer him a chance to complete our questionnaire."

At the lectern, Deb Holt, president of the Pecan Point Humane Society and Rotary Club secretary, called the meeting to order. The tall, conservatively dressed, dark-skinned woman appeared in her element, joking with the audience and owning the room. It was a side of her I hadn't seen before, as I'd only known her in the animal rescue environment. When I joined the organization as a community service volunteer, she'd viewed me as a typical, uncommitted short-timer. But after my extra-curricular work on the ordinance reform, I'd earned her respect. Now that I'd stayed on as a PPHS volunteer despite having completed my mandatory hours, she treated me as one of the group. I smiled at Deb, no longer uneasy in her presence.

After leading the audience in the Pledge of Allegiance, Deb gave an overview of the Rotary Club's mission and explained the purpose of the event. "As the moderator of this forum, I'll let each candidate tell you about their qualifications, and then give them one minute to explain their stance on what they see as the most important issue facing Pecan County. Once the candidates have made their pitches, we'll have a question-and-answer session."

Victoria had the floor first. Articulate and polished, she had the eye contact thing down, focusing on individual audience members just long enough to make a connection, then moving on, all-inclusive. If I didn't know what a witch she was, I'd have bought her bill of goods. How could Barry not see through her after all she had done to him?

"Ms. Barton, what do you see as the major issue for our county?" Deb asked. "In other words, what's the main thing you hope to accomplish if you're elected to the Board of Commissioners?"

Victoria adjusted the microphone, projecting confidence. Obviously, she had anticipated the questions and prepared thoughtful answers. "This county needs more recreational opportunities. The old Patel Shopping

Center would make an excellent location for a new rec center, and the county can buy the land at a reasonable price. We'll border the plot with a row of affordable townhomes that my brokerage predicts will sell out quickly, at top dollar, bringing the county additional revenue in property taxes. I plan to put in a pool, pickleball courts, and bike paths along Pecan Creek."

"And how much are you going to raise our taxes to do this?" yelled a voice from the audience. I didn't see who asked the question, but I was glad someone who was not me challenged Victoria.

"We'll have time for questions later," Deb assured the heckler. "Write them down and hand them to one of the Rotarians circling the room."

Jill passed me an index card, and I wrote mine. *Trap-Neuter-Vaccinate-Return (TNVR) has been proven to be the most effective way to control the overpopulation of free-roaming cats, but the wording of the Pecan County animal ordinance makes TNVR illegal. Will you support a change to the law to protect those who care for community cats and strive to humanely limit their reproduction?* I showed it to Jill. She nodded and handed the card to the stodgy Rotarian passing down the aisle.

Victoria demurely took her seat, and Dr. Smythe was up. He struggled with the microphone, alternating between no sound and eardrum-piercing reverberations. "Uh," he began, holding the mouthpiece way too close. "I'm Dr. Steven Smythe, a proud conservative and follower of Jesus Christ, and I've been practicing family medicine in Pecan Point for over twenty years."

After polite applause, Deb asked, "Dr. Smythe, what do you see as the major issue for the county, and how do you plan to address it if you're elected?"

The doctor cleared his throat. "Uh… Pecan County is a great place to live, work, and raise a family. And I hope to keep it that way."

Deb nodded diplomatically but pressed him further. "So, you don't see any major problems that need work?"

He adjusted the microphone, although it didn't need adjusting, paused, and swallowed loudly. "Uh, the traffic."

Murmurs echoed through the audience, and several people clapped.

Deb smiled. "I agree. At certain times of day, I've had to wait through several cycles of the light before I can get through the intersection of Main Street and Loop Road. How do you intend to fix that?"

"Well, uh…" The doctor scratched his head. Clearly, he didn't have a plan. "If I'm elected, I'll form a committee to study the issue and come up with the best solution."

Twitching in her seat, Victoria activated the microphone in front of her. "Madame Moderator, if I may?"

Before Deb could grant permission, Victoria leaned in. "The Board of Commissioners has already met with the Georgia Department of Transportation to discuss the growing traffic problem in Pecan Point. They've submitted several proposals for solving the gridlock at that intersection. I have contacts at the G.D.O.T., and if elected, I pledge to spearhead this project. But Dr. Smythe, forgive me for interrupting. I'm sure you have a plan, too. Let's hear it."

The doctor's eyes darted around the room, searching for a sympathetic face. "Uh… the committee…"

Deb came to his rescue. "We'll get into more details during the question-and-answer session. I think everyone has an opinion about traffic." She beckoned to the stage a tall, gangly, ginger-haired man who resembled Conan O'Brien. "And now, let me introduce our final candidate, Zach Kirkpatrick, property manager for Oakwood Studios."

My breath caught. Zach and I had only spoken on the phone and communicated by email, so I didn't know what he looked like. Or that he was running for office. Why would someone so new to the area want to serve on the Board of Commissioners?

Chapter Twelve

I wondered if Zach's generous grant to the LifeSaver Spay & Neuter Clinic to support Trap-Neuter-Vaccinate-Return had been motivated by his political ambitions rather than his concerns about cat overpopulation. But whatever his motivation, I viewed him as a favorable alternative to Victoria or the pathetic Dr. Smythe.

After Zach introduced himself, Deb asked her standard question, "What do you see as the major issue for the county, and how do you plan to address it if you're elected?"

Zach adjusted his microphone and flashed a magnanimous smile at Deb, then at the audience. "Transportation. My opponents talked about the traffic woes and how to solve them by adding lanes or strategically timed stoplights. But the root of the problem is the lack of adequate public transportation." His eyes swept the audience as if gauging their reception. "Too many cars on the road with only one driver. I'm sure you've seen the gridlock heading into Atlanta during rush hour, which is practically all day."

Murmurs rippled through the audience, punctuated by a few weak claps.

"I propose putting in a light rail from downtown Pecan Point to the Atlanta airport, intersecting with Atlanta's MARTA system. We could add several Pecan County stops, such as Oakwood Studios and a park-and-ride on Loop Road." He smiled again. "The light rail would connect to a bus system covering downtown Pecan Point, and it would be free within the city limits, cutting down congestion considerably."

"Free?" scoffed a gruff voice. "With our tax dollars, you mean?"

"Might reduce traffic," someone else said. "And the parking shortage downtown."

The murmurs grew louder. Not everyone shared Zach's vision, and small arguments broke out among audience members. Dr. Smythe's face had turned beet purple; his cheeks puffed as if he would explode any minute.

Deb retook the floor. "Thank you, Mr. Kirkpatrick. You've certainly given us something to think about." She turned to the audience. "Now it's time for our question-and-answer session. If you haven't already, please write your questions on the index cards we provided. Rotarians are coming down the aisles to collect them. After the Q and A, the candidates will be back at their tables if you want clarification on their positions or need more information."

A short, bespectacled man delivered a stack of cards to the stage and handed them to Deb. She flipped through them and drew one out. "Several of you have proposed new projects under the guise of 'improving' our county." She made air quotes around "improving" to illustrate the author's intent. "How do you plan to pay for these projects, and what is your policy about raising taxes?"

Victoria held up a finger and leaned closer to her microphone. "Pecan County prides itself on having one of the lowest tax rates in the state, and I pledge to keep it that way. But if we want to grow and maintain a high quality of life for our residents, we need better recreation facilities and more robust services. A lot of these improvements can be paid for through the increase in our tax base from new residential construction. If we continue to make Pecan County a desirable place to live, more people will move here and contribute to our economy." She tilted a shoulder toward Zach. "Maybe my opponent is not aware, since he's new in town, but the Pecan County Board of Commissioners and Whitehead Realtors—of which I am a part—were responsible for bringing Oakwood Studios to our county. That project created hundreds of jobs and boosted our tax base."

A few grumbles about Oakwood Studios emerged from the audience. One man hopped to his feet. "Most of the Oakwood employees don't even live in Pecan County, so where's that tax revenue you promised?"

"And isn't the movie company getting a tax break from the state?" jeered a deep voice.

Victoria held up her hand. "My solution to raise additional revenue would be to add a one-percent SPLOST." She flashed a condescending smile at the man complaining about Oakwood employees not living in the county. "That's a Special Purpose Local Option Sales Tax. It would have to be approved by the voters, of course; everyone has a say. But think about it: people from other counties who pass through to shop or dine in our restaurants—or use our new recreational facilities—people who don't own property here, such as many of the Oakwood employees, would be subject to the SPLOST, thus taking the tax burden off Pecan County property owners."

"Oh, great," I whispered to Jill. "She wants us to vote ourselves a tax increase."

Jill rolled her eyes. "Pecan County has done it before. The residents eat up that propaganda."

Dr. Smythe cleared his throat, a guttural sound amplified by his microphone. "If we didn't build these unnecessary recreation centers and light rail systems, we wouldn't need a SPLOST. Pecan County is great the way it is, and people live here for the low taxes, peace, and quiet."

A round of claps erupted.

Zach took the floor. "Putting in a light rail system wouldn't require a SPLOST or higher property taxes for Pecan County residents. There are grants available from the state for transportation projects, and ridership fees will cover the expenses once it's operational."

"Bull," bellowed one of the men who'd protested earlier. "You're new to Georgia. What do you know about us?"

"Do you even live in Pecan County?" shouted a woman.

"Yes, ma'am, I do." Zach addressed the naysayer, "Sir, I'd love to talk about my light rail proposal after the program and show you my research."

Dr. Smythe cleared his throat again; whatever was lodged down there wasn't coming out easily. "I'm against putting in a rail system because crime will increase in our bubble. Public transportation will make it easy for the undesirables from Atlanta to come to Pecan Point, commit robberies, and jump back on the train to escape our jurisdiction."

Applause rang out, punctuated by a few indignant mutters.

"That's a crock," cried a man near the front row. "Hop on the train with a flat-screen TV?"

Laughter tittered through the audience.

Dr. Smythe gave a thin-lipped smile and sat back down.

Zach held up his hand. "Many cities in the Northeast have bedroom communities like Pecan Point connected by light rail, and their crime rates are low. With proper security and community buy-in, public transportation can be a safe and economical service for our citizens."

"Yankee!" someone called out. "Carpetbagger."

"Go back to the Northeast," yelled a companion.

"Or Hollywood," muttered a throaty female voice. "With all the movie liberals."

Shooting a sharp look at the detractors, Deb stepped in and drew another card. "Time for a new question." She looked my way and winked as she read my words.

Victoria smirked. "Someone needs to get a life," she murmured to Dr. Smythe, apparently not realizing her microphone was on.

"What was that, Ms. Barton?" Deb asked.

You go, girl. I grinned at Deb, watching Victoria try to compose her horrified face.

My nemesis straightened in her chair, breathed deeply, and pasted on the fake smile. "Of all the issues facing Pecan County, cat overpopulation is low on the list." She pointed at Deb. "You folks at the humane society do incredible work to find homes for stray cats and dogs. I'm not sure tinkering with our animal ordinances, which have been in place for decades, is the best use of the Board of Commissioners' time when there are so many ways we can enhance the lives of our *human* residents." She waved her hands to encourage a round of applause, then continued, "Like providing healthy recreational opportunities for families and children."

"Children?" I muttered to Jill. "Victoria wants to build that court because she and Roy Don play pickleball, and now they have to drive to Atlanta to do it."

Dr. Smythe grabbed his microphone with an ear-splitting screech. "We have a perfectly good pound to handle the stray cat problem."

Boo, hiss! I wanted to scream. It was all I could do to keep from throwing something at the stage.

Zach activated his microphone. "I've been reading a lot about this issue lately, and pet overpopulation is a huge national problem. Even today, close to four million healthy, adoptable cats and dogs are put to death in shelters every year, simply because they don't have homes." His eyes roved the sea of shocked faces as he waited for his point to sink in. "Until communities wake up and pass spay/neuter laws, this atrocity will continue."

Jill and I stood up and clapped. The hint of a smile threatened to crack Deb's poker face. I looked around, wondering if Sandra Larson, director of Pecan County Animal Control, was here. Last year, she had proposed a spay/neuter law and was shut down by the Board of Commissioners. I'd promised to help her revive her proposal in exchange for her support of my ordinance changes to legalize TNVR. She'd be pleased with Zach's position.

Zach beamed in our direction. "When Oakwood Studios came to town, we inherited a colony of free-roaming cats already living on the property. We've been working with PPHS to do the trap and neuter." He smiled at Deb. "I've looked at the Pecan County animal ordinance, and I agree with this citizen that it's outdated. The way it's written, someone who traps a cat to be neutered and vaccinated becomes its owner. So, returning it to its outdoor home after the procedure can be construed as animal abandonment, which, if enforced, could deter potential volunteers from helping the humane society with population control."

Grinning, I nudged Jill. Zach was my man.

Scarcely listening to the rest of the program, I took out my phone and googled him. He had a LinkedIn profile, a Facebook page, and an Instagram account, which I immediately followed. His profile showed lots of experience in the film industry. He'd served on city councils in three of the towns where he'd previously lived.

Most of his recent posts were about Oakwood Studios: its construction, upcoming movies being made there, and funny employee antics. One post showed several feral cats bent over a dish of food near the side of the building, and the caption read, "Working with the local humane society to TNVR our resident cat colony." I smiled.

I navigated to Facebook and sent him a friend request. Scrolling through his list of friends, none of whom were mutual, I stopped on a familiar face. *What?*

I stared at the picture, wondering if it was the same person. What did these two have in common?

Zach Kirkpatrick and Kwintone Johnson were Facebook friends.

Chapter Thirteen

fter the program, I made my way to Zach's table in the lobby. The candidates were slowly filing out of the auditorium, detained by voters asking them questions.

A smartly dressed man in his twenties busily fanned colorful campaign brochures across the black tablecloth at Zach's station. He straightened the frame of a large glossy photo of Zach in its stand and turned to face me.

My breath caught. Although he was slightly shorter, darker, and had a shaved head instead of long hair, the young man could have been Kwintone's twin.

"Hello, ma'am." He extended his hand. "Eddie Fenton." His slightly lop-sided grin with a gap between his two front teeth furthered his resemblance to Kwintone. "What questions can I answer about Zach's platform?"

I shook his hand, studying his face. He had the same penetrating hazel eyes as Demi and Kwintone. "You… you remind me of someone."

A dimple formed in his left cheek as his smile widened. "Probably my dad. Fenton Motors in Atlanta?" In a singsong voice, he recited a jingle from the obnoxious TV commercials, "Feel more alive with your brand-new drive."

I giggled. "Those silly lyrics pop into my head whenever I pass that lot." One of the Fenton Motors dealerships was on my route to the LifeSaver. Its towering billboard featured a jolly, light-skinned Black man above the infamous slogan. Edward Fenton was a former Major League Baseball player who had invested the proceeds from his multi-million-dollar contracts in a profitable chain of automobile dealerships. Gazing at Eddie again, I could now see the resemblance. "So, Eddie, do you work at the dealership with your father?"

Eddie picked up a brochure. "I help out sometimes, but selling cars isn't my dream gig." His eyes strayed to the lanky redhead striding toward us, and his whole face brightened. "My place is in the film industry."

Zach slid behind the table and squeezed Eddie's shoulder. "Thanks, man, for setting all this up. Great job." He turned to me. "Aren't you DeeLo Myer? So glad to meet you in person."

Not dwelling on how he recognized me, I shook hands with Zach. "Likewise. It's good to put a face with a name. What made you decide to run for the Pecan County Board of Commissioners?"

He nodded as if he'd foreseen the question. "I'm new to the area and bring a fresh perspective. That might worry some long-time residents, but I have a track record of diving into community affairs wherever I live and getting things done."

"Which will bother some people. Like expanding public transportation." I gave him a knowing glance. "You could probably tell Pecan County voters aren't sold on light rail to Atlanta."

He shrugged. "I don't expect a proposal like that to pass right away. I've done my homework. Pecan County is quite conservative, and the current Board of Commissioners reflects that attitude. But if I can get people to envision new possibilities…" He seemed passionate; now, if I could channel that passion toward animal welfare issues…

My gaze shifted to Eddie, who hung on the candidate's every word, then focused back on Zach. "I like the way you answered the question about feral cats. I want to believe you were sincere."

"Of course, I'm sincere." He frowned as if a cloud had cast a shadow over his face; then it passed as quickly as it had come. "I'm not a politician who tells people what they want to hear. I'm a concerned citizen who wants to help make things better."

His words were exactly what I wanted to hear.

A cluster of professionally dressed women strolled over, picked up brochures, and asked Zach questions about light rail. I stepped back and observed how he interacted with them, spouting facts and figures and giving examples of communities that had benefited from similar projects. His warm smile appeared to win them over.

When the women had gone, a middle-aged couple came to the table. The man grilled Zach for several minutes about his ideas on taxes, development, and traffic. For a newcomer, Zach seemed well-informed about the community's issues, with a thoughtful answer to every question. While Zach engaged with voters, Eddie worked the crowd, passing out brochures and promoting the virtues of his candidate.

After another flurry of visitors, we were alone again. Zach smiled. "Where were we?"

I cleared my throat. "I don't remember how much I told you over the phone about the county's animal ordinance. If you didn't guess, that question you answered on stage was mine."

He grinned. "I suspected."

"I have an agenda." I lowered my voice. "Last year, I tried to get the Board of Commissioners to revise the county animal ordinance to exempt feral cats and their caretakers from the laws governing pet ownership. I'm sure you can agree that feral cats are not pets."

He nodded. "I didn't know much about TNVR before I came to Pecan Point, but now I've seen it working firsthand. Our receptionist, Merilee Jones, volunteers with you guys at PPHS, and she brought me up to speed."

I didn't know Merilee but appreciated her efforts. "If you're elected, will you help me change the ordinance?"

"I'll have to review your proposal, but it sounds like a cause I would support." He studied me. "You said you tried to pass it last year. What happened?"

I sighed. "Roy Don Whitehead was the first commissioner I approached, and he was behind it. But then he decided to tack on some controversial clauses that would have lost us the support of some of our advocates."

"I see." Zach stroked his chin. "Sounds like your proposal got mired in unnecessary bureaucracy. What did the other commissioners say?"

I closed my eyes; the memory was still painful. My neck hurt, and my throat closed up whenever I thought about my last meeting about ordinance changes, when everything went terribly wrong. "Another commissioner seemed very interested, but then… You must have read what happened with him. That's why we're having a special election."

Zach winced. "Yeah, I heard some of it."

"I also promised Sandra Larson, the animal control director, that I'd help her add a spay/neuter requirement for animals adopted from the shelter. She presented the proposal last year, but it failed by one vote."

Zach shook his head. "I was surprised to learn Pecan County didn't already have mandatory spay/neuter. That's a project I'd definitely support."

I smiled. "That position should win you the votes of the PPHS volunteers. And we can be very persuasive."

"Good to know. I've always had a soft spot for animals."

I searched his face for the sincerity I craved. "If you can promise to get my ordinance changes on the agenda, I'll support your campaign. I'll help however I'm needed."

He straightened. "Well, DeeLo, that's wonderful news. As you can see, I entered the race late, so I'm behind. I could use the help to catch up."

"You have to beat Victoria Barton."

He grimaced. "That lady's a smooth talker. It will be hard." He cocked his head. "Do you have something against her?"

"Let's just say we're not each other's biggest fans."

He didn't ask why. Maybe he already knew.

I glanced around the room to check if anyone else was vying for his attention. "You need a better social media presence. In addition to your personal Facebook page, you should have a separate one for Zach Kirkpatrick, Candidate. And you need to be active on Instagram, TikTok, and Twitter—or uh, X."

"DeeLo, how would you like to be my social media manager?" Zach suppressed a laugh. "It sounds like you have some great ideas, and you can probably tell that social media is not one of my strengths."

I wondered what Barry would think about my working on an opposing campaign, but I quickly dismissed my guilty feelings. He already knew I wouldn't support Victoria. "Thought you'd never ask. If you have any logos or slogans, send them to me, and I'll get started tomorrow."

"Sounds great." Zach eyed the waning crowd. "Guess it's time to pack up."

"I'm excited. When I came here tonight, I was concerned about how this election might go." I watched Eddie pick up the glossy photo of Zach, admire it for a moment, and then carefully place it in a box cushioned by the tablecloth. I turned back to Zach. "By the way, when I browsed your social media earlier, I noticed we have a friend in common: Kwintone Johnson."

Zach knitted his eyebrows together. "Kwintone Johnson?" He touched his smooth chin. "Oh, yeah, Kwintone. He's a friend of a friend. I've only met him a couple of times." He tilted his head toward Eddie, who was closing up the boxes. "He and Eddie are tight."

Chapter Fourteen

I stared at Eddie as he finished packing Zach's stuff. His resemblance to Kwintone haunted me. Friends? Or brothers? If Eddie was Kwintone's brother, he might also be Demi's brother. If Eddie and Kwintone were brothers, did that mean Car King Edward Fenton was Kwintone's, and thus Demi's, father? Could I solve her mystery for her?

"Eddie." Zach put a hand on his assistant's shoulder. "Did you meet DeeLo Myer? She's going to help build our social media presence."

Eddie grinned. "Welcome aboard, DeeLo."

"Pecan County, get ready for the Zach Attack," I quipped.

"Ooh, I like it," Eddie gushed. Zach chuckled.

I picked up my phone. "Let's take a selfie of the team. I'll post it on your social media."

The men leaned in, and I stretched my arm until we all fit into the viewfinder. After inspecting the results, I texted the photo to Demi with the caption, "Does anyone look familiar? Could this be another brother?"

* * *

Barry was waiting beside my SUV when I came out of the community center. "DeeLo." He spread his arms and enveloped me in a bear hug. "I didn't see you all night."

Did you look for me? I stiffened, resisting the embrace, unable to enjoy the comfort of his arms around me. "I saw you when I came in, but you were busy talking to people at Victoria's table, so I sat with Jill."

He stroked my hair. "You should have come over. I missed you. Victoria was asking about you."

Sure, she was. I leaned my head back to study his face. "Where'd she go? I figured you two would go out and celebrate after the debate."

He scowled. "She left with Roy Don."

There had never been any love lost between those two men; Victoria's affair with Roy Don Whitehead had been the catalyst for the Bartons' divorce. But the expression on Barry's face bore a closer resemblance to jealousy than the usual disgust he showed for the county commissioner and real estate mogul.

As we pulled back from our embrace, I pushed aside the puzzling emotion on his face. "You know I can't support Victoria's campaign."

"You'd be pleasantly surprised if you gave her a chance." Without a doubt, starstruck admiration for his ex-wife had replaced the jealousy over her relationship with Roy Don. "Didn't you hear her tonight? Her ideas are fresh and innovative. She'll be good for Pecan County. And wouldn't you like to see a woman on the BOC for a change?"

Not that woman. With a hand on my car door, I faced him. "I've decided to support Zach Kirkpatrick. I agreed to help with his campaign."

"Zach Kirkpatrick? But he's so new in town. What does he know about Pecan County?"

"Quite a bit, actually. I was impressed with all the research he's done."

"He can't know as much as Victoria. She's lived here all her life."

"Sometimes an outsider's perspective can be refreshing."

Barry narrowed his eyes. "What do we really know about him? He came out of nowhere. Wants to put in a light rail, for God's sake."

"Zach said he'd help me pass our revisions to the animal ordinance."

"And that's the reason?" Barry shook his head. "What makes you think Victoria wouldn't?"

Somebody needs to get a life. I sniffed. "Were we in the same meeting tonight?"

"Victoria's a reasonable person. Once she's in office and gets a chance to read the proposal, see how much support you've garnered, I think she'll get on board." He winked. "You can be very persuasive."

"Yeah, right. She's immune to my charms."

Barry put a hand on my shoulder. "Want to get dinner?"

"Kind of late, isn't it?"

"Have you eaten?"

"Well, no…"

"Come to my place. You know I make a mean grilled cheese."

I searched his face, hoping for confirmation that we were okay despite Victoria's renewed interference and our political disagreements. "Okay. But then I have to go home and feed Manny."

* * *

Barry's cooking was hard to resist. Dinner would be a simple grilled cheese sandwich with my favorite five-grain bread, slivered jalapeño peppers, and a generous portion of flavorful Jarlsberg. Crispy on the outside and gooey in the center—just the way I liked my go-to comfort food.

While he prepared our sandwiches, I excused myself to the bathroom. En route, I made a surreptitious check of the apartment for evidence of Victoria. No women's clothing hung in the bedroom closet, no feminine toiletries in the medicine cabinet or by the sink, no lingering scent of her strong, floral perfume. All good signs. Barry's apartment always looked like he'd just moved in: bare walls, stark furnishings, boxes still partially packed. Like he was camping out until I asked him to move in with me, or until Victoria invited him back into their as-yet unsold mansion.

That monstrosity had been on the market for over two years, ever since their divorce was final. Recently, Whitehead Realtors had begun renting it out for weddings, office parties, and other events.

"DeeLo, are you okay?" Plates clattered against the counter. An aroma of toasted bread and melted cheese filled the air.

"Coming." After checking my hair and make-up, I returned to the kitchen. "Smells great."

We sat on tall stools at the breakfast bar and dove into our sandwiches.

Swallowing his first bite, Barry asked, "Can I get you something to drink? I bought some of that Sauvignon Blanc you like."

I shook my head. "I have to drive home. Manny hasn't had dinner yet."

Barry's smile dimmed. "Manny can fend for himself for a night. Doesn't he have that automatic feeder and water dispenser? As if it would hurt him to miss a meal."

"Yeah." My cat was quite independent, and I'd often left him alone overnight. Before he was mine, he lived in a bookstore, usually staying by himself from closing until the store opened again in the morning. He'd be fine. Maybe I responded that way because I enjoyed cuddling with Manny, confiding my problems, and listening to him purr as if he understood.

The fact that I was thinking about cuddling with my cat instead of staying overnight at Barry's gave me pause. Briefly.

Barry walked to the refrigerator and removed the chilled bottle of wine. "I'm going to have a glass. Let me know if you change your mind."

I watched him pour, eyeing me, a knowing smile on his face, gauging how long I could resist. He'd untucked his shirt, undone the top two buttons, and taken off his glasses, now looking less like Clark Kent than his alter ego.

"Oh, all right," I sighed. It wasn't about the Sauvignon Blanc or my pledge not to drive after imbibing; it was about nurturing our relationship, defending it against the ever-present threat of Barry's ties to Victoria. Before I could change my mind, he'd set a goblet in front of me and filled it.

We toasted and took a sip; the tartness of the wine complemented the rich flavor of the cheese melted onto crispy, whole-grain bread.

And then our arms encircled each other. Our lips met hungrily, and we moved in tandem toward the bedroom. If Victoria popped over at midnight again, no one would answer the door.

Chapter Fifteen

The next morning, Barry and I straddled our barstools, drinking coffee before leaving separately for the office. "I have to stop by my house and check on Manny, so I'd better go. Don't want to disappoint the boss by being late." With a grin, I set my empty cup on the counter and gave him a peck on the cheek. "Thanks for last night."

He gathered me into his arms for a deeper goodbye kiss. "Thank *you*."

We walked together to the parking lot. He opened my car door and waited while I rolled down the window, foggy from the dew, for another farewell kiss.

I had just pulled onto the road when my phone vibrated with a text. I glanced down at the seat where it lay. *Demi.* I'd answer when I got home.

Manny greeted me at the door, rubbing against my calves, weaving himself between my legs, and scolding me with sharp meows for my prolonged absence. I petted his furry head, freshened his water, and fed him a can of his favorite tuna. He gobbled it down greedily, playing the poor, starving cat despite an almost full bowl of kibble sitting on the kitchen floor.

While Manny ate, I read Demi's text: "Rerouted. Will have a 5-hour sit at ATL. Pick me up at 4:30 p.m. and let's go find Kwintone."

"You know where to find him?" I typed back.

I waited for a response, but nothing more came.

* * *

During my lunch break, I stayed at my desk to create Zach's business

Facebook page, using his brochure as a guideline. He'd emailed me his logo, which I made as the header. I pinned the photo I'd taken of the three of us last night and a summary of his platform. I included reminders about the November election day, early voting locations, and instructions on how to vote absentee. Links to articles about the benefits of light rail and its success in other communities fleshed out the feed.

Wondering if I was pushing too far too soon, I posted a photo of an ear-tipped cat exiting a trap, captioned by a vow to amend Pecan County's animal ordinance. I then added links to articles about TNVR and respected animal advocacy organizations that supported the practice.

Holding my breath, I sent Zach the Facebook page link for approval. Almost immediately, he returned a thumbs-up and asked me to add Eddie as another administrator.

There were several Eddie Fentons on Facebook; I selected the only one who was on the list of friends for both Zach and Kwintone. I almost didn't recognize the account by the picture because he had hair; shaving his head must be a relatively new look for him. After sending Eddie an invitation to become an administrator, I checked out his profile. It would be good to know something about the people I'd be working with on this campaign.

Again, Eddie's resemblance to Kwintone struck me, even more so with his face framed by long, thick hair. The arresting hazel eyes. Similar-shaped nose and mouth. And the tooth gap.

Were they related? I couldn't wait to talk to Demi about Eddie.

I smiled to myself. I'd resisted acknowledging Kwintone as her brother, even though their DNA had matched. But now I was trying to force another brother on her without scientific proof.

Eddie was active on social media; he posted almost every day, and his profile was public. Shots of friends at sporting events. Selfies with other guys acting silly at parties. Photos with his father at the dealership, standing beside his proclaimed latest dream car. An advertising ploy, or a genuine wish list?

There were posts from work: movie sets, flattering pictures of a smiling Zach, lots more pictures of Zach, some posed, some candid. But no photos of Kwintone, not even a mention.

I glanced at Eddie's profile again. He was employed at Oakwood Studios, which explained his connection with Zach. His occupation was listed as "apprentice animal trainer." There were pictures of him walking dogs and teaching them tricks. And a few close-ups of just the dogs.

Eddie also shared numerous petitions pleading for animal rights. From the Humane Society of the United States: "End the Export of Live Horses for Slaughter," "End the Suffering of Farm Animals." From Change.org: "Drilling in the Arctic National Refuge Threatens Wildlife." From the ASPCA: "Stop Puppy Mills! Support Cruelty Victims." From the Physicians Committee: "End Testing on Monkeys."

Oakwood Studios. Animal testing. Aiden Lee Green, stabbed on studio property.

Eddie Fenton. Detective Ross had asked if I knew him. Was Eddie on the detective's radar because of his animal activism?

"DeeLo?" Barry's voice broke my concentration.

I looked up from my computer. "What can I do for you, boss?"

He grinned sheepishly, as he often did when I used formalities in the office. "Can you pull together the investment statements for Catherine Foster's foundation? She's coming in at two this afternoon."

"I'll get right on it." I navigated to our electronic file system and printed the necessary documents in minutes. The new database I had set up had brought Barry's firm out of the Dark Ages when their system consisted of piles of paper documents crammed into overstuffed file cabinets and dusty cardboard boxes.

Several years ago, Catherine had won a huge settlement in a wrongful death suit, and Barry had been managing the proceeds for her ever since. He'd recently helped her set aside most of the fortune into a small nonprofit foundation for cat rescue, with a focus on funding TNVR activity.

I pressed Print, sending the necessary documents to the office copier. "By the way, Demi wants me to help her with an errand this afternoon, so I'd like to leave around four."

"Four?" His brow creased.

"I can come in early tomorrow if—"

"No, it's fine. If anything comes up, I'll get one of the interns to handle it." He headed back to his office.

By the time Catherine arrived, I had everything set up for her appointment with Barry. "DeeLo." Not a hugger or a handshaker, she greeted me with a faint smile. Her attire for the meeting with her attorney didn't look much different from what she wore to trap ferals.

"Hi, Cat. Barry's ready for you."

"Thanks." She tried to shove a strand of dirty blond hair behind her ear, but it flopped back in her flat face. She'd had her hair cut short recently, and pushing the stray bits behind her ear no longer worked. "Hey, how did it go with that guy? You know, the speeder with the weird name."

"Kwintone."

"Yeah, that's the one. Did he show up?"

"Sort of." I opened the door to the conference room where I'd laid her paperwork on the table. "He still has hours to complete."

She plopped her short, stubby body into a leather armchair. "Not our problem. Did you catch many cats the other night?"

"Four, but they say at least six more have been hanging around Oakwood Studios. None of them have ear tips."

"I'm not surprised. But I'm relieved management is willing to let them stay. Merilee Jones is a receptionist there now, so she probably had something to do with it."

"Yes, Zach Kirkpatrick, the property manager, mentioned that one of our volunteers works at the studio and suggested TNVR. Did you know Zach is running for county commissioner?"

Catherine shrugged. "I don't get involved with local politics."

"But you should this time. At least, make the effort to vote. If he gets elected, Zach will help us get the animal ordinance changed."

Catherine raised her bushy brow.

"DeeLo." Standing by the open door, Barry cleared his throat. "The office is not the place to campaign." With a sweep of his arm, he cued me that it was time for me to leave the room.

Chapter Sixteen

emi was waiting outside baggage claim when I navigated the line of cars cruising the arrivals level. I pulled over to the curb, and she hopped in. She doffed her uniform jacket, laid it across the back seat, and fastened her seat belt.

"So, where are we going?" With a glance in my rearview mirror, I eased back into traffic.

Demi rattled off a midtown Atlanta address.

"Can you put it in my GPS?"

In a moment, Siri was bossing me around, telling me how to exit the airport and enter the freeway.

"Did you bring Kwintone's phone?"

Demi held it up.

"After you left, I wished we'd checked his search history."

"I did. Cleared."

"Cleared! What's he trying to hide? Searches for animal testing? How to kill someone?" With a sidelong glance at my niece, I changed lanes to comply with Siri's directions.

"DeeLo, we don't know if Kwintone had anything to do with that poor man."

"Would he tell you if he had?"

Demi made a face like she used to when we were kids, when she'd made up her mind and couldn't be convinced otherwise. "How is the victim, by the way? Have you found out anything more?"

I shook my head. "Last I heard, Aiden Green—that's his name—was still unconscious." I'd called Jill earlier, and she didn't have any updates. Neither did the hospital. "But I found out something interesting about Kwintone."

"What?" Demi looked up from the phone.

"Did you get the picture I sent?"

She scrunched her face. "Of you with those two dudes?"

"Both of them are Kwintone's connections on social media."

She shrugged. "I accept a lot of friend requests from casual acquaintances. Some from other flight attendants who are friends of friends. Did either of those guys tell you how they know Kwintone?"

"Zach says Kwintone is Eddie's friend. I haven't asked Eddie yet how they know each other, but I plan to tomorrow. We're having lunch to talk strategy about Zach's campaign for the Pecan County Board of Commissioners."

Demi laughed. "You're going up against Victoria?"

"Someone needs to."

"What does Barry say?"

"He supports Victoria. We've agreed to disagree. But I didn't send you that picture to keep you in the loop about Pecan County politics. Did you take a good look at Eddie's face?"

Demi found the photo on her phone. "Hmmm."

I'd expected her to be more excited. "He and Kwintone could be brothers. And Eddie was raised by his biological father. Maybe Eddie's father is Kwintone's father… and yours."

My niece studied the photo again, then stared out the window. "Let's not get ahead of ourselves."

Her statement was so un-Demi-like that I almost missed my exit.

* * *

Kwintone lived in a townhouse in an upper-middle-class neighborhood near Centennial Park that had been gentrified after the 1996 Olympics. I wondered how a kid his age could afford that real estate; his property value was at least double mine.

I parked on the curb in front of his unit. His Mustang was nowhere in sight, but perhaps it was housed in a garage somewhere. Or maybe his car was still missing. If it was stolen, had he reported it? Was he the one who drove it off? Demi had not shared much information—if she had any.

We got out of the car, and I followed my niece up the steps to his front door. "Do you think he'll talk to us? If he's even home."

"He'll talk to us." Demi rang the bell. "He knows I have his phone."

"How does he know? Have you been in touch with him?"

Her non-answer told me she had. No wonder she didn't want me to report her alleged brother missing. He wasn't.

No sounds came from inside the townhouse. Demi rang the bell again.

"Does he know we're coming over?" She'd been so maddeningly close-mouthed about her mysterious possible relative. "Have you heard from him since he disappeared the other night?"

"He—" A loud VROOM cut off her words. Hip-hop music blared from the rolled-down windows of a red Mustang driving by.

Guess it wasn't stolen.

Demi ran down the walkway waving her arms. "Kwintone!"

The Mustang stopped. Demi rushed over and jiggled the handle of the passenger door. I followed but hung back at a safe distance, too far away to view the driver or decipher their conversation over the cacophonic beat.

In a moment, Demi stepped back onto the sidewalk, and the vehicle parked in front of my Lexus. The music stopped. Kwintone unfolded himself from the driver's seat. Alive and well. I didn't know whether to be relieved or furious.

We followed him up the walkway to his front door.

"Where did you go the other night?" I demanded. "We were afraid you'd been hurt."

Kwintone unlocked the door and stepped aside to let us enter. "No, I'm fine."

"Did you hear what happened? You must have heard the sirens," I tried again. "We thought someone stole your car."

"No, it's right here."

"You could have told Demi you were okay."

"I didn't have my phone." His condescending look might as well have said, "Chill out, Karen." He motioned us toward a leather sectional facing a rustic brick fireplace. "Have a seat. Would you ladies like some coffee?"

"No, thanks." I sat on the couch and scanned the framed photographs on the wall.

"That would be great." Demi followed him into the spacious kitchen opening to the family room, separated only by a granite island. "I'll be up late tonight." She set his smartphone on the counter. "Sorry, we took this. We were trying to find you."

He snatched the device from the counter and quickly scrolled through it as if searching for something. Frowning, he stopped to read a message and then typed a reply. In a moment, he sighed and set down the phone.

I got up from the couch for a closer look at one of the photos on the wall that had caught my eye. It appeared to be a teenage Kwintone standing beside a petite blonde woman who, from a distance, could have been Desiree. I turned, gesturing toward the photo. "Is that you with your mom?"

"Yeah." His voice sounded husky. Demi had said his mother recently passed away from cancer, so perhaps the memory was still too painful to talk about.

I joined them in the kitchen. "Where did you go when you left me? After that phone call?"

Still ignoring my questions, Kwintone opened a cabinet stocked with pods for his single-serving coffee maker. He glanced over his shoulder at Demi. "What would you like?"

Demi selected a medium roast, and Kwintone placed it into the Keurig. From another cherrywood cabinet, he removed two ceramic mugs. While her coffee brewed, he chose a dark roast for himself. "Sure you don't want anything, DeeLo?"

"I'd rather have some answers." I gazed around the ultra-modern kitchen with stainless steel appliances and a sleek induction range in the center island. "But I'll take a water if it's cold."

Kwintone put on his charming host smile, revealing the dimple in his cheek and the gap between his front teeth. He pulled a bottled water from the Sub-Zero refrigerator. "Here you go, ma'am." Before closing the door, he took out a pint of almond milk.

I uncapped the water while Demi removed her cup from the coffee maker so Kwintone could prepare his. Why wasn't she asking him questions? I felt like the bad cop.

Demi poured almond milk into her coffee. "So, Kwintone, we're glad you made it home okay."

A start, but lame. "We were worried about you," I added.

Kwintone took his steaming cup from the Keurig. "Yeah, I wasn't sure what was going down, so I hustled out of there. Didn't notice my phone was gone until I went to call you."

"What do you mean by 'what was going down'? Who were you with?" I fiddled with my water bottle while staring at Kwintone, willing him to look at me.

He took a deep sip of his coffee, swallowed, and cleared his throat. "There was a guy who said—"

Demi's Taylor Swift ringtone interrupted us. She picked up her phone. "Hello?" Her eyes widened, and she raised her wrist to check her watch. "Yeah, okay. I'll be there." She disconnected and grabbed her handbag. "Gotta go. That was Flight Attendant Scheduling. I've been rerouted again." She turned to me. "How fast can you get me back to the airport?"

In a flurry, we gathered our things. I tried one more time to glean information from Kwintone. "How did you get away so fast?"

Smiling, he cleared the coffee cups from the counter and propelled us out the door. Maybe it was my imagination, but he seemed relieved by the diversion and reprieve from our questions.

I lifted my water bottle. "Thanks for the refreshments."

As I stepped onto the walkway, I murmured to him, "The Pecan Point police are looking for you. You need to call them." When he failed to react, I added, "Or you could at least talk to me."

He held up his hand and waved goodbye just as his phone rang.

Chapter Seventeen

I zipped through traffic like a NASCAR driver, changing lanes and exceeding the speed limit as much as traffic would allow. Focused on returning Demi to work on time, I couldn't concentrate on how little we'd learned about her newfound brother's activities. Had he crossed paths with the man who was stabbed?

After I dropped Demi at the airport, I got a text from Jill. Aiden Green had regained consciousness and had been moved from the ICU to a private room. No one had been able to talk to him yet, though.

I headed for the Pecan Point Hospital. After I pulled into the lot and parked, I glimpsed a red Mercedes S-class sports car backing out of a nearby spot. *Victoria.* Gripping the wheel and staring straight ahead, she didn't appear to notice me.

Visiting hours were in progress, and Jill had given me Aiden's room number, so I didn't check in with the front desk. Since he was awake, maybe we could get some answers. For Demi's sake, I hoped Kwintone wasn't responsible for the man's injuries. But if he was, she needed to know before she became too attached to the idea of having a brother.

I took the elevator to Aiden's floor. The smell of disinfectant burned my nose as I stepped onto the polished tile.

Turning into the hallway, I almost collided with Lisa Ross, head down, face flushed, furiously typing on her phone.

Straightening to her full five-foot height, the detective's wife shoved her phone into her purse. "DeeLo Myer. Long time, no see." Even though Lisa must be in her mid-thirties, there was something childlike about her demeanor—perhaps her squeaky Minnie Mouse voice, perhaps her diminutive size and Shirley Temple curls.

"How've you been?" I smiled, feeling a stab of self-consciousness as I attempted to make small talk. If she knew I'd come to see her boss, she might wonder why.

"Oh, the cats are fine." Her eyes darted to the closing elevator doors, trapping her in our conversation for a while longer. "No more wild kittens, thanks to you."

"I saw your husband yesterday. He said you have a new job."

She blinked, startled. "Uh, yeah. Neuroscience Laboratories."

"How do you like it?"

Lisa pushed her bangs off her forehead, grimaced, and wiped away a few beads of sweat.

I studied her face. The building wasn't hot; why was she perspiring? "It's terrible what happened to the CEO. Do you know him well?"

"Uh, no, but I heard he's here in the hospital somewhere. So awful!" She peered over her shoulder. "I was visiting my … uh… my grandmother." She maneuvered past me and pressed the elevator call button.

A ding announced the elevator's arrival. As the doors opened, a food service worker pushed a cart of meal trays, bumping slightly over the gap as he steered it onto the floor, emitting a whiff of bland, overcooked vegetables.

"I hope your grandmother will be okay," I called as Lisa slid past the cart and disappeared behind the closing elevator doors.

Aiden's room was down the hall and around the corner. A uniformed guard dozed in a chair outside, his barrel chest heaving rhythmically.

I stared at the guard for a moment, wondering if I should wake him and ask permission to enter or just go in. What if the guard was there to restrict visitors?

But I needed to find out if Demi should be worried about her alleged brother. With no gatekeeper challenging me, I entered the room.

On the inside wall hung a whiteboard with cryptic notes, nurses' names, shifts, and extension numbers. Before trying to decipher any clues, I snapped a photo of the whiteboard with my phone.

Aiden appeared different from the figure I'd seen sprawled on the ground in the dim moonlight; his skin was paler, his hair darker, his shut eyes more sunken. Clear plastic tubes ran from underneath a bandage on the back of his hand to a bag suspended from a metal pole next to his pillow. A monitor beside him steadily beeped, displaying numbers on a screen.

I took a step toward his bed. He looked more like a corpse than a living human being.

"Mr. Green?"

The monitor flashed wildly, and its beep became a piercing screech. I froze.

"Excuse me, ma'am." A nurse rushed into the room and brushed me aside. She stared at the monitor, pressed some buttons to silence it, and then checked the IV.

Another person in scrubs rushed in. He held a stethoscope against Aiden's chest and listened.

I stepped further out of their way.

Other personnel hurried into the room, pushing a crash cart. The security guard, now awake, hovered in the doorway. His eyes flitted in my direction. "Hey, who are you?"

The nurse turned to me. "Ma'am, you need to leave."

"I…" What was happening? Had I caused it? What had I done?

Someone else nudged me out. I gazed curiously inside the room before the door closed behind me.

The security guard was back in his chair, his attention diverted by a nurse. She gestured toward Aiden's room. "Probably another false alarm. Don't worry about it."

I stopped. "So, he'll be okay?"

The nurse turned my way. "Ma'am, no visitors now."

The guard's brow furrowed as if he were trying to place me amid all the recent chaos. Before he could figure it out, I strode swiftly down the hall and rounded the corner without looking back.

* * *

Rattled about the episode with Aiden Green, I escaped into the elevator and pressed the button for the ground floor. I obviously wasn't getting any information from him tonight.

The elevator descended, and in a moment, the doors slid open. In the middle of the lobby, chatting with a gray-haired woman wearing a business suit and a hospital badge, stood Zach and Eddie.

"DeeLo." Zach beamed as I approached. "What brings you here?"

I could have asked him the same question. "Oh…visiting a friend."

His face grew solemn. "I hope it's nothing serious." When I didn't respond with a story of woe, he turned to the woman. "DeeLo Myer is our social media guru."

I smiled at the acknowledgment.

Zach laid a big hand on my shoulder. "DeeLo, this is Helen Carlyle, the hospital administrator. She just made a big donation to our campaign."

"On behalf of the hospital?" *Can they get involved in local politics?*

"From her personal funds," Zach clarified.

Helen shook my hand. "Pleased to meet you, DeeLo. I love Zach's ideas for improving the hospital's volunteer program. What a great way to get more high school kids to give back. This county needs an innovative commissioner who really cares about the community."

Volunteer program to put kids to work at the hospital? Zach hadn't told me about that one yet. Was it a bona fide plan he'd thought through or a spur-of-the-moment, kiss-up idea to solicit a donation? I smiled again, like I knew what she was talking about, and held up my phone. "If you don't mind, Helen, can I get a photo of you with Zach so we can announce your support on social media?"

Helen and Zach leaned in for a grip-and-grin pose. I centered them on my screen, ensuring the check-in desk filled the background to convey the hospital setting. A woman in scrubs hovered nearby, which added to the authenticity. I clicked several shots in rapid succession.

The hospital administrator excused herself, and I started for the exit.

"DeeLo." Zach stopped me. "Eddie and I were about to grab a bite to eat. Can you join us? Maybe have a little impromptu strategy session?"

I hadn't made any plans with Barry yet and couldn't think of an excuse not to go. Besides, I had questions for both men that had nothing to do with the campaign.

Chapter Eighteen

Eddie had a craving for lasagna, so I recommended Leonardo's. Neither he nor Zach had been there before.

"They have a great vegetarian lasagna in addition to one with grass-fed beef," I said as we strolled up the walkway to the entrance. "You won't be disappointed."

The hostess led us across the terracotta tile to a table overlooking the nature preserve. Both men gazed around at the Tuscan décor, and Zach pointed at a mural depicting a quaint hillside village surrounded by vineyards. "They've done a good job evoking Italy."

I smiled, pleased that my restaurant recommendation was a hit. "I think the owners are from Italy." I wasn't sure that was true, but it felt true.

After studying the wine list, Eddie ordered a glass of Chianti. Zach and I stuck with ice water.

Zach closed his menu. "You don't drink wine, DeeLo?"

"I do, but I have to drive home."

He nodded. "Smart."

"One glass won't make you impaired," scoffed Eddie as he accepted his wine from the server. "Especially with food."

"I don't like to take chances." I sipped my water. "Shall we talk campaign strategy?"

"Sure." Zach rested an elbow on the table. "I want to hear your ideas."

"First of all," I held up a finger, "the *Pecan County News* publishes a candidate questionnaire. It's great publicity, and the paper has a wide circulation because it's free. Almost every business has a rack of them.

Answering the questions is a way for the public to get to know you and learn more about your ideas. Victoria is the only candidate who has taken advantage of the opportunity so far."

Eddie frowned. "A free local newspaper? One of those throwaway rags?"

"The people who read it are voters."

Zach raised his glass. "Let's do it. How do I get this questionnaire?"

I took out my phone. "My friend Jill Hernandez is a reporter for the *Pecan County News*. I'll ask her to send you the form." I typed a note to Jill and then looked up. "Let's go over your answers together before you return it." I navigated to the newspaper's website, found Victoria's completed questionnaire, and emailed Zach and Eddie the link. "Before you start, look over your opponent's responses that the paper published last week. You'll get a feel for what they're looking for. You want to embrace Victoria's more popular ideas but differentiate yourself and highlight how you can do better."

"Sounds like a plan." Zach grinned.

Eddie picked up his phone when it dinged with my message. "We're supposed to copy her?"

I wasn't sure where Eddie's negativity was coming from; he'd been so amiable when we first met. "Not copy. Observe how she answers the questions. Victoria jabbers a lot about her vision without really committing to anything controversial. You can subtly call her out for that, show the chips in her veneer."

The server returned to take our food orders. Zach and Eddie chose the vegetable lasagna, and I requested linguine with shrimp in a lemon cream sauce.

"After your questionnaire is published, I'll monitor the newspaper's website for comments because we must respond to them all. There will be naysayers who are critical no matter what and like to stir up trouble. We have to be respectful but show they can't bully you." I counted off tasks on my fingers. "Let's try to send a letter to the editor once a week, clarifying any issues that might not be resonating with the voters."

Zach and Eddie exchanged glances. Zach seemed to hang on to every word, but Eddie knitted his brow.

I held up another finger. "We'll post on social media at least once a day. I already put up the shot of you and Helen with news about her donation. Send me some bullet points about your volunteer program for the hospital, and I'll get those up tomorrow with another copy of the photo. I'll also check with some of the regular columnists and bloggers; maybe they'd like to interview you. They're always looking for interesting content. And I think I can get you a spot on the local radio station. The owner is one of our firm's clients, and he likes me."

"All this great information is making my head spin." Zach smiled at me, then gazed at Eddie. "What do you think, Hon?"

Hon? I sat up straighter, regarding Zach and Eddie in a new light.

Eddie turned to me. "What's your background again?"

His tone conveyed resistance, and I couldn't tell if he disliked my ideas or resented sharing Zach's attention. Or both. "I've never worked on a political campaign. But I handled public relations for my ex-husband's film production company back in Los Angeles."

Eddie's eyes lit up at the words "film production company," and some of the negativity evaporated. "You have a background in cinema?"

"Public relations. Those skills can transfer to any industry. Including politics."

Zach covered my hand with his. "We're lucky to have you, DeeLo."

Feeling Eddie's scrutiny, I moved my hand. "Thanks. But I've been doing all the talking, and I don't want you to feel like I'm shoving my ideas down your throat. Tell me what you had in mind."

Zach shrugged. "I only filed last week, right before the deadline. We're just getting started. We created those brochures you saw at the candidate forum and ordered yard signs, but apart from that, we'd be lost without you."

Like poor, clueless Dr. Smythe.

"What about you, Eddie? What made you get involved in this campaign?" As I stared at his petulant face, I pondered his uncanny resemblance to Kwintone and wondered how I could steer the conversation in that direction.

Eddie turned to Zach with the dreamy admiration I'd seen several times before. *More than admiration.* "I wanted to do whatever I could to help Zach."

"Do you live in Pecan County, Eddie?" Votes were the goal, and I recalled the assertion someone made at the Rotary forum that most Oakwood employees didn't reside in the county.

Zach's eyes shifted between our faces as if reading my thoughts. "We're renting a condo here in Pecan Point, looking to buy a house. Eddie registered to vote in time for the election. We're keeping our relationship low-key because I wasn't sure how Pecan County voters would feel."

"Your instincts are probably correct. Unfortunately." I took another sip of water. "But if your personal life stays private, it shouldn't be a problem. People here are conservative, but most of them are reasonably tolerant."

The server brought our food, and conversation ceased as we dug in. Maybe Eddie's snippy mood would improve after a plate of lasagna and another glass of wine. The meal break allowed me an opportunity to change the subject.

I twirled some pasta around my fork. "So, Eddie, how do you know Kwintone Johnson?"

Eddie stopped chewing and gave Zach the side-eye.

Zach cleared his throat. "He did a good job with our brochures."

I pictured Kwintone's card lying in the Oakwood Studios parking lot. The name "Digital Design" didn't give much of a clue to what his company did. Was creating brochures part of their business? Or had Kwintone made the brochures as a favor for a friend? I wondered how—and when—his card had found its way to the studio parking lot. And apparently, so did Detective Ross.

"How do *you* know Kwintone?" Zach asked me.

Touché. "He was helping me trap cats for PPHS Monday night." To Eddie's furrowed brow, I explained, "The Pecan Point Humane Society." I elected not to mention Kwintone's "community service," a distinction that made me uncomfortable when I was still volunteering by court order. "We were on the Oakwood Studios lot the night someone stabbed Aiden Green."

Both men paled at least a shade.

"Surely you heard about the stabbing?" My eyes scanned their faces like a security camera recording their reactions.

Zach flagged a passing server. "May we please have our check?" When she nodded, he turned back to me, his color almost normal again. "Of course. Senseless tragedy. The attack hit Oakwood employees particularly hard since it happened on our property."

"People are afraid to walk to the parking lot alone, especially after dark," said Eddie.

"We've increased security to make employees feel safer," Zach added.

"Does the parking lot have cameras?" If so, someone could pull the footage, and the mystery of Aiden Green's stabbing would be solved.

"Not in the area where he was found, but now it does," said Zach.

"Did Green have business at the studio?"

"No," Zach replied, too quickly.

"Have the police told you anything more?" I continued to search the men's faces, seeking to read between the lines of dialogue. "I'm the one who found Mr. Green, so I'm interested in how he ended up stabbed on the Oakwood Studios lot."

Eddie straightened. "What did Kwintone say?"

I turned in his direction. "Haven't talked to him about it yet. Kwintone left before I found the victim."

Another surreptitious glance passed between Eddie and Zach.

What's that about?

Before I could open my mouth to comment, Barry and Victoria bounced into the restaurant, laughing noisily. His hand lay against her waist, and as she caught my eye, she flipped her hair and smirked.

Chapter Nineteen

T he server brought our check, and Zach insisted on paying. My eyes shifted to my boyfriend and his ex-wife, our political opponent, toasting each other at a table across the room. Unlike Victoria, Barry was still oblivious to my presence.

Eddie followed my steely gaze to the competition. "Looks like we better watch what we say."

Zach signed the credit card slip, took his receipt, and closed the leather cardholder. "Shall we call it a night?"

I rose. "Thank you for dinner."

"Thank you for all your help, DeeLo." Zach smiled as he and Eddie headed for the exit. From the way they'd clammed up when I mentioned the stabbing, I suspected one or both knew more about what happened to Aiden Green than they'd disclosed. And they certainly hadn't been very forthcoming about their connection to Kwintone. The challenge would be getting them to trust me enough to talk about it. All of it.

I strolled past the table where Barry and Victoria sipped red wine and sat side by side instead of across the table from each other, much more amicable than mere campaign colleagues. Barry looked up. "DeeLo." He fiddled with the frame of his eyeglasses the way he did when taken by surprise.

"Strategy meeting?" I smiled, attempting to appear casual and mildly curious rather than accusatory and jealous.

"This seems to be a popular place for that." Victoria nodded toward the front entrance as Zach and Eddie disappeared behind the closing door.

Barry edged a little farther away from Victoria and pointed to the chair across from him. "Please join us, DeeLo."

Victoria gripped her wine glass, sloshing some of the liquid over the rim. "Yes, please tell us what that fool Zach Kirkpatrick is up to."

"He has some good ideas." I strained to keep my tone civil and noncombative.

Victoria covered her mouth to suppress a giggle. "I can't believe that…" She rolled her eyes and gestured with a limp wrist. "…. thinks he even has a chance to become a Pecan County commissioner. Can you imagine?"

Barry cringed, and his eyes darted to a nearby table where a couple stopped talking to stare.

It was time to leave before I said something I'd regret. I hoisted the strap of my handbag higher over my shoulder. "Well, I don't want to interrupt your meeting. Have a good evening."

"DeeLo…" Barry made a feeble attempt to call after me, but he didn't get up and follow.

Without looking back, I marched for the exit.

I sat for a moment inside my locked car. My hands were shaking. Why was Barry spending so much time with Victoria lately? Was it just about her campaign? Would working toward a common goal like that bring them back together?

Taking a series of deep breaths, I checked my phone. I'd missed a call from Kwintone.

* * *

I didn't return Kwintone's call right away. I was still fuming and processing my feelings about running into Barry and Victoria together. Again.

When I got home, Manny greeted me with his usual starving, neglected cat routine. After eating a few bites from his fresh bowl of dry cat food, he followed me to the couch to snuggle while I phoned Kwintone.

"Hey, Auntie Dee," he answered in a voice way too casual for a man who might be wanted by the police. Had Detective Ross ever contacted him? If not, what was he waiting for?

I ignored the cutesy nickname Kwintone had given me. "It's DeeLo. Did you do what I suggested?"

"And what was that?"

"Talk to the Pecan Point police." I struggled to retain control of my phone as Manny headbutted me, demanding attention.

Kwintone paused so long I thought he'd hung up. Then he let out a breath. "Why would I do that? Are they mad that I haven't finished my community service?"

Is he kidding me? "Did you know a man got stabbed on the Oakwood Studios lot the night we were there? About the time you left for your mystery meeting. They questioned Demi and me. We were the ones who found him while we were looking for you. I can't believe they haven't tried to contact you, too."

"Stabbed?" Kwintone sounded genuinely surprised. I wondered if the expression on his face matched his tone.

"Haven't you listened to the news?"

"I don't follow the news much." His remark sounded too flippant for someone who had been so close to a violent crime scene.

"Who were you meeting that night? After you left early from your community service assignment?" I stroked Manny's thick, black fur while he purred and kneaded my leg.

Another long pause. I expected Kwintone to tell me it was none of my business.

"The police are going to ask, and they might not be as nice as I am."

Just when I thought he was going to hang up, Kwintone murmured, "A guy named Eddie."

My hand stopped on Manny's head. "Eddie Fenton?"

"You know him?"

"How do *you* know him?" Unhappy that the petting had paused, Manny nuzzled my hand.

"It's about my father."

The phone slipped from my grasp, earning a yowl from the cat as he jumped off the couch.

I picked up the device from the floor. "Kwintone?"

The line had gone dead in the scuffle. I hit redial.

Ringing. Then voicemail.

"Kwintone, I'm sorry we got disconnected. My cat... Please call me back."

I hung up and waited. Nothing.

Manny crept back onto the couch and, with a satisfied glance at me, curled into a ball.

I composed a text: "We have more cats to catch. Meet me at nine tomorrow night. Same place."

In a moment, Kwintone's response came. "See you tomorrow night."

Chapter Twenty

Unlike our last foray into TNVR, Kwintone showed up on time. He wore jeans, athletic shoes, and a light jacket over a T-shirt advertising some band I'd never heard of.

Trying almost too hard to play the gentleman, he helped me unload the traps from my SUV and scout suitable locations for them. He muted his phone without being reminded and listened while I explained how to set up and bait the traps. He even handled the slimy, stinky sardines. A complete 180—did Kwintone have a benevolent twin?

When we were done, I offered him paper towels and sanitizer. "Thanks, Kwintone."

He wrinkled his nose at the fishy odor and then grinned, exposing the dimple. "At your service, Auntie Dee."

"DeeLo," I corrected him. "And I'm not your aunt."

"DeeLo." He gestured toward the woods where we'd set up. "What's next?"

"We wait for a cat to smell the sardines and venture into a trap. Hopefully, not one we've caught before."

"How do you know if you've caught a cat before?"

I pulled out my phone and showed him the image of an ear-tipped feline that I'd posted on Zach's Facebook page. "When we take them to the clinic for neutering and vaccinations, the veterinarian clips off the tip of the left ear while the cat is under anesthesia. So, if an ear-tipped cat ventures into a trap, we let it go. Saves everyone an unnecessary trip to the clinic."

Kwintone nodded. I couldn't determine if his expression was mocking or reflected real interest.

"Fortunately, most cats who've been trapped before have become savvy enough not to get caught again. But every now and then, there's a daredevil who's hungry enough to think he can snatch the food before the door comes down."

Kwintone gestured around the area; some of our traps were barely visible in the moonlight. "How can you even tell if there's a cat in one of those contraptions?"

I pointed to the closest one. "See the fluorescent pink ribbon tied to the entrance door? Flapping in the wind?"

Squinting, he nodded.

"When a cat goes into the trap and steps on the trip plate, the door comes down, along with the ribbon. As long as the ribbon remains aloft, the door is open, and we haven't caught anything yet."

"Anything? You mean, a cat?"

"That's what we're going for. Not the occasional possum or raccoon."

He made a sour face. "I hate possums. They're so ugly."

"They won't hurt you. And they're good for the environment. It's best to just let them go and leave them alone." A chilly breeze had whipped up, and I hugged my torso. "Let's sit in my car while we watch the traps, and you can tell me about Eddie Fenton and your father."

It felt good to be out of the wind as I settled into the driver's seat. Kwintone reclined the passenger seat and took out his phone.

"Eddie Fenton," I reminded him. "What's your connection?"

Sighing, he put down his phone and turned toward me. "It's complicated." He sounded like Demi.

My eyes made a quick scan of the traps. All the ribbons were still aloft. "We have time."

Kwintone sighed again. "I don't know why I'm telling you this."

"Because I'm trying to help you. And Demi." *Mostly Demi.*

He stared out the window into the darkness. "I always thought my dad died when I was seven. I mean, the man I called 'Pops,' who read me bedtime stories and showed me how to throw a spiral. We were tight, a strong military family, blessed. But all that came crashing down when he was killed during a training exercise. Afterward when the calls and condolences faded, it was just me and my mom, holding it down and pushing through without him."

"I'm sorry for your loss."

Kwintone cut his eyes at me. "It was a long time ago, so lose the platitudes. You don't have to pretend."

"I'm not… I know how it feels." It had been years since I'd thought about that kind of loss. "My father died when I was five." I remembered the love, but could hardly picture his face. "My mother remarried when I was seven, though, so my stepfather helped raise me. He was always there for me and Demi." *Desiree and our brother, David, not so much.* It sounded like Kwintone's only memories of a father figure were from early childhood. "I guess your mom didn't remarry?"

"Nope." Kwintone stared back out the windshield. "After Pops died, it was just the two of us. When Mom passed last year, and I went through her papers, I found out she'd been lying to me all my life."

"Lying? What do you mean?"

"The man I knew as my dad…wasn't. And he knew it too."

I arched my eyebrow even though the reveal was not a surprise. "Maybe they were protecting you… She never mentioned this?"

"Never. She lied to me."

Lie was a strong word. I doubted Kwintone's mother concealed the information out of malicious intent, although it might seem that way to him. "Did she leave any clues in her papers about who your biological father is?"

"Not exactly. But I was able to put it together from the letters."

"Letters from whom? Love letters?"

"Emails from him that she had printed out. And I wouldn't call it love. The opposite."

I twisted my mouth, not sure what to say, hoping he'd elaborate.

"She threatened him."

"Threatened? Like asking for money?"

Kwintone winced. "Mom accused him of leading her on and went ballistic." Our breath had fogged up the windshield, and he rubbed the condensation away with his cuff. "Maybe she misunderstood his intentions."

"I'm sorry."

He turned to me, his face almost a snarl. "Why? It's not your fault."

"But I can still feel sad for her. My sister, Desiree, was in a similar situation—apparently with the same guy." *Alone, pregnant.* Except Desiree had a loving family to lean on—a mother who would practically raise her daughter for her. "Demi never knew who her father was; she still doesn't. Her mom refuses to talk about him."

Kwintone frowned. "The guy—'Fen1999' at gmail.com—was engaged to be married to someone else. He never loved my mother."

Again, I thought about Desiree and what she must have felt like when she found out she was pregnant. "But it sounds like your mother did find someone who loved her... and you. My sister never got married."

"Yeah, Pops was a good guy. Unlike the *sperm donor* who fathered me." The words "sperm donor" came out like a hiss.

"Then why do you want to find him?"

Kwintone shook his head, his hazel eyes flickering with fury. For a moment, I was afraid he meant the man harm. A vision of Aiden Green bleeding on the ground flashed before me.

"I want to know if he's the same person who set up my trust fund."

My mouth dropped. That wasn't what I'd expected him to say.

A streak of movement outside drew my attention to a slamming trap door. I tapped Kwintone's shoulder. "Come on. We caught a cat."

* * *

I showed Kwintone how to cover the trap to calm the panicked cat, who, fortunately, did not have an ear tip. "Congratulations. I think that's one you baited all by yourself."

He gave me a modest half-smile, but his eyes lit up at the compliment.

"A trust fund?" I asked as we carried the occupied trap to the car.

He tightened his jaw. "Another thing my mother never told me about while she was alive. The money could have helped with college. I'm still paying on those student loans I had to take out."

By the time we loaded the trap into my SUV, we'd captured another cat, also without an ear tip.

"How did you find out about the money?" I asked as we loaded the second cat into the back of my vehicle and adjusted the traps to make more space.

"Going through her papers with the lawyer."

Back inside the car to escape the wind, I reclined in the leather seat. "You only learned about the trust fund after your mom's death?" Why would a mother keep a windfall like that from her son? "Was there an age requirement to tap into the account?"

"Twenty-one." He gave me a sad puppy look. "Four years ago. I could have used the money to help with her medical bills. We were struggling after she got sick."

I didn't have an answer. Pride? Bitterness? Had she forgotten about the nest egg? Couldn't believe it was real? Maybe there were strings attached. The woman was dead, so we couldn't ask her. "You think your biological father might have set it up."

"Who else would have? Maybe he felt guilty. Or maybe he was afraid she'd come after him for more." Kwintone buried his face in his hands. "She was a wounded woman on the warpath."

I stared at the once-cocky young man beside me, now drained of bravado. "The bank should be able to tell you who opened the account."

"They did. It was Edward Fenton."

Chapter Twenty-One

Edward Fenton, Car King. Eddie's father, Kwintone's connection to Eddie.

I knew I was right about the family resemblance. *Demi's other family.* Had I solved the mystery of her paternity?

"So, have you been in touch with Mr. Fenton?" I watched Kwintone's face as he stared out the window. "Is that why you were meeting Eddie Monday night?"

Kwintone snorted. "Eddie. What a coward."

"Coward? What do you mean?" I twisted in my seat to read his expression better. "About what happened at Oakwood Studios?"

"Puh…lease."

There were so many directions this conversation could go, so many secrets to uncover. I waited to see which way he would head.

Just when I thought he'd clam up, Kwintone tossed his long tresses and spoke again. "A few months ago, I went into the dealership, hoping to confront the famous Car King. Mr. Atlanta Braves Big Shot." He winced. "*Confront* isn't the right word. I just wanted to meet the man and get some answers. See if he even remembered Mom."

"What happened?"

"Mr. Big Shot, the Car King, wasn't there, of course. But Eddie was working that day. He was quite the salesman." A smile flickered across Kwintone's full lips. "I ended up buying my car from him."

I chuckled. "Eddie's a little go-getter."

"We vibed. Started hanging out together. I tried to get information about his dad without making it too obvious."

"Did you get to meet the famous Car King?"

"A few times. But I could never get him alone to really talk, to ask him anything. If he recognized me, or my name, he never let on."

"That's not surprising. From what you've told me, it sounds like he wasn't in touch with your mom after you were born." I glanced at his face; if my words had stung, he was hiding the pain. How many more out-of-wedlock children did this man sire apart from Kwintone and Demi?

Kwintone shut his eyes. "It's hard not to think about that whenever I see him. Whenever I drive by one of his billboards. I don't want to think my father's a jerk, but…"

"Maybe not a complete jerk if he set up that trust fund for you."

"Blood money. Blackmail." Kwintone's face contorted as if in anguish.

"You don't know that." I put a tentative hand on his shoulder. It felt like I was comforting Demi's little brother, not being vulnerable with an arrogant pretender and possible killer. "Have you discussed your suspicions with Eddie?"

"Eddie!" Kwintone spat.

"What did—"

Headlights behind us lit up the car. With a squeal, I reached for the glovebox, where I kept my pepper spray.

"What the—" Kwintone touched something in his pocket.

There was a tap on the glass.

Whipping around toward the driver's window, I blinked into a flashlight's beam, illuminating the face of Detective Paul Ross.

* * *

The police cruiser had eased up behind my car without strobes or sirens, and we'd been so engrossed in our conversation that we hadn't heard the engine or noticed the headlights.

Kwintone's eyes grew wide. He abandoned whatever was in his pocket and put his hands on the dashboard.

I fumbled with the switch to roll down my window, then remembered I had to press the start button to get any of the electronics to work. Detective Ross waited with crossed arms while I lowered the glass.

One of the cats in the back started growling, and another hissed in response.

"Yes, Detective?" I pasted on my sweetest, most innocent smile.

"DeeLo Myer. Thought I'd find you here." Squinting, he leaned into the window, invading our space. "Is that Kwintone Johnson with you?"

Hands still on the dashboard, Kwintone replied, "Yes, sir."

"We need to talk. I guess seeing 'Pecan Point Police Department' on your caller ID sent you into hiding." Detective Ross straightened up. "Both of you, please get out of the car."

I started to ask why, then thought it best to comply.

At least the detective didn't frisk us like on those TV cop shows. Kwintone seemed resigned to it and surprised when it didn't happen.

When we were outside my car, Detective Ross said, "It's about Aiden Green."

Clunk!

The detective put a hand on his holster.

Out of the corner of my eye, I glimpsed a trap door close, its fluorescent ribbon down. "Excuse me, Detective. I have to…"

The detective's mouth dropped. "DeeLo…"

I held up my hand and pointed toward the trap. "A cat…You remember when Lisa and I…"

"You can't…" Perhaps he recalled the times I'd trapped cats for his wife because he didn't stop me from rounding the car, opening the hatch to retrieve a towel, and rushing to the trap to cover the newly captured feline.

After positioning the trap beside the others amid a chorus of yowls, I closed the hatch and dutifully rejoined the detective and Kwintone. "Sorry about that. It's inhumane not to cover them—"

"I remember." Detective Ross's voice was stern, all business.

"So, what were you saying about Aiden Green? Did he wake up?" Maybe the man had identified Kwintone.

"He's dead."

I clasped a hand over my mouth. "Dead?"

Kwintone's eyes grew wide, and his lips formed an O.

"Oh, my God!" My knees wobbled. *When did it happen? What was that sound I heard from the machine?*

Detective Ross fixed his eyes on me. "And what were you doing in his hospital room last night?"

Chapter Twenty-Two

I bit my lip. *Aiden Green is dead?* Had that screeching monitor not been a false alarm after all?

"He died shortly after you left his room." Detective Ross's eyes had not left my face.

"I…" Gulp. *Does he think I had something to do with it?*

"What were you doing in his hospital room?"

"I…I stopped by to see if he was awake. I…" It dawned on me how flimsy my excuse for being in the man's room sounded. What I'd really wanted to find out was whether Kwintone was involved in his attack, and I couldn't very well say that to Detective Ross with Kwintone standing right beside me. And now, my motive for the visit looked suspicious.

The slam of another trap door interrupted us again. Kwintone glanced at me.

I gestured toward the captured feline. "Is it okay if I—"

"Go ahead." Detective Ross shook his head and let out an exasperated puff of air. "But come down to the station tomorrow and make a statement."

"I'll help." Kwintone took a step to follow me.

The detective turned to him with a palm out. "Mr. Johnson, I need you to come with me now."

"Tomorrow would be better." Kwintone's expression was hopeful with a touch of defiance.

"Now." The detective clenched his jaw.

"Detective, that's not…" I felt guilty being allowed to tend to my trapping like a free citizen while Kwintone was about to be detained.

He glared at Detective Ross. "Not without my lawyer."

Detective Ross shrugged and steered Kwintone toward the police car. "Give him a call then. Ask him to meet us there."

I should call Barry. He wasn't a criminal attorney, but he was good at sorting out problems and would give us both valuable legal advice.

Kwintone was on his phone while Detective Ross escorted him to the police car.

By the time I'd covered the trapped cat, they were gone.

I sent Demi a text. "The police have Kwintone."

My phone vibrated moments after I'd pressed Send. "What are you talking about?" she shrieked.

I explained how we'd been trapping at Oakwood Studios again when Detective Ross found us. "He told us Aiden Green is dead."

Demi gasped. "They think Kwintone hurt that man? Does he need to be bailed out?"

"He said he was calling his lawyer."

"Well, that was good thinking. But why did you let them take him?"

I tucked the phone in the crook of my neck while I carried the trap to the car. "You're kidding, right? What was I supposed to do?" We didn't even know for sure that Kwintone was innocent.

"That detective has a crush on you. You could have talked him out of taking Kwintone."

I felt my cheeks flush; fortunately, no one was around to see. "Yeah, right. That would probably get me into more trouble. Demi, he's a married man. With a kid. And I'm dating Barry."

"Well, still… what about Barry? Can't you ask him to bail Kwintone out? I won't be home until tomorrow."

I set down the cage and popped open the back of the SUV. "Kwintone wasn't under arrest, so he might not even need to be bailed out. And besides, he was on the phone with his own lawyer when they left."

"Are you sure about that?" Not waiting for my reply, Demi continued, "I'm calling my brother. Talk to you later, DeeLo."

I stared at my now silent phone. Praying he wasn't with Victoria, I called

Barry. I might be in more trouble than Kwintone was.

Chapter Twenty-Three

Barry's voice was husky when he answered on the third ring, as if he'd been asleep. Alone, I hoped. *He'd better be.*

"Barry, I need your help." I climbed into the driver's seat and locked the doors.

"What's wrong?" He sounded more alert.

I cleared my throat. "I have to make a statement to the police tomorrow."

"DeeLo!" Barry was fully awake now. "What have you done?"

"Nothing. But they think—"

"Where are you?"

"Still at Oakwood Studios. I just finished trapping."

He paused for a moment as if computing what kind of trouble I could have gotten into while trapping at Oakwood Studios. Probably looking at the bedside clock and realizing it was almost midnight. "All right. Come on over, and we'll talk about it."

He must be alone, thank goodness. "Can you come to my place? I have cats in the car, and I need to keep them in the garage overnight."

I could hear him breathing, so he hadn't hung up.

"Please…" I should be applying some feminine wiles, but under the circumstances, it didn't feel right.

"Are you heading home now?"

"Yes, I'm all packed up."

"All right. I'll meet you at your house."

* * *

True to his word, Barry showed up about fifteen minutes after I arrived home. His hair was mussed, and the faded purple T-shirt from the Alzheimer's Walk we did together last year was inside out.

I threw myself into his arms. "Thanks for coming. Sorry to wake you in the middle of the night."

Gently, a bit stiffly, he extricated himself from my embrace. "Tell me what happened."

Was he just sleepy, or did he wish it had been Victoria who woke him up at midnight this time?

We moved to the couch and sat down.

Not leaving anything out, I told him about Kwintone's reappearance, my visit to Aiden Green's hospital room, and Detective Ross's interruption of our trapping.

Barry kneaded his forehead. "DeeLo, why on earth did you go to that man's hospital room?"

"I thought he might be awake. I wanted to ask—"

"That wasn't your place."

"Demi needs to know if Kwintone was involved. Or if he's innocent…"

Barry shook his head. "That's the job of the police. Haven't you learned amateur sleuthing can be hazardous?"

I closed my eyes, remembering my near-death experience last year. But in the end, I had exposed a killer.

"I'm surprised Detective Ross didn't take you to the police station on the spot, instead of trusting you to come by later to make a statement." Barry scrunched his face as if still trying to decipher the detective's reasoning.

"Guess he had his hands full with Kwintone. And he knows how to find me." I smiled, picturing Paul's baffled expression while he watched me tend to the traps. I would never have been that bold with another officer. "He must remember something about TNVR from when I helped his wife catch their ferals."

Barry took off his glasses and wiped them on his shirt. "A bit unconventional, but it's a good sign. He must not think you're dangerous. Or a flight risk."

Manny, who'd been napping on my bookshelf, leaped down and hopped onto my lap. I stroked the soft fur on his big head.

Barry reached a tentative hand toward my cat. Manny sniffed it, then turned his attention back to me. Barry gave up with a shrug. "We need to prepare what you'll say tomorrow. I don't think it's wise to admit you were hoping to interrogate the patient."

"What do you mean by 'interrogate'? I just wanted to ask him a question or two."

"You know what I mean. Sticking your nose where it doesn't belong. Interfering with an investigation. The police don't appreciate that."

I let out a puff of air. "Should I go with the 'good Samaritan wanting to check on the person I helped save'?"

"The less information you volunteer, the better. But whatever you do, don't lie to the police."

I never intended to lie, but sometimes my stories could sound untruthful when I attempted to leave out something irrelevant that could be construed as misleading.

"Just stick to the facts, and don't offer anything unless asked. Was anyone else around?"

"There was a guard outside the room."

Barry raised his eyebrows. "And he let you enter?"

"Well, he'd dozed off, so I didn't ask him." I winced. A detail I'd neglected to mention that now made me sound guilty.

Barry rolled his eyes at the ceiling, as if seeking help from above, then focused back on me. "No one else was in the room?" When I nodded, he continued, "How was Mr. Green while you were there? Awake? Sleeping? In distress?"

"I assumed he was sleeping. He didn't seem to be in any distress. He didn't even move."

"Did you touch him?"

"No."

"Did you touch anything? Say anything to him?"

I shook my head vigorously. "Nothing. As soon as I approached his bed, the monitor started beeping, and the cavalry came running."

"Did anyone speak to you? Ask why you were there?"

"They told me to leave, so I did." I swallowed. *Eventually.*

Barry eyed me. "You didn't stick around? Try to find out what was going on?"

He knew me well. "For a minute. But then I heard one of the nurses talking to the security guard about it being another false alarm." I met his gaze. "When Detective Ross told me Aiden Green was dead, I was absolutely shocked."

Nodding, Barry shifted gears. "So, Kwintone Johnson is alive and well. His car wasn't stolen; he must be the one who drove it away from the scene of the crime. What did he tell you? Why was he there, and what did he see?"

I shrugged. "We hadn't gotten that far yet. Kwintone can be as evasive as Demi." My amateur sleuthing skills needed refinement. Inevitably, I tended to wander off-topic. I'd delved into Demi's paternity mystery instead of trying to find out who assaulted Aiden Green.

Barry narrowed his eyes as if he didn't believe me. "What did you two talk about all evening?"

"It's complicated." Before I could catch myself, the words of Demi and Kwintone had slipped from my lips, and I stifled a chuckle despite the seriousness of our discussion. "Besides TNVR? The search for his father."

Barry peered at me over his glasses.

I explained about meeting Eddie Fenton and noticing his resemblance to Kwintone. Apparently, Kwintone's research had also led him to Eddie and the possibility that they shared a father.

"*The* Edward Fenton? The Car King might be Demi's father?"

"Looks like it."

Barry pushed his glasses back up his nose. "I think Edward Fenton was once a client of ours. My father set up a trust for him over twenty years ago. Fenton was a big baseball star before he became *The Car King.*"

"A trust?" *Kwintone's trust fund?*

"I believe so. Victoria might have taken over the account. I remember her mentioning a meeting last year with the Car King. Might have been a real estate deal, though, not the trust fund."

"Do we still have the paperwork?"

Barry's eyes widened. "DeeLo, that file doesn't concern you. Let's talk about what you're going to say to the police tomorrow."

"Okay." *But would it hurt to run a quick search later?*

"So, Kwintone said he met with Eddie Fenton. Did either of them see Aiden Green?"

"I don't know. As I said, we didn't get that far. Detective Ross showed up and interrupted our conversation."

"Well, I guess the police will sort that out with Kwintone. And I imagine they've talked to Eddie and the other people at Oakwood Studios."

I would have liked to be a fly on the wall while Kwintone made his statement. Would he be truthful with the police? Or would his lawyer advise him not to answer any questions?

"What do you plan to say if they ask you about the night Aiden Green was stabbed?"

I sat up straighter, which caused Manny to lift his head. "I've already made my statement. That night, at the scene."

"But you didn't tell them everything, did you?"

I lowered my eyelashes. "I told them what was relevant…"

Barry gave me that scathing look again, like a teacher about to issue a reprimand. "After Kwintone makes his statement, they might have more questions. What are you going to tell them?"

"I—"

"I suggest the truth." He reached out and pushed a strand of hair away from my face. "The whole truth."

"But Demi—"

"Let Demi take responsibility for her own actions, and you take care of yours."

I bit my lip. He was right. But I hoped the detective would only ask about my visit to Green's hospital room.

"Is there anything else you can remember about either night? Anything you haven't told me?"

My phone lay on the coffee table in front of us. I picked it up and scrolled to the photo I had taken in Aiden's room. "There was a whiteboard hanging on the wall with notes. I snapped a picture in case something on it might prove valuable later. Like maybe the names of nurses I could talk to…" I zoomed in on the photo and tilted the phone toward Barry.

He squinted at the screen. "Looks like a list of nurses with their hours and phone numbers. And a couple of squiggles that might have something to do with administering his medications."

I pointed at the top entry. "Evangeline is an unusual name, don't you think?"

Barry shrugged. "I've never known one, except from the Longfellow poem."

"There's a nurse named Evangeline at the Pecan Point Memory Care facility. She takes care of Mom sometimes. I wonder if she moonlights at the hospital?" I set my phone back on the coffee table.

"I suppose it's possible. Some employees are only part-time, so they have to work other jobs."

I stroked Manny's coat and kissed his head. "How about we visit Mom tomorrow and see what we can find out?"

Manny's answer was a purr.

Barry groaned. "DeeLo…"

I tugged at his T-shirt. "Do you know you put that on inside out?"

He looked down. "Oh…"

"It's okay. Just take it off." I pulled it over his head.

Twisting away, he rose, then bent and gave me a peck on the forehead. "I'd better go. I know you have to get up early to take the cats to the clinic."

Stung, I persisted and touched his arm. "That's hours from now."

He kept moving like he was late for an appointment. Reluctantly, I followed him to the door. "But you'll go to the police station with me tomorrow, won't you?"

"Of course." He gave me the kind of goodnight kiss he might give his grandmother. "See you at the office." And with that, he was gone.

Chapter Twenty-Four

I hauled the cats into the LifeSaver clinic and set their traps one by one against the wall. One kitty was yowling at the top of his lungs, in contrast to the other two, who were deadly silent, traumatized... like they were about to face a police interrogation.

I set my paperwork on the counter and asked the receptionist, "Do we still have credit on the Oakwood Studios account?"

"Oh, yes." She grinned. "In fact, Zach Kirkpatrick added another two thousand to the grant to cover *any* cats or dogs in Pecan County, not just the ferals from Oakwood Studios."

My eyebrows shot up. "That was certainly generous of him."

She took my paperwork and thumbed through it. "Yes, I heard he's running for Pecan County commissioner. My grandparents live in Pecan Point, and I told them they should vote for him."

"Thanks. They won't regret it." I smiled. "Pecan County needs someone like him." *Zach's a better politician than I thought.*

On my way out, I snapped a photo of the clinic and posted it on Zach's Instagram with the caption: BOC candidate Zach Kirkpatrick supports spay/neuter assistance for Pecan County pets.

* * *

When I arrived at the office, I checked in with Barry, who was sitting at his desk. "Oh, good morning, DeeLo. Do you mind following up on these?" He handed me a list of wealth management clients who were missing documents.

So much for having time to search for the Car King's file. If it was one of Victoria's, it might not even be in our database.

"Sure, boss." I glanced at the client names. "You're still coming with me to the police station today, right?"

He looked up and adjusted his glasses. "Of course. I said I would. What time?"

Detective Ross had texted me a reminder this morning while I was at the LifeSaver. "The detective won't be in until this afternoon. He suggested two o'clock. Does that work for you?"

"Any time after lunch is fine."

"Sounds good." I retreated to my cubicle and texted Catherine Foster, asking her to pick up the cats, hoping I was only delegating the task on the side of caution. She didn't work, so she was usually available and well-equipped to house them overnight and release them the next day. After getting her affirmative reply, I plunged into my assignment, trying not to stress about the impending police interview.

* * *

Demi called during my lunch hour. I was nibbling a sandwich and updating Zach's other social media channels with news about the Oakwood Studios grant to the LifeSaver to benefit Pecan County pets, trying to stay busy and not think about the police interview.

"Did you speak to Kwintone?" I asked.

"You were right," she replied. "They didn't hold him."

"What was his story? Does Kwintone know Aiden Green? Did he meet with him Monday night?"

"He couldn't talk."

Why was I not surprised? "And you didn't press him?"

Her long pause indicated she knew more than she was telling me. Maybe. "Demi..."

"He said we'd catch up later."

"When?"

"I thought we'd come to your place tonight. I told Kwintone about our Fettuccine Alfredo, and he offered to bring the wine."

I straightened in my chair. "You didn't think to ask me first?"

"Oh, sorry. Do you and Barry have plans?"

Not yet. And foremost, I hoped I wouldn't be staying on as a guest of the county after meeting with Detective Ross this afternoon. "I'm taking Manny by the memory care home to visit Mom." *And talk to Evangeline about Aiden Green.*

"Well, how long will that take? You're not going to eat dinner there."

"Why don't I call you later, and we'll figure something out?" All I could focus on was my statement to Detective Ross—and not screwing it up.

"Got it. Barry might make you a better offer, and I'll have to question Kwintone all by myself."

Demi was taking advantage of my curiosity, and she knew it. I'd have to figure out a way to get some answers out of Kwintone.

* * *

Barry wasn't in his office when I was ready to head for the police station. I turned to the intern who was playing receptionist this week. "Where's Barry?"

She smiled cheerfully from her almost paper-free desk. "He left for a lunch meeting about an hour ago. With Victoria, I think."

Lunch meeting? With Victoria? It was the first I'd heard of those plans. "Thanks," I muttered through pinched lips.

"No problem." With a swish of her long, brown ponytail, she smacked her gum and returned to painting her nails.

I sent Barry a text. "Just a reminder that we have to be at the police station at two." I punctuated it with a heart emoji.

Dots appeared.

I watched, waiting for the response.

Then nothing.

I was about to drop the phone into my purse when the reply came: "Lunch running late. Meet you there."

As I headed out alone for the police station, I hoped Barry wouldn't stand me up again, but I had a sinking feeling he might.

* * *

Barry's SUV wasn't in the parking lot when I arrived at the police station. I was a few minutes early, so maybe he would still show up. I sat for a moment, taking deep breaths, checked my phone again, then eased out of the vehicle and made my way toward the one-story, gray brick building.

The tiny lobby had straight-backed metal chairs lined against the wall and a gray tile floor that hadn't been swept lately. A uniformed policeman stood in a corner, taking a report from a balding, middle-aged businessman who reeked of cigar smoke.

A desk officer shuffled papers behind a plexiglass barrier. She looked up when I approached and spoke into a thin microphone. "May I help you?"

"DeeLo Myer to see Detective Paul Ross."

She consulted a calendar. "Oh yes. He's ready for you." She hit a buzzer that unlocked the gray metal door off to the side.

"I..." Where was Barry?

My phone dinged with another text. Shuddering, I read: "Meeting still going, so I can't make it. Just remember what we talked about last night, and you'll do great!" He followed his feeble excuse with a smiley-face emoji.

I would have loved to tell him what to do with that stupid smiley face.

Chapter Twenty-Five

Maybe because I was mad at Barry, Detective Ross appeared especially handsome sitting behind his big metal desk. Clean-shaven, sandy hair neatly trimmed… and those emerald eyes had always mesmerized me.

"Thank you for coming in, Ms. Myer."

So, we were back to a business relationship.

"You said you wanted to see me." I sat down in the chair across from the desk. "Did you get the information you needed from Kwintone Johnson?"

He pressed his lips together. "DeeLo, we're not here to talk about Kwintone Johnson. I need you to tell me about your visit to Aiden Green's hospital room on Wednesday evening."

My heart pounded, and I tried to remember my conversation with Barry last night, which only made me angrier that he'd stood me up today. Having lunch with Victoria had been more important than helping me stay out of jail.

"DeeLo?" the detective prompted, pencil poised over a clean sheet of paper.

I inhaled deeply, then let the breath out too fast. "You know that my niece and I saved Aiden Green's life. We're the ones who found him and called the paramedics."

Detective Ross just stared at me. Did he believe I could transform from savior to killer in only a few days?

Under the spell of those deep green eyes, I rambled on. "I wanted to see how Mr. Green was doing. It's hard to get information from the hospital staff if you're not a relative."

"Do you know how Mr. Green made his living?" The detective's eyes had not left my face.

I flashed back to our conversation a few days ago in the Oakwood Studios parking lot. "Neuroscience Laboratories." I couldn't deny knowing the man did scientific tests on cats; I'd already tipped my hand. Did Detective Ross think my concern for cats gave me a motive to assault the lab's CEO? "But how does that—?"

"Was that what you planned to talk to him about when you went to his room?"

"No!"

My forceful denial must have gotten through to the detective because he shifted his gaze from my face to his paper and scribbled something.

"I mean, I'm against animal testing, but I'm not a radical activist. I've never participated in a protest and certainly wouldn't resort to violence."

"Okay." His pencil hovered over the paper. "So, the only reason you went to Mr. Green's room was to check on his well-being?"

He's not buying it. I averted my eyes, embarrassed at how flimsy that excuse sounded. "Well, I also wanted to ask who hurt him." I recrossed my legs. "Isn't that what you've been trying to find out, too?" Demi would have a fit that I was bringing this up and perhaps giving the police the idea that Kwintone was involved.

"And you didn't think the police were doing their job?"

"I thought I could help. Some people don't like talking to the police."

"Do you have a theory about who might have stabbed Mr. Green?" Detective Ross was staring into my eyes again.

"No." I'd had my suspicions at first, but I must not have believed Kwintone was a killer, or I wouldn't have invited him out trapping with me again at night in a lonely parking lot. "I just wanted to know what happened to the man I helped save."

Detective Ross nodded and wrote some more. Did he believe me? His expression was unreadable.

"How did Mr. Green die? It sounds like you don't think he succumbed to his injuries." Jill had told me Aiden was out of intensive care and seemed to be recovering, which was why I thought I'd have a chance to talk to him.

"We're investigating."

"Do you suspect foul play? Did something happen at the hospital?" Why else would the detective be questioning me about my visit?

"DeeLo, you know I can't tell you."

"Well," I tried. "I—"

"Tell me about going to his room. Did you ask the guard if you could enter?"

I swallowed. "The guard had dozed off, so I didn't disturb him."

Detective Ross cast his eyes upward and let out a puff of air, reacting the same way Barry had last night.

"I knew pretty quickly that I wouldn't be able to speak to Mr. Green," I continued. "He appeared to be sleeping."

"Did you touch anything?"

"No. As soon as I took a step toward his bed, the monitor started beeping. Before I could do or say anything, hospital staff came running, and a nurse told me to leave."

"And did you?"

"Well… I was concerned. Wanted to make sure he was okay and that I hadn't done anything inadvertently to cause the monitor to go off. Then I heard a different nurse tell the security guard it was probably another false alarm." Glancing down, I realized I had been gripping the edge of the desk and let go. "Apparently, it had happened before?"

Detective Ross shrugged. Maybe that was news to him. "So, the commotion woke up the guard?"

"I guess so. He was awake when I left."

"And did he come into the room to see what was going on?"

"Maybe. It had grown so crowded I couldn't tell you who all was in there."

The detective wrote some more.

I tried to peek at what he was writing, but I was too far away, and the angle was off.

"Did you see anyone else in the hallway when you arrived? Pass anyone on the way to his room?"

I replayed the scene in my head. "There was a food service worker delivering meals. But he didn't come into Mr. Green's room."

The detective nodded and wrote. "Anyone else?"

"Oh, I ran into Lisa when I got off the elevator."

"Lisa?" His face had lost some of its color.

"Your wife."

Detective Ross still seemed confused. Maybe his wife hadn't told him about her trip to the hospital.

"Yeah, she'd been visiting her grandmother. How's she doing, by the way? Lisa seemed worried."

"Her grandmother?" His lip curled as if he didn't believe me.

How much do they communicate? "You didn't know your wife's grandmother was in the hospital?"

"Lisa was with our son last night. Her grandmother died two years ago." The look he gave me insinuated I was lying.

"But maybe—"

"No, the other one died when Lisa was twelve." He twirled his pencil.

Then what was Lisa Ross doing at the hospital? "I know what I heard. She said she was visiting her grandmother. Maybe yours?"

Detective Ross stared past me, focusing on a point behind my head.

I turned to see what had fascinated him, but it was a bare wall. I twisted back around and faced him. "Do you have any more questions for me, Detective?"

Shaking his head as if awakening from a trance, he set down his pencil. "No."

Chapter Twenty-Six

Feeling lighter, relieved from my fear of incarceration, I almost skipped out the door. Still, I pondered what had just happened. Why did Lisa lie? And would her lies impact her husband's investigation? I decided not to go back to the office. Let Barry worry whether I made it out of the police interview a free woman. Besides, he probably assumed I'd gone to pick up the cats at the clinic; no use telling him I'd asked Catherine to do it.

Sitting in my car before leaving the station's parking lot, I called the Pecan Point Memory Care facility and inquired if Evangeline was on duty.

"Evangeline Powers?" asked the woman who answered.

I'd never known her surname. "Is there another Evangeline?"

"No… She's here until five. Would you like to speak to her?"

"No, thanks. I'll see her when I get there."

I hung up and sent Demi a text: "If you and Kwintone still want to come over for dinner, I should be home by six."

Next, I drove home to fetch Manny. As soon as I brought out the cat carrier, his eyes grew wide, and he leaped off the bookshelf.

"Manny!" I cried, trying to intercept him as he dashed for my bedroom. His instinct was to hide under the queen-size bed, right in the center where I couldn't reach him without moving furniture.

I managed to head him off before he made it to his destination. Scooping up the cat, I stroked his furry body and murmured, "You know you like to visit Mom. I'm sorry, I have to put you in that carrier to get you there."

My reassuring words didn't stop Manny from squirming and resisting my efforts to wedge him into the carrier. He splayed his four legs across the opening and dug his claws into the plastic sides. After thwarting several escape attempts, I managed to stuff all his limbs inside. He wailed like a torture victim as I latched the door and lugged the carrier to the car.

His howls didn't cease during the entire ride to the memory care home.

I peeked at him through the holes in the carrier as I drove. The frightened cat stared back at me, pupils wide, his gold irises reduced to a thin rim. "Manny, you always enjoy seeing Mom and her friends. Lots of people to pet you."

His answer was a plaintive meow.

When I pulled the bouncing carrier out of the car, Manny continued his caterwauling. I bumped into a middle-aged man passing through the parking lot. "Sorry," I muttered.

He eyed me quizzically. "Do you need some help, ma'am?"

"No, thanks, I'm good."

"What's in there?" He peered into the carrier as Manny let out another wail. "You know, the vet's office is down the road. This is a senior center."

I straightened and smiled. "Manny is a therapy cat."

"Yeah, right. And my dog's a magician." Shaking his head, an amused smile on his face, the man continued to his car.

I headed inside and, with a nod to the woman at the front desk, made my way to my mother's room.

"DeeLo! You brought Manny."

As soon as I freed Manny from his carrier, he jumped onto Mom's lap and transformed back into his usual lovebug self. Her face was radiant as she stroked the cat's silky black fur.

Even though my mother suffered from Alzheimer's, she still remembered my name and my cat's. Something to be grateful for.

I gazed around her room, making a quick visual check for her most cherished belongings. Her spoon collection on its wooden rack appeared intact. Her books and rows of ceramic elephants seemed undisturbed on their shelf. Occasionally, something went missing, but overall, security was good. "Mom, have you seen Evangeline today?"

"Who?" Mom often struggled with staff names.

"Evangeline Powers, the nurse who teaches you yoga."

My mother knitted her brow. "Yoga?"

"Don't you still do yoga? I thought you went a couple of times a week."

"I do?" She twisted her mouth in concentration. "Maybe."

"Anyway, have you seen Evangeline today?"

"Angie's not a nurse."

Angie? "No, Evangeline. Maybe she's a nursing assistant. Your yoga instructor."

Mom got a faraway look in her eyes as she continued to pet Manny. "Who?" Before I could try again to jog her memory, she added, "She loves cats. Tell her Manny is here. Do you know who brought him?"

Blinking back the tears that came whenever I thought about how this horrible disease was slowly taking my mother, I bent over and kissed her forehead, then gave Manny a pat. "Will you two be okay for a few minutes? I'm going to find Evangeline."

"She might be at the hospital." Mom kept stroking the cat's fur. "Thank you for coming, DeeLo. You can leave Manny with me while you go on your date."

I closed the door to her room in case Manny decided to wander.

* * *

I located Evangeline in the courtyard, holding a Styrofoam cup of black coffee and puffing on a cigarette. Not exactly the healthy habits I'd expect of a yoga instructor. Her scraggly, above-the-shoulder, light brown hair was heavily streaked with gray, and her craggy face made her look older than she probably was.

"Evangeline." I sidled up next to her. "How have you been?"

She dropped the cigarette into the almost empty coffee cup and coughed. "Same old."

"Still teaching those yoga classes for the residents? My mom loves them." *Well, what she can remember of them.*

"For real?" Evangeline smiled, revealing a missing incisor. She wrinkled her already wrinkled forehead. "Diana Myer is your mom, right?"

I nodded. "And I'm DeeLo."

"Did you bring Manny today?" Evangeline's eyes swept the area around me, perhaps in search of the cat.

I jabbed a thumb behind me. "He's in Mom's room."

"I'll have to stop in before I leave. I love that kitty, and my landlord won't let me have pets. Maybe in the next place."

"Moving soon?"

"End of next week." She grinned. "Getting out of Dodge."

"Leaving Pecan Point?"

She pantomimed a swaying palm tree. "Headed to Florida."

"Oh, I'm sorry to hear that. Mom will miss your yoga classes."

She shrugged. "It's been a good gig."

"Are you getting off soon?" I asked even though I already knew the answer.

She glanced at her watch. "Five o'clock. Can't come soon enough."

"Do you get to go home and relax, or do you have to go to your other job?"

"My other job?" Evangeline tossed the Styrofoam cup into a trash can as we walked toward the door to the interior.

"I thought you also worked at the Pecan Point Hospital." I could still picture her name on the whiteboard in Aiden Green's room.

She scrunched her face. "What gave you that idea? This job is plenty. I'm here six days a week."

"Oh." I backtracked. "I just figured…"

"I used to pick up an extra shift there every now and then, but… Why?"

I tilted my head to get a better read of her body language. "Do you know a man named Aiden Green? CEO of Neuroscience Laboratories."

She stiffened, and her hand on the sliding glass lever began to tremble. The door froze in its tracks. "Aiden Green?"

I studied her face. No way she would react so viscerally if she didn't know the man.

"He's my ex-husband. What about him?"

Ex-husband? Not what I was expecting. "Did you know he was in the hospital?"

She sniffed. "The morgue now."

I couldn't tell if the emotion on her face was regret or something else. "You were listed as one of his contacts on the whiteboard in his room. It was mostly nurses, so I just assumed…"

"Yeah, he kept me as his emergency contact. I don't know why. Too lazy to change it, I guess. No one else cares a whit about him. Lucky for me, I'm still his beneficiary. That's how I'm getting out of here."

I flinched. The police might view being a beneficiary as a motive.

She contorted her face into a cross between a prune and a snarl. "How did *you* know Aiden? Were you one of his—"

Before Evangeline could finish her question, the nursing home director stuck her head through the partially open door. "Oh, there you are, Powers." She slid the glass door the rest of the way open. "Can you come to the conference room? We're having a quick staff meeting."

Evangeline gave me a cursory nod and followed her boss inside.

Trying to decide if I'd learned anything useful, I closed the door to the courtyard and headed back to Mom and Manny. It seemed like my sleuthing was generating more questions than answers.

Chapter Twenty-Seven

Word had gotten out that Manny was in the building, and when I returned to my mother's room, it was like a petting zoo for senior citizens. Mom let her friends take turns caressing Manny, and he tolerated their handling like the therapy cat he'd been when his former owner used to bring him here.

Among the visitors was Vaughn Henry Connors, Victoria's father. I had nothing against the old man, but seeing him prompted me to check around the corner for Victoria lurking nearby. She claimed her father was allergic to cats, and she blew a gasket whenever she saw him reach for Manny. I'd never observed the old man suffer any adverse symptoms from handling Manny, so perhaps the allergy was only in Victoria's mind. Otherwise, the staff would have made an effort to keep him away from the therapy cat.

Mom passed Manny to a scrawny woman with Coke-bottle glasses and looked up at me. "Did you get the bad man?"

I flashed a sheepish grin as murmurs arose from her visitors and they focused their attention on me. How was I supposed to answer that?

"Not yet, Mom." I patted her shoulder.

"Have you met my daughter DeeLo?" Beaming at her friends, Mom stretched an arm toward me. "She's come to take Manny back to the bookstore."

Not correcting my mother, not wanting to dredge up memories of what happened to Manny's former owner, I pried my cat from the stick-like arms of a wizened lady in a wheelchair. "Manny will be back soon," I assured her.

Fortunately, the cat went into his carrier with much less fuss than before.

Even though he was a perfect gentleman around the residents, he probably craved some quiet time after an hour or so of being manhandled. And maybe he didn't want to ruin his image by being a brat in front of his admirers.

****

When I got home and freed Manny from his carrier, I straightened the place and took inventory of my refrigerator.

I texted Demi. "If you want Fettuccine Alfredo, pick up some heavy cream on your way over. And jalapenos."

In a moment came the reply. "No jalapenos."

I texted back. "Shrimp?"

"Chicken." She followed with three exclamation points and an emoji of a bird that looked more like a turkey than a chicken.

I smiled to myself. We'd both modified Mom's recipe but disagreed on the added ingredients. Since Demi had promised to cook and was buying the ingredients, we'd have to go with her version.

I ran the vacuum cleaner over the living room carpet to get rid of the daily accumulation of black cat hair. Fortunately, the stain from Demi's last wine spill was barely visible.

Manny perched on the bookshelf, where he had an unobstructed view of the room.

"Keep an eye on Kwintone," I told my cat. "We need to find out what he was really up to that night." Manny was an excellent judge of character.

The vroom from the downshift of a turbocharged engine announced my guests' arrival. I peered out the window just as Kwintone emerged from the red Mustang. He pecked something on his phone and then slipped it into his pocket. Reaching behind the driver's seat, he retrieved a brown paper sack.

Demi got out of the passenger side, handbag slung over her shoulder, and a white plastic grocery bag in each hand. She shut the car door with her hip and joined Kwintone on the walkway to my steps. Laughing and chatting amicably, the tall, newfound siblings had a similar gait and flair.

I opened the door before they could ring the bell and pointed to my niece's bulging shopping bags. "Looks like you got more than cream."

"Wanted to make sure you have everything I need." Demi pushed past me en route to the kitchen.

Kwintone stopped on the threshold. "Should we take our shoes off?"

I wish. I glanced back at my freshly vacuumed, light beige carpet. "Nice of you to offer, but it's not necessary. Demi never does."

Kwintone came the rest of the way inside and held the bag toward me. "I brought a Cabernet and a Chardonnay. Do you have a corkscrew?"

"What kind of hostess would I be if I didn't?" I closed the front door and led him to the kitchen, where Demi was already rattling pans and assembling ingredients.

Kwintone set the wine on the counter, and I located a corkscrew for him. "I'll get some glasses."

I headed into the dining room and selected three crystal goblets from my wedding collection in the china cabinet. When I returned, Kwintone had opened the Cabernet and was about to uncork the Chardonnay.

I put a hand on his wrist. "I have some cold Chardonnay in the fridge. Why don't we drink that while yours is chilling?" I brought out an open bottle and filled one of the glasses. "Who wants white?"

"Red for me." Demi unwrapped a package of fresh mushrooms.

Kwintone picked up one of the empty glasses and tilted it toward me. "I'll have the white, but only half a glass." He watched me pour and held up his hand when I'd reached his invisible mark. "I'm driving."

I searched Kwintone's face for a hint of smugness, a jab at my infamous DUI mistake. But if it was there, he hid it well. I turned to my niece. "Demi, what can we do to help?"

She waved the chef's knife at me. "Pour me a glass of Cab, and then go sit down. I have everything under control."

"What about a salad?" Kwintone set a glass of Cabernet on the counter beside her. "Can I help with that?"

"Shoo." Demi flicked her wrist at us and carried the mushrooms to the sink to wash. "DeeLo, I know you want to interrogate Kwintone."

I winced and cut my eyes toward her half-brother, wondering how he'd react. *Interrogate* was such a strong word. Why did people keep using it with me? I just wanted to find out what happened the night Aiden Green got stabbed.

Chapter Twenty-Eight

Kwintone and I settled on opposite ends of the couch. As we sipped our wine, Manny watched us from his perch.

Kwintone pointed. "Did you know there's a cat on your bookshelf?"

"Oh, really?" I glanced at Manny, gold eyes glowing, body still as a taxidermy specimen.

"Is it real?" Kwintone flinched as Manny blinked. "Oh, my God, it's real."

I shrugged. "Manny was raised in a bookstore. He feels most comfortable sleeping among books."

"He's staring at me."

"He's checking you out. Manny is an excellent judge of character." I cupped the cool goblet in my hand.

Kwintone took another sip of wine. "Well, those gold eyes give me the creeps."

Like a ninja, Manny leaped from the bookshelf and sauntered over to the couch, bushy black tail in the air. He sniffed Kwintone's athletic shoes and then the leg of his khaki pants.

Kwintone set his glass on a coaster and bent to stroke Manny's large head. "Hey, buddy."

Manny sniffed his hand, mouth slightly open, then head-butted it to encourage more petting. No growling, no hissing.

Really, Manny? "I guess he thinks you're okay."

Manny crouched, then jumped into Kwintone's lap. I watched for his reaction—the moment of truth. Was he a cat person? Would he recoil?

Although slightly startled, Kwintone adapted quickly and ran a hand along Manny's spine. With the other hand, he pointed to Manny's ear. "Why does your cat have an ear tip? He's obviously not feral."

"He was born in a feral colony but got injured as a kitten, so the woman who found him—the bookstore owner—brought him inside to heal. He decided he preferred living indoors."

"How did *you* end up with him?"

"His owner died."

"Aw." Kwintone scratched the cat's chin. "Sorry, buddy."

"She was murdered." I hadn't meant to blurt that out. No need to add that I'd found her body on my first night doing community service.

"What?" Kwintone dropped his hand from Manny's chin.

"DeeLo!" called Demi from the kitchen. "Where's your nutmeg?"

I set down my wine and rose. *Good timing, Demi.* I headed for the kitchen and the enticing aroma of sautéing garlic.

Demi clattered around in a sea of pots and cutting boards in various stages of food preparation. Bacon sizzled in a small frying pan on one burner, the garlic in a larger pan on another. Water had begun to boil in the spaghetti pot. Sliced mushrooms lined the cutting board, awaiting their turn to join the sauce. She dumped a cup of diced chicken into the pan with the garlic, which sputtered as it hit the hot mixture.

"Smells good." I inhaled the aromatic blend. "Sure you don't need help?" I located the nutmeg in a cabinet and brought it to her.

"Thanks." She took the spice bottle from me and set it beside the stove. "No, go see what you can find out."

So, this was her plan? I'd assumed Kwintone had already told her everything. But maybe she'd tried and failed to get him to talk, and now it was my turn.

"Manny seems to like your brother."

Demi sprinkled nutmeg and herbs onto the chicken. "Of course he does. He likes everyone."

I lowered my voice. "Except murderers."

"Yeah…" She winced. "But Kwintone isn't a murderer."

"As far as we know," I said over my shoulder on my way back to the living room. I wanted to believe that.

Kwintone was still petting Manny when I returned to the couch. He looked up. "Does Demi need any help?"

"She says she has everything under control." I sat down and picked up my glass. "By the way, how did it go at the police station the other night? Did your lawyer make it?"

Kwintone smiled, showing the tooth gap that reminded me so much of Eddie. "You see that I'm not locked up."

"What did the detective ask you?"

"He found one of my business cards in the parking lot of Oakwood Studios and wanted to know how it got there. I told him I created some campaign brochures for Zach Kirkpatrick, the property manager. I gave Zach a stack of my cards to pass around the office in case anyone else was interested in my services."

"And Detective Ross bought it?"

Kwintone's nostrils flared. "Why wouldn't he? It's the truth."

"What else did the detective ask you?"

Manny lifted his head and stared accusingly at Kwintone, perhaps because the neck massage had stopped.

"Did he ask if you met with Aiden Green?"

"He did, but my lawyer advised me not to answer any more questions."

"Did you?"

The familiar cocky expression was back. "Did I answer more questions? Or did I meet Aiden Green?"

"Was Aiden Green the person you left to meet on Monday night?" I patted my lap, beckoning Manny, who left Kwintone and crept across the couch to me.

"I told you it was Eddie Fenton."

"You met in the parking lot?"

"No, we met in an office building next to the Oakwood Studios sound-stage."

I had to adjust my mental picture of this clandestine rendezvous. An office sounded like a less sinister location than a parking lot. And maybe the sedans I'd seen parked behind the soundstage weren't connected to whoever met with Green. "But Aiden must have been there too. Wasn't he the one who called you?" I rubbed Manny's head as he settled on my lap. I flashed back to that fateful night when Demi and I followed the ringing phone to the fallen body.

"Green was there." Brow furrowed, Kwintone took a sip of wine. "But he didn't call me."

My breath caught. *Then why was that number in your call log?* "What did you meet about?"

Kwintone set down his glass and fingered his thick mane of hair. "Eddie was using me to help him set a trap."

Chapter Twenty-Nine

"DeeLo, can you set the table?" Demi called from the kitchen before I could ask Kwintone to explain about Eddie's trap. "Dinner's almost ready."

Kwintone shrugged. "You heard the boss."

Just when I was making headway. I rose and led him into the dining room.

We stood in front of the hutch while I handed him three china plates and counted out utensils from the silverware chest. Laying Irish linen napkins beside the plates, I admired how the flecks of gold in the cloth picked up the gold on the rims of the bone china.

"Nice stuff." Kwintone set the plates on the table. "Expecting royalty?"

"Wedding gifts," I replied, my voice more bitter than intended. Memories arose of compiling my bridal registry with Desiree and Demi since my fiancé couldn't be bothered. One of many red flags I'd ignored. "Might as well get some use out of them."

"I guess the marriage didn't take?" Kwintone glanced at me with a faint smile.

I needed to stop mentioning that my china, crystal, and silverware were wedding gifts, as the conversation inevitably gravitated to my failed marriage. And the lying, cheating jerk I'd almost managed to forget. I just needed to reinvent myself as someone who would purchase these beautiful items for herself. *Because I'm worth it.*

With a deep sigh, I placed a fork onto a napkin. "No. I tried, but the marriage didn't take." *Interesting way to put it.*

Kwintone nodded. "Maybe it was for the best. Demi says you've hit the jackpot."

He was referring to Barry, of course. Although the two had never met, Kwintone had undoubtedly heard Demi sing praises about our relationship, which was infinitely more stable than any of hers. And Barry had provided advice about community service as a solution to the speeding ticket, so he was a semi-hero in Kwintone's eyes. Unfortunately, I wasn't swimming in confidence anymore about my future with Barry, so Kwintone's remark didn't reassure me.

I called to Demi, "Should I fill the water glasses?"

Her response came in an equally raised voice. "Someone can refill my wine."

"I'll do it." Kwintone laid the last napkin on the table and headed into the kitchen.

In a moment, he returned with a crystal pitcher of ice water.

I took it from him and filled a glass. "You were telling me about your meeting with Eddie Fenton. And how he was using you to set a trap for Aiden Green. What kind of trap?"

Kwintone sighed. "The cats."

Pitcher poised over a glass, I stopped pouring. "The cats? What cats?"

Kwintone took the pitcher from my hand and set it on the table. "You know about Neuroscience Laboratories? Where Green ... worked."

I nodded. "They do neurological tests on animals. Mostly cats. Medical research." Trembling with revulsion, I recalled those photos circulating in petitions from animal rights groups—pictures of drills penetrating the skulls of innocent cats.

"Eddie is a big animal advocate," Kwintone was saying. "Radical with a capital R. He was in a protest at the lab a couple of years ago that turned violent—broken windows, destroyed equipment, and a security guard beaten into critical condition. A lot of the protesters went to jail, but the Car King bailed Eddie out, got him off with a slap on the wrist, and the arrest has been expunged from his record. Eddie's dad has connections all over the state."

Jill had told me about the protest that had happened long before I moved to Pecan Point. From reading Eddie's social media posts, I wasn't surprised he'd been involved. "I gather there's no love lost between Eddie Fenton and Aiden Green, if only philosophically."

"That's an understatement." Kwintone pulled out a chair and sat down. I did the same. "Green didn't know Eddie from a cockroach on the lab floor, but Eddie has been keeping tabs on Neuro Labs ever since the protest. Last year, the company applied for a grant from an animal advocacy foundation to change their testing procedures so they don't have to use cats. They got the money, and there was a big news story about their progressive approach to research."

Kwintone may have been talking about Jill's story. Perhaps others were written as well.

"But they never stopped using cats. According to Eddie, Neuro Labs never implemented the new procedures. If they even existed. Eddie thinks their whole grant application was a fraud."

"How does Eddie know?" Perhaps Eddie and Jill had the same sources.

"He's kept in touch with some of the lab workers who look after the animals, ones who don't agree with the testing. Spies, I guess Green would call them."

"What does all that have to do with *you* setting a trap for Aiden Green?"

Kwintone drummed his fingers against his water glass. "Neuro Labs used to get their cats from the local animal shelter. But about a year ago, the old director retired—or died, maybe—and a new chick from somewhere up north—Wisconsin, I think—took his place. She won't give Green any animals."

Sandra Larson. *Good for her.*

"But why did Eddie think *you* could help?" As I spoke, it dawned on me. "Wait. From TNVR? He thought you could trap some 'extra' feral cats?" I used air quotes to emphasize "extra," my voice shaking with outrage. "Is that what this is about?" I could have been a part of this scheme. If Kwintone had behaved more responsibly that night, if he'd driven a bigger car, I'd have assigned him the trip to the spay/neuter clinic. And he might have taken the cats to a laboratory instead of the LifeSaver.

Kwintone placed a hand on my shoulder, which was tight with tension. "Of course, Eddie didn't want that. He was just baiting Green, seeing if he'd admit that he still tortured cats in the name of science."

"So, Eddie wanted you to *pretend* to negotiate with Aiden Green about selling him cats? You weren't *really* going to give him any?" My heart kept pounding.

"Something like that."

"And did he take the bait?"

A crash sounded from the kitchen.

"Dinner's ready," called Demi.

Chapter Thirty

My hands shook as I carried the Italian pottery serving bowl of steaming Fettuccine Alfredo from the kitchen to the dining room table. The noise we'd heard happened when Demi was rummaging for a serving dish, and a pot fell out of the cabinet.

Demi followed me to the dining room with a large green salad, and Kwintone brought the wine.

"Smells as good as Leonardo's," said Kwintone. "Demi, Girl, who knew you could cook?"

As I set the dish on the table and sat down, I couldn't stop thinking about Aiden Green and his research. *Poor cats.* I felt bad enough trapping them, keeping them locked up and famished overnight, then taking them to a strange place where they were anesthetized, operated on, and their ears were snipped. But at least their torment was short-lived, and soon they were returned to familiar territory, vaccinated against deadly diseases, and free from the cycle of bearing litter after litter, watching their babies fall victim to predators or starve to death. But to think I could have sent them to a worse fate: a laboratory where they were maimed, poisoned, and subject 24/7 to cruel, painful experiments, after which they were discarded to die. "You never seriously considered selling those cats to Neuro Labs?" I eyed Kwintone, remembering when Demi told me he'd bragged about making money from community service. Whose side was he really on?

"No way." Kwintone topped off my wine. "I told you Eddie was setting a trap. He recorded Green trying to buy cats for his lab, proving he still experiments on them."

Demi arched her eyebrows. "Ooh… a secret recording like in one of those spy movies?"

I picked up my glass. Had Demi forgotten what happened that night? All that blood? We'd both thrown away the clothes we'd been wearing. We were talking about something much more serious than some spy scheme. "How did it go so wrong? How did Green get stabbed?"

Kwintone set the bottle on the table and seated himself. "No idea." He could be as maddeningly cryptic as Demi.

"But you were there. Didn't you see what happened?"

"It got… weird."

I couldn't read his face. "What do you mean, *weird*?" I glanced at Demi to see if she was as baffled and bothered as I was. She was busy dishing pasta onto her plate.

Kwintone picked up his fork. "Green was on to us. He snatched Eddie's phone and stopped the recording."

"What did Eddie do?" *Did Aiden keep Eddie's phone?* I recalled the ringing that had led us to Aiden Green. Was the last number in Kwintone's call log Aiden's? Or Eddie's? He'd insisted he hadn't ever talked to Green.

"Eddie grabbed for his phone, but Green wasn't having it. Got this sadistic grin and twisted Eddie's wrist around till he jerked it away." Kwintone grimaced. "I got a bad vibe and split."

Demi twirled strands of cream-coated fettuccine around her fork. "You deserted your friend?"

He swallowed. "I…"

"But you didn't leave. You went back." That must have been when I found Kwintone's Mustang parked beside the road, windows rolled down, cellphone on the seat. "In a hurry. On foot. Why didn't you just drive back to the parking lot?"

Kwintone took a deep drink of water. "I was pissed that Eddie set me up and was done with his fool scheme. But after I drove away, I got a feeling he might be in trouble. Then, out of the corner of my eye, I saw someone running toward the woods, so I stopped and rushed to check it out."

My pulse raced. Had Kwintone gone for a weapon? A knife? "Why didn't you take your phone?"

"I didn't realize I left it. Must have slipped out of my pocket."

I glanced at Demi. Was she buying his story? "What happened in the woods?"

"I didn't find whoever was running, and by then, I was closer to the building, so I just walked back there."

"Who else was at your meeting?" Demi brought her fork to her lips.

"Eddie's boo." Kwintone set down the glass. "Zach."

"Zach was there, too?" I shouldn't have been surprised after the way he and Eddie had dodged my questions the other night. And Zach, ever the gentleman, would not have wanted Eddie to handle a perilous clandestine encounter alone. "What did Zach do when Aiden grabbed Eddie's phone?"

Kwintone shrugged. "I told you, I split. But I think Zach tried to get everyone to chill."

No wonder Eddie had seemed peeved with Kwintone whenever I brought up his name. Eddie must have thought Kwintone deserted them.

Demi set down her fork and fixed her eyes on her brother. "What happened when you went back to the building?"

Kwintone stared at his plate.

"Kwin, what happened?" Demi's voice had become sharper, more insistent; I was glad she'd stepped into the role of "bad cop." Maybe she'd do a better job than I had so far.

Still not meeting her eyes, he toyed with his food. "The door was locked. Everyone was gone."

"Gone?" Her finely plucked eyebrows shot up. "What do you mean?"

"Eddie and Zach were heading to their car, so I knew they were good."

"Where was Green?" I asked.

"I didn't see him." Kwintone's voice had grown soft in contrast to Demi's shrill tone. "I assumed he left, too."

"Did you look?" With one elbow on the table, my niece rested her chin in her palm and continued to stare at her brother.

"Why would I look for him?" Kwintone stared back at her.

"Kwin..."

"Was Green's car still there?" I shoveled pasta around on my plate but didn't take a bite.

Kwintone turned to me. "Dunno which car was his. When I showed up, there was a black Camry next to Eddie's Accord." Kwintone closed his eyes as if thinking back to that night. "Mighta been someone in the passenger seat."

"Did you get a good look at the person in the Camry?" I couldn't believe I was hoping for another suspect in Aiden's attack. "Man or woman?"

Kwintone shrugged.

Demi studied her brother with more skepticism than I'd seen so far. "When you went back to the building and saw that everyone had left, what'd you do?"

"I bounced, too. That place creeped me out." Kwintone held her gaze, but his mouth twitched, telling me he might not have spoken the whole truth.

"So, you went back to your car but didn't see mine? And DeeLo's? Parked right in front of yours on that access road?"

Kwintone hung his head like a scolded little boy.

I let out an exasperated puff of air. "I'd been there at least twenty minutes." When I tried to reconstruct the timeline, many of his statements didn't add up. "You left our trapping site long before that."

"Want to try again, Kwin?" Demi's tone was harsh. "The truth this time, not the version you made up for the cops."

"I… Okay." He lifted his head to meet her gaze. "I caught up with Eddie and Zach. I told them I didn't vibe with being used like that. Eddie agreed it was a bad idea. Zach didn't say anything, but he didn't have to."

"Did Eddie get his phone back?" I drizzled dressing on my salad.

Kwintone turned to me. "I didn't ask about his phone, but I don't think so."

"Was Aiden Green around?" I speared a leaf of lettuce with my fork.

"Didn't see Green, but the Camry was still there. With no one inside, though. Coulda sworn someone else was in the car earlier."

I raised my eyebrows and exchanged a glance with Demi. Straining to picture the Oakwood lot while we were searching for Kwintone, I couldn't recall seeing a Camry, but maybe it was on the other side of the building.

"You still haven't told us why you drove away when you must have seen our cars," Demi said. "You and I were planning to meet at Sam's Bar, remember?"

Without making eye contact, Kwintone took a bite of pasta, chewed slowly, and swallowed. "Okay. I didn't drive my car."

Demi rolled her eyes. "What kind of—?"

"Eddie did." Kwintone set down his fork. "I told him my car was making a weird sound—it was about time for maintenance anyway—and Eddie said he'd take it to the dealership for me the next day. I handed him the key so he could drive it and check out the noise. But honestly, that noise was just my excuse to get a minute alone with Zach."

If Eddie was the one who drove Kwintone's car away from its spot along the road, he wouldn't have recognized Demi's and my vehicles, so that part of Kwintone's story made sense. "Why did you want to talk to Zach alone?"

Kwintone traced the condensation on his water glass with his finger. "I needed Zach to convince Eddie to take a DNA test to see if we're related."

The abrupt switch from one mystery to another jolted me. "Did you tell Zach about the trust fund the Car King set up for you? Does Eddie know about it?"

Kwintone bobbled his head; I couldn't tell if his answer to the trust fund question was yes or no. "Zach said it's up to Eddie, but good luck with that. Eddie claims his dad's no cheater and wouldn't disrespect his mom that way. He thinks I wanna scam his family."

"Eddie really looks up to his father," I said. "He might be having a hard time accepting the idea that the Car King might have another child." *At least two more.*

"Eddie's an only child and doesn't want to share. He's a spoiled rich kid." Kwintone scowled.

I'd seen evidence of Eddie's jealousy when I was around him and Zach; he didn't want to share Zach's affections with anyone else and seemed afraid I'd get too close.

Demi appeared to still be processing all the revelations. "Do you seriously think Eddie Fenton is our brother?"

Kwintone shrugged. "There's gotta be a connection. Why else would the Car King fund a trust for me? How does he know me?"

"But without DNA evidence, how will we know for sure?" Demi poured herself more wine.

I tapped my finger against my jaw. "Barry said our firm did some work for the Car King back when his father ran the day-to-day, before Barry's time. Maybe it was Kwintone's trust fund."

"So?" said Demi.

I should ask Barry's father if he remembered the transaction, but he'd had several surgeries recently and hardly ever came into the office anymore. "If the file doesn't give me any clues, maybe I can call Mr. Fenton. Say we need to clarify something with the paperwork." Already, I was planning my phone conversation.

Kwintone snorted. "After all this time? No way he'd buy it." He shook his head. "I've gone through all the nonsense the bank handed over. Edward Fenton doesn't claim me as his son. He doesn't deny it either, but there's nothing in there that says I'm his kid."

I snapped my fingers. "I've got it!"

Demi and Kwintone turned to me, question marks on their faces.

I rapped the table to simulate a drum roll.

Chapter Thirty-One

Glancing up from drumming the table, I announced, "Desiree."

Demi scrunched her face as if I'd told her we were out of wine. "Do you really think my mom will admit Edward Fenton is my father after all these years?"

"Think about it, Demi." I thumped my forehead. "Shouldn't she have some reaction when she comes face-to-face with the man who fathered her child?"

"If she even knows who my daddy is. That's always been debatable." Demi sighed. "How will we get Mom in the same room with the Car King?"

I tapped my fingers on the table again. "What if we hold a big fundraiser to kick off Zach's campaign?"

"Fundraiser?" scoffed Kwintone. "Isn't it kind of late? When's the election?"

I ignored their skeptical expressions. "I'll put Eddie in charge of the planning and ask him to invite the Car King. He wants his dad to be proud of him, and he believes in Zach."

"But what about Mom?" Demi shook her head. "She won't go to a fundraiser for someone she doesn't know. Besides, she's not into politics."

"Desiree likes parties, though, doesn't she?"

Demi shrugged. "Sure."

"We can hold our event on the day Desiree comes to the memory care home to visit Mom. You can go with her and then bring her to the fundraiser afterward. Tell her she needs to support her baby sister."

Kwintone smirked. "Look at you, DeeLo. A little puppet master."

I placed my hands on my hips. "Do you think either the Car King or Desiree will come to an event because *I* asked them to?"

"Wouldn't your big sister come to your event if you invited her?" His smirk remained.

Demi glanced at her brother and shrugged.

I sighed. "She probably would, but she might question my motive. If we make it seem spur-of-the-moment, Desiree won't figure out she's been set up."

"Where do I come in?" Kwintone asked.

"You can be in charge of catering." When his mouth flew open, I patted his shoulder. "Kidding. Just be there. Prepare your questions for the Car King. Or, you could offer to help Eddie. Get on his good side. Remember, I'm putting him in charge of planning the event for Zach."

"Might want to ask him first," Demi muttered.

Kwintone turned to Demi. "How big do you think the explosion will be? What if they parted on bad terms? Lord, help us if my mom came face-to-face with that dude. May she rest in peace."

We bowed our heads for a moment of silence out of respect for Kwintone's deceased mother.

"Does Desiree know you've been searching for your father?" I asked Demi. "Did you tell her you found Kwintone?"

Demi shook her head. "No, and no. And don't say a word."

"Hey." Kwintone held up a hand. "If the Car King comes, maybe we can just snag a DNA sample ourselves. Plan B. We could—"

My phone, which was plugged into a charger on the hutch, started ringing. I rose to answer, thinking it could be Barry. "Excuse me."

Catherine Foster's name appeared on the screen. My pulse quickened. Had she remembered to pick up the cats from the LifeSaver this afternoon?

"Catherine." I held my breath. "Is something wrong? Did you get the cats from the clinic?"

"They're fine." Her tone sounded peeved that I would even ask. "Gave everyone food and water, and they should be ready for release tomorrow."

"Do you want me to—"

"No, I got it. But I need you to go see that witch, Sandra What's Her Face, tomorrow. Early, because the animal shelter closes at noon on Saturday."

"What—?"

"Animal Control picked up the cats at the Patel Shopping Center, and they're scheduled to die on Monday."

I pictured the cats I'd trapped at that shopping center where Catherine had first introduced me to TNVR. Even though they weren't pets like Manny or the cats I'd grown up with, they had names and personalities. Big Mack, the first feral I ever trapped—so huge and ferocious-looking—was possibly Manny's father. Octomom, the elusive kitten factory, who delivered three litters of eight before we shut it down. Mittens, the protective older sister from Octomom's first litter, who showed maternal instincts toward her young siblings even though she was spayed before she ever bore a litter. Now, these and other healthy, innocent cats were sentenced to death?

"Why did Animal Control pick them up? Isn't Natalie Wojcik still feeding them?" Wojcik Dry Cleaners was one of the few remaining businesses in the distressed shopping center where the cats roamed. When Azmina Patel died last year, the title passed to her sister, who lived out of state, and I suspected the property would eventually be sold.

"Natalie's been evicted. Sparks Development Corporation bought the land, and they're planning to bulldoze the place to build townhomes. Now the cats have nowhere to go."

"That's awful," I said. "What's going to happen to Natalie?"

"I don't know." Catherine sounded impatient, as if Natalie's fate was not her concern. "They'll find a new location. Someone said she was moving to a strip mall off Loop Road."

"What can we do about the cats?"

"Talk to Sandra. Buy some time until we can make a plan."

"But—"

"She likes you. She won't give me the time of day." Catherine was probably right. She lacked social skills and made no effort to develop any.

"What can I tell Sandra? Do you have any ideas?" My mind's wheels spun. Could I ask Lisa Ross to take the cats? She had three acres backed up to woods, and her feline family had accepted a newcomer last year. But five more?

"Talk to Merilee Jones at Oakwood Studios. She runs our barn cat program; maybe she can place them. Or move them to the Oakwood lot if there are no available barn jobs."

Catherine had told me how dangerous it could be to try to relocate feral cats. Rather than adjust to a new, potentially hostile environment, their homing instinct often propelled them to leave, perhaps crossing highways, construction sites, or natural hazards en route to the original, now unsafe location. "Won't they try to find their way home? Oakwood Studios isn't far from the Patel Shopping Center."

"Let Merilee explain the assimilation process. But DeeLo, first you have to get to Sandra. Those cats' lives are in your hands." Catherine hung up without saying goodbye.

* * *

My guests had cleared the table and were washing dishes by the time I finished my call with Catherine. They'd set the leftovers on the kitchen counter. I transferred the food to Tupperware. "You guys take some of this. I'll never eat it all."

"Don't mind if I do." My niece plucked one of the Tupperware containers.

"Dinner was delicious, Demi." I put my portion in the refrigerator and closed the door. "Thanks for cooking."

"Thanks for hosting," chimed in Kwintone, picking up his bag.

"When do you think you'll hold this fundraiser?" Demi asked. "Isn't the election in a couple of weeks?"

"Yes. We'll have to do it soon. I'll talk to Eddie and Zach tomorrow."

"Mom and I will be down here to visit Grandma on Friday," suggested Demi. "Just sayin.'"

I crossed my fingers. "Hope we can pull it off with the Car King."

As they prepared to leave, I chided myself for not digging deeper, for allowing my focus to be hijacked again by the mystery of Demi's paternity.

There were still unanswered questions about the night Aiden Green was stabbed, and I suspected Kwintone had not told us the whole story.

Chapter Thirty-Two

As I promised Catherine, I arrived at the animal shelter when it opened. The sprawling, one-story building dated from the mid-twentieth century, with mud-brown wood panel siding and several nonmatching wings that had been added in various decades. Dogs barked fretfully, one-upping each other in volume.

Sandra Larson sat behind her large, gun-metal desk, thumbing through paperwork and sipping coffee from her I-Heart-New York mug. The large-boned woman in her mid-forties had short, spiked, auburn hair and so many freckles that they seemed to be holding hands.

No one manned the front desk yet. I rapped on her doorframe. "Hey, Sandra."

She looked up with a smile that said *I'm busy; make this quick.* "DeeLo, how are you?"

Sandra's tone said she didn't really want to hear about my health, so I launched right into the purpose of my visit. "I understand your officers picked up some cats from the Patel Shopping Center this week."

She blew at a wisp of hair that had crept onto her forehead. "Had to. That property's been sold, and the new owners want them gone."

I pressed my lips together. "Those cats have lived on that lot for years. They're all fixed and vaccinated, and they're not hurting anyone. Couldn't you talk some sense into those people?"

Sandra snorted. "Do you think Randall Sparks would listen? The same commissioner who slapped down my spay/neuter proposal because it might interfere with pet owners' 'individual liberties'? He's clueless."

"But does that necessarily mean he wouldn't be sympathetic to the plight of a group of community cats? Don't they deserve personal liberty?"

Sandra's chuckle erupted in a guffaw. "Go ahead and ask him. But keep in mind, they're getting ready to raze the shopping center and build a forest of townhomes. The cats wouldn't be safe around all that construction, anyway."

I winced, picturing the bulldozers crushing anything in their path. She was right; the felines couldn't stay. It seemed unfair. "Don't kill those cats. And don't send them to Neuro Labs."

Sandra rolled her eyes. "I've already told those people I won't be a party to animal testing. I knew they wouldn't stop when they got that big grant." She sighed. "But no one is going to adopt a feral cat. And they're miserable in cages. One of them has already scraped most of the fur off his face, trying to get out. If I release them, they'll wander into the green belt to hunt, and Nick Norton from the Pecan Creek Nature Foundation will be the first to complain. We'll have to pick them up again."

"We need time to find them another place."

"How much time?"

I shrugged. "I have some ideas. PPHS has a barn cat program…"

Sandra shuffled the papers in front of her as if she was itching to get back to them. "I'll give you until Friday. Now, if you'll excuse me…"

Before I could respond, the phone on her desk rang, and she picked it up, waving me out.

* * *

Back in my car, I tried to call Lisa Ross with my plea that she take the cats, but got her voicemail. I decided not to leave a message. My plan needed more explanation than I could convey without a two-way conversation.

My next call was to Zach. We had lots to talk about: cat relocation, party planning, and maybe I could glean a little more insight into what happened the night Aiden Green was stabbed. According to Kwintone, Zach and Eddie were the last people to see Green before he was attacked. They knew more than they'd admitted.

Zach answered on the second ring, and his voice was cheery enough to reassure me that I didn't wake him up.

"Can you talk?" I ventured. "I have a proposal… actually, a couple of proposals."

"Sure. Hang on a sec." Muffled voices, followed by a "Thanks, Hon," and then sipping. "Sorry, DeeLo. Eddie just brought me my coffee."

"I know the election is only a few weeks away, but have you thought about having a fundraiser? Invite the movers and shakers of Pecan County and really get your message out."

Zach was quiet for a moment. Was he mulling over my proposal or trying to think of a polite way to tell me I'd lost my mind? "A fundraiser this close to the election? Would that help? What would we use the funds for?"

In the light of day, my plan to get Desiree and the Car King together sounded even crazier. What had I been thinking? "I don't know… maybe it should be more like a Meet-and-Greet rather than a fundraiser. No pressure for people to donate. Of course, if they want to, we could defray our event costs and maybe pay for some ads."

"Hmmm…I like the idea of a Meet-and-Greet." There was a pause, and it sounded like he took another drink of his coffee. "But can we pull it off in time to do any good? Early voting starts in two weeks."

"We'd need to hustle. Maybe Eddie could help with the planning?" I crossed my fingers. "He must have a lot of contacts. Son of the Car King and all."

Again, it sounded like Zach had put his hand over the mouthpiece. *Conference with Eddie?* When he came back on the line, Zach replied, "Eddie is intrigued. Tell you what, DeeLo. Do you have some free time today?"

Barry still had not called.

"My schedule's wide open."

"Wonderful. Why don't you come over for brunch, and we'll talk more about it? Eddie just put a mushroom quiche in the oven."

"I'll be there shortly." My stomach rumbled; I hadn't eaten breakfast before heading to the animal shelter.

Zach gave me the address, and I put it in my GPS.

* * *

Zach and Eddie shared a newish two-bedroom condo overlooking the Pecan Creek Nature Reserve. They'd said they were renting, planning to buy a house, but they appeared much more settled than Barry, even though they'd only lived in their place for a few months, whereas Barry had been in his undecorated apartment for over two years.

Artwork and family photos hung on the custom-painted walls; the shelves were filled with books and knick-knacks from tourist destinations around the U.S. and abroad. The furniture, rugs, and accessories were color-coordinated as if the men had worked with an interior decorator.

A savory aroma of fresh-baked quiche teased my nose as I walked in. "That smells great," I said.

Eddie beamed. He wore a red and white gingham apron over his gray sweats. "Good morning, DeeLo. Would you like coffee?"

"I'd love some. Thanks."

Zach took my bag and jacket and set them on a chair. Eddie poured coffee into a blue Oakwood Studios mug and handed it to me.

In a moment, we were all seated around the table in a dining alcove between the open kitchen and the family room. Greenhouse windows provided a prime view of the forest.

The table was set for three with bright Fiesta dinnerware on woven-grass placemats, finished with stainless steel flatware and gingham napkins that matched Eddie's apron.

"So, DeeLo." Zach drained his coffee cup. "Tell us more about your idea for a Meet-and-Greet event. Eddie was just talking about how we need to do more to build awareness of my campaign."

"Great minds think alike." Eddie grinned. The sunlight from the window shone on his shaved brown head as he got up to check the quiche.

"We should hold our event before people start early voting." I poured half-and-half into my coffee. "An opportunity for Zach to address the group. It doesn't have to be fancy. Some finger foods and soft drinks. A cash bar to keep our costs down, and so people aren't as tempted to overindulge."

"Makes sense." Zach nodded.

"I'm not sure about the venue, though." I gestured around the room. "This place is too small, and so is my house. One of the parks might work if we could count on nice weather, but I'm finding fall in Georgia is fickle. Maybe—"

"I know the perfect place." Eddie set the steaming quiche on a trivet in the middle of the table. "113 Peachtree Lane. It has a beautiful ballroom they rent out for events, plenty of parking in the circular driveway and the cul-de-sac…"

Barry and Victoria's house. The marital mansion they had been unable to sell after their divorce. I'd never been inside and had no desire to change that. On second thought, it might be fun to stick it to Victoria by holding a campaign event for her opponent in her house.

"Uh… I've heard the rental fee for that place is quite expensive. What's our budget?" If Victoria knew I had anything to do with the event, she'd probably double the price.

Eddie waved dismissively as he sat down. "I'll get my dad to pay for it."

The Car King? This was my opening. "Eddie, could you persuade your father to attend? The Car King is a local celebrity. I know he doesn't live in our district—"

"But my grandparents do." Eddie flashed a gap-tooth grin. Just like Kwintone's. "I'll be sure to invite them too."

Even better.

Zach cut the quiche and motioned for my plate.

He loaded a generous slice and handed it back. Next, he served Eddie, then himself.

Eddie picked up his fork. "Yeah, I'll get Dad to endorse Zach and show up at the event. That should bring some people out."

"Super." I smiled. "What does your calendar look like? Do you think we could organize something for next Friday?"

"Friday?" Zach jerked toward Eddie. "What do you think, Hon? It's awfully soon. Can we put everything together that fast?"

"Let me make some calls. I'll see if the venue is available and then check with Dad, get him on board." Eddie seemed to be in his element. I hadn't even asked him to plan the event, but he was already running with it.

Eddie contacting Whitehead Realtors about renting the venue was ideal, so maybe Victoria wouldn't connect the transaction to me. "Once you firm up the plan, let me know, and I'll put out a blast on social media." I took a bite of quiche, savoring the creamy blend of Gruyere, mushrooms, and herbs.

"Eddie, this is delicious," Zach said after he swallowed. "You've outdone yourself."

"I concur." I scooped another bite onto my fork. "I hope you can plan an event as well as you cook."

Eddie's answer was a smile.

"I'll announce the Meet-and-Greet in our PPHS newsletter," I said. "It goes out to all the humane society volunteers, plus adopters and donors. I'll let them know how Zach plans to support animal-friendly initiatives, like TNVR ordinance reform and spay/neuter." I watched their faces to assure myself that Zach was still committed to my agenda.

"That sounds great." Zach's smile didn't waver. "I appreciate all your support. I'm not supposed to campaign at work, but if Merilee wants to tell her friends and colleagues about the event..." He gave a *what-can-I-do* shrug.

I set down my fork. "While we're on the subject, I have a favor to ask. About relocating some feral cats."

Eddie shook his head. "The ferals on the Oakwood property? Those cats aren't going anywhere. I made sure of that."

Chapter Thirty-Three

I blinked, wondering what Eddie meant. How had he "made sure" the cats weren't going anywhere? By getting rid of the threat—Aiden Green? "Actually, I wasn't talking about the Oakwood colony. We're glad you're letting them stay. But another group is in trouble."

"Another group of feral cats?" Zach's brow creased.

"Yes. There used to be a large colony behind the Patel Shopping Center. When their feeder died last year, a lot of the cats scattered. In fact, some might have come to the Oakwood Studios lot. But most wandered into the nature reserve and crossed the creek to Leonardo's restaurant. The owner allows his employees to feed them."

"That's good," Eddie chimed in. "I knew I liked that place."

"About five stragglers stayed behind," I said. "One of the business owners was looking after them, but now she's been evicted, and they're about to bulldoze the site and build townhouses."

"Oh, no," said Zach. "Although I'm not surprised. That place was barely hanging on. Mostly empty storefronts."

"Anyway," I continued. "Animal Control rounded up the cats, and they'll put them down unless we can find another place for them by Friday."

Eddie's mouth dropped. "We can't let that happen! They can come to Oakwood." He glanced at Zach. "Right, Babe?"

Zach shrugged, his eyes scanning our pleading faces. "I… I guess so. What's a few more feral cats roaming in the woods?"

"They're already fixed and vaccinated," I assured him. "However, relocating cats is not as easy as it sounds."

"Will they try to go back to the shopping center?" asked Eddie. "That homing instinct, right?" The anger had faded as quickly as it came, replaced by a tenderness I'd seen on the faces of many of the humane society's most diehard volunteers.

"Very likely. Also, the resident cats might chase them away. Cats can be territorial."

Zach picked up the leftover quiche and started for the kitchen. "So, what can we do?"

"I don't have experience relocating feral cats, but your colleague, Merilee Jones, is in charge of the PPHS barn cat program." I gathered my utensils and laid them on my empty plate. Before I could rise, Zach took it from me while Eddie picked up his plate and Zach's. "Merilee coaches people who adopt working cats; it takes several weeks to get them acclimated to their new environment so they won't take off." I turned in my seat to face my hosts, who were both in the kitchen now.

"Working cats?" Zach's brow creased.

"Cats with a job to keep the rodents away. People who own barns, warehouses, breweries—places that attract a lot of mice—hire working cats." I folded my napkin and set it on the placemat. "Although cats are great hunters, the caretakers still have to feed them. Interestingly, most of the rodents take off on their own once the cats arrive."

Eddie put away the leftovers while Zach rinsed plates and loaded the dishwasher.

"What can I do to help you?" I gathered our napkins and started to get up.

"Sit," said Eddie, taking the napkins from me. "You're the guest. Would you like more coffee?"

"No, thanks." I drank the last cold drops from my mug and handed it to him.

"Looks like we need to talk to Merilee," said Zach. "And see if she thinks we can successfully move these cats to Oakwood."

"That would be great, and I'll do whatever I can to assist." I twisted in my seat again to converse better with them in the kitchen. "Relocation would certainly be preferable to sending the cats to Neuro Labs."

"What?" Eddie slammed the coffee pot down on the counter so hard I was afraid he'd break it.

"Neuroscience Laboratories, the medical research facility. Where Aiden Green worked."

"I know what it is," Eddie muttered. "They should have shut that place down years ago."

I took a breath, watching his mercurial face. "Kwintone said that you—"

"Kwintone!" Eddie's face reddened.

Zach turned to me. "DeeLo, how do you know Kwintone Johnson? You've mentioned him several times before."

I met Zach's gaze. "Kwintone matched with my niece as a sibling on one of those DNA sites. She's been trying to find her father, and so has he."

Zach shot Eddie an alarmed glance.

Eddie glared, stone-faced. "Tell your niece not to trust a thing *Kwintone* tells her."

I furrowed my brow. "Why would you say that? Don't you think those ancestry sites are reliable?"

But both Eddie and Zach had said all they were going to about Kwintone Johnson and Aiden Green.

* * *

After I left Zach and Eddie's condo, I headed to our local PetSmart store to purchase cat food for Manny. A white plastic A-frame sign next to the entrance announced "Pecan Point Humane Society Pet Adoptions Today." I couldn't resist stopping by to see what cats and dogs our organization had on display, and besides, I knew Merilee often worked the adoptions. Maybe she'd be there today.

I hardly ever worked at adoption events, and I didn't know many of the regular volunteers, including Merilee. Some of them recognized me as one of the TNVR gurus; I was the go-to volunteer when someone reported stray cats that needed to be trapped and fixed. Most preferred dealing with me rather than Catherine Foster, the true leader of the program, who'd been my mentor. She could make a volunteer feel stupid for asking a perfectly valid question. Fortunately for our organization's image, Catherine never worked at events where she'd have to interact with the public.

Exuberant barking led me to the corner of the store where our group was conducting operations. A teen volunteer, plastic bag in hand, struggled to control an eager, oversized mongrel puppy as he tugged at the leash en route to a needed walk. I stepped aside to let them pass.

The cat team had set up crates atop folding tables where cats and kittens waited to meet potential adopters. Some slept, some meowed, and some tried to climb the bars of the cages, looking for a way out. One volunteer had sewn colorful cotton hammocks that were suspended via metal clips from the bars of the upper part of the cages, creating a sort of loft bed—very popular with the kittens. I watched one pair jockeying for position in the hammock; the victor ultimately pushed his sibling out of the makeshift bed to the towel-covered floor of the crate. After righting herself, the energetic calico jumped back into the hammock, ready to resume the fight.

I picked up a plastic fishing pole from the top of one of the cages and dangled the feather bait in front of the kittens inside. A little tortie cocked her head and strategically batted it, then leaped after the toy as I yanked the line away.

"Cute, aren't they? Are you looking for a kitten?"

I turned to face the pencil-thin, thirty-something woman behind me. Her long, straight, light brown hair was pulled back in a clip, and she wore a loose-fitting red PPHS T-shirt that hung past the waistband of her jeans. Her nametag read: Merilee Jones.

Just the person I needed to see.

Chapter Thirty-Four

Ipointed to the young woman's name tag. "Merilee Jones? Glad to finally meet you. I'm DeeLo Myer, the volunteer who's been doing TNVR at Oakwood Studios."

She held out her hand, which was cool to the touch. "DeeLo, it's a pleasure. I'm not much of a trapper, so we really appreciate what you're doing."

"But you're the one who convinced management the cats should stay, right? We could certainly use more advocates around town." I smiled sincerely.

Merilee beamed. "It didn't take much convincing. Zach Kirkpatrick is the best. He listens, and he's very forward-thinking." She stuck a finger into one of the cages to pet the calico kitten rubbing against the bars. "And his boyfriend, Eddie, was already feeding the cats. He's given them all names: ZsaZsa, Lady Gaga, The Divine Mr. M."

I chuckled. It was reassuring to hear Merilee's positive assessment of Zach, confirming the traits I so badly wanted to be real. She knew him a lot better than I did. Sometimes, I wondered if I could be walking into danger, blinded by Zach's promise to support my animal ordinance reform proposal—especially after I'd learned he and Eddie had been in the vicinity when Aiden Green got stabbed. They'd also been in the lobby of the hospital the evening Green died. It wouldn't be the first time I'd trusted a killer.

I followed Merilee's finger to pet the needy kitten. "You do know Zach's running for the open position on the Board of Commissioners?"

"Oh, yes. We're not allowed to campaign at work, but I'm trying to get the word out to all my friends and the PPHS volunteers. I think he'd be great for Pecan County."

"I've been helping with his campaign, and we're planning a—"

"Excuse me, ma'am." A plump, curly-haired woman holding a chubby toddler's hand pointed to the cage next to us. "Are these kittens dog-friendly?"

Merilee threw me an apologetic smile and turned to the customer. "Ma'am, they haven't ever been around dogs, but these others in the next cage live in a foster home with two Labs, and they all get along. Would you like to hold one?"

I tapped Merilee on the shoulder. "I know you're busy now, but could we get together later? I'd love to pick your brain about the barn cat program."

"Give me a call; I should have some time tomorrow." With a smile, she handed me a business card and escorted the woman and her child to the Meet-and-Greet room.

* * *

I paid for my cat food at the register and left the store. My phone vibrated while I was crossing the parking lot to my car. I glanced at the screen: Barry. Letting the phone continue to ring, I unlocked my door and placed the bag in the passenger seat. I settled into the driver's seat and answered in a deadpan voice right before the call went to voicemail. "Hello?"

"Thank God," he said. "Where are you?"

"Just leaving PetSmart. I had to get cat food for Manny. Why?"

"How did it go at the police station yesterday?"

Seriously? Now, he's concerned? "It worked out okay. I called Demi to bail me out."

"Bail you out?" His tone rose an octave. "What happened?"

I was silent. He deserved to be worried.

"DeeLo?"

I relented. "Kidding. The questions went pretty much the way we rehearsed. And after I told Detective Ross that I saw his wife on Green's floor, he got all flustered and ended our interview."

Barry was quiet for a moment. "You didn't mention seeing Lisa Ross when we were going over your statement."

I let out a puff of air. "And I didn't mention seeing Victoria drive out of the hospital parking lot just as I arrived. Or ask you where she'd been Monday night before she came to your apartment at midnight."

"DeeLo! Are you seriously trying to make Victoria out to be a suspect?"

Okay, that was petty. But wouldn't it be nice if she were guilty? "Seeing Lisa didn't cross my mind until the detective asked me if I saw anyone outside the room before I went in." I leaned against the seat back and switched the phone to my other ear. "It was a strange encounter. She seemed agitated, kind of discombobulated. Told me she was visiting her grandmother in the hospital, but Detective Ross said Lisa's grandmother died two years ago. So, what was Lisa really doing there?"

There was a pause, and for a moment, I thought we'd been disconnected.

"I'm sure the detective will get to the bottom of it. It's not something you need to be concerned about." Barry's mind-your-own-business attitude was starting to annoy me. And maybe he was touchy because I'd brought up his precious Victoria.

"I hope I didn't cause a rift in their marriage." I tried to sound sincere; I didn't mean to cause the Rosses trouble. I just wondered why Lisa had lied. Did it have something to do with Aiden Green? If she'd gone to visit her boss in the hospital, why not say so? She claimed she barely knew the guy, so why would anyone think she'd do something nefarious to him? Was she afraid her husband would be jealous if she visited another man in the hospital?

"Well, I'm relieved you were able to convince the detective that *you* had nothing to do with Green's death," Barry said. "Of course, I knew you'd handle the interview fine. But I thought you'd call me after you were done, and I got worried when I didn't hear from you."

"Not worried enough to call and check on me, though." The words slipped out before I had a chance to edit them.

There was a long pause. I could hear Barry swallow. "I—"

"I had things to do. And I wasn't sure how long you'd be tied up with

Victoria." Saying her name always left a bitter taste in my mouth.

"Yeah. She was a mess at lunch yesterday. I stayed with her a lot longer than planned. She thinks Roy Don might be seeing someone else."

"Oh, that's a shame." It was hard to keep the Seinfeld-esque sarcasm out of my voice. What did Victoria expect? When she and Roy Don got together, they were each married to other people. Why did she assume he wouldn't cheat on her one day?

"I never understood what she saw in that guy," Barry continued. "And if they break up, it will be awkward for her to work with him on the Board of Commissioners after she's elected. I hope they don't let it affect their decision-making."

"*If* she gets elected," I couldn't resist adding. "But regardless, they'll still have to work together at Whitehead Realtors." I hoped Victoria wouldn't consider returning to Barton & Barton if her relationship with Roy Don ended.

"Let's not talk about them. What are your plans for this evening?"

"Why? Do you have something in mind?"

"I'd love to take you to dinner if you're free."

Are you sure Victoria doesn't need you to hold her hand? I wanted to sneer. Instead, I replied, "I can arrange that. What time should I be ready?"

* * *

As soon as I hung up with Barry, my phone dinged. "WELL???!!!" was all Catherine's text said. *Typical Catherine.*

Chapter Thirty-Five

Rather than reply to her cryptic text, I called Catherine.

"Did you go to the animal shelter this morning?" she demanded before I could utter a word. "What happened with the cats?"

"Relax, they're fine. Sandra gave them a reprieve until Friday."

"And then what?" Catherine was still shrieking.

"I think we might have found a place at Oakwood Studios. I met Merilee Jones at PetSmart today, and we're going to discuss logistics tomorrow."

Catherine breathed a heavy sigh. "Tomorrow? Where are you meeting?"

I wondered why she cared. Did Catherine want to join the meeting? That was the last thing I'd expect of her. "I don't know. We didn't get that far. Merilee was working adoptions, and it got busy."

"You guys could come over here."

"For real?" *Who are you, and what have you done with Catherine Foster?*

"I'd like to learn more about the barn cat program. And maybe I can help."

"Okay. I'll suggest it to Merilee. I'm sure she'd be happy to have your assistance."

"I wish I'd kept Octomom." Catherine's voice softened. "Remember? She lived in my basement for over six weeks while she nursed that last litter. By the time I had her spayed and released, she was practically tame."

Now I understood Catherine's motive. Octomom was one of the cats at risk.

"After I talk to Merilee, I'll circle back to arrange a meeting time," I promised as we ended our call.

* * *

While I waited for Barry to pick me up for dinner, I googled "Aiden Green and Evangeline Powers divorce." Several salacious-looking articles appeared. Each party had threatened to kill the other in front of the harried judge who was deciding their fate.

I clicked on the first story and skimmed through the boring sections; the headline was the juiciest part. Theirs was the second marriage for both spouses, and neither had children, so the proceedings should have been relatively simple.

But they weren't. Evangeline accused Aiden of serial adultery, mental cruelty, and narcissism. He accused her of "shirking her wifely duties," which were never clearly defined in the article.

She'd signed a prenup, which she tried to get out of, saying that his adultery negated the agreement. He had the better lawyer, and the prenup stood. The divorce was granted. Evangeline got nothing except the paltry assets she'd brought into the marriage.

No wonder she hadn't seemed saddened by his death.

* * *

Our favorite Thai restaurant was under renovation. The line at the new Mexican place was out the door, and they weren't seating anyone without reservations. So, Barry and I ended up at Leonardo's.

And there on the patio sat Victoria Barton and Roy Don Whitehead, huddled together as if they were in their own private dining room. Whatever trouble in paradise she'd poured out to Barry must have passed. Surely, he must see how she was using him.

I nudged Barry. "Let's get a table inside. It's a little chilly anyway."

The hostess clutched the menus to her chest. "Are you sure? I don't have anything inside available right now; it will be about a half-hour wait. Or you could sit at the bar."

"Can we—"

"Outside is fine," Barry replied firmly. "It's a nice night, and they have heat lamps on the patio."

The hostess showed us to a table with a full view of Victoria and Roy Don. My appetite seeped away. Sensing my displeasure, the hostess handed us oversized menus and made a quick getaway. "Your server will be right over."

I picked up a menu and peered over the top at Barry. His eyes were fixed on Victoria rather than the dinner selections.

I slapped my menu closed. "Maybe we should go somewhere else."

He jerked his head away from ogling his ex-wife and opened his menu. "No, this is fine. My taste buds are primed for a good lasagna."

The server came for our drink orders and recited the evening's specials. Barry ordered a bottle of his favorite Chianti without consulting me.

As soon as the server left, he noticed my open-mouthed expression. "I'm sorry, DeeLo. I thought you liked Chianti. And it goes well with…"

I picked up my water glass and took a sip. "It's fine. But you could have asked me."

He turned his attention back to the menu. "What looks good to you?"

I thought about what might taste good with Chianti. "That Shrimp Fra Diavolo special she mentioned is tempting."

"Get it. I know how much you like shrimp." He closed his menu. "I'm going to stick with my usual lasagna."

The server returned with our wine. She and Barry went through the ritual of opening the bottle, pouring him a sample to approve, and then filling our glasses. "Are you ready to order?"

"I'd like the Shrimp Fra Diavolo," I announced, even though she was looking at Barry.

"Beef lasagna for me, and Fra Diavolo for the lady," he said, as if he hadn't heard me.

The server jotted our orders on her pad. "Good choice." She nodded at me.

Barry's eyes had strayed to Victoria's table again. Their body language projected tension. Roy Don's face grew red, and Victoria leaned forward, pursing her collagen-infused lips and squinting accusingly at him.

"How's your father doing?" I asked in an attempt to regain Barry's attention. The old man hadn't come into the office since his gallbladder surgery several weeks ago. I usually didn't cross paths much with him, but I would have liked to ask about his interaction with the Car King when he set up Kwintone's trust fund.

"What's that?" Barry had just realized I'd spoken.

"Your father. How's he doing?"

"Oh." Barry shrugged. "Taking it easy. We haven't talked since last week." He savored a sip of wine. "Mom's been pestering me to come over for dinner. What night's good for you?"

"I'll have to check my calendar." I reached for my phone to consult my trapping schedule, wondering if this proposed dinner with his parents would even happen.

A thud from the next table distracted me from my phone. Roy Don rose, sliding his chair across the terracotta floor with an ear-piercing scrape. "Enough," he bellowed, tossing his napkin at the table as he stalked away.

Victoria's eyes filled with tears, and she blotted them with her napkin, partially dislodging one of her fake lashes, now suspended like a butterfly alighting on her cheek. With a sniff, she looked around the room, straightened her shoulders, and forced a public relations smile.

Barry leaped up, almost crashing into a server who approached, juggling a tray with our food. She managed to rescue the plates before they fell and eased them onto our table as he swerved around her and made a beeline for Victoria.

"Enjoy," mumbled the server, looking too embarrassed for me to meet my eyes.

"Thank you. It smells great." I pretended to focus on my steaming shrimp while watching my so-called boyfriend comfort his treacherous ex-wife. She was bawling now, playing on his sympathies as she'd perfected after their eighteen years of marriage.

One bite was all I could manage; my stomach was in knots. I pulled my napkin off my lap and stood. But since Barry had driven us, I couldn't easily leave. I headed for the haven of the ladies' room—fortunately, in the opposite direction from Victoria's table—to cool off and think.

A dark-haired woman was touching up her lipstick at the mirror when I bounded in. She turned around, and our eyes met. It was my friend Jill Hernandez. "DeeLo! I didn't know you were here."

"We're on the patio. Are you with Scott?"

She nodded with a dreamy smile and fingered her diamond engagement ring. The restroom's fluorescent lighting amplified its sparkles like a prism, reminding me of the different stages we'd reached in our romantic lives.

Before she could ask me about Barry, I moved to a different topic. "Any new developments in the Aiden Green story? I understand it's a murder investigation now."

She put away her lipstick. "According to my sources, the police don't have any new suspects. I'm going to Neuro Labs on Monday to interview some of the employees. From what I hear, Green's second-in-command, Gregory Thompson, is the real proponent of using animals in their research instead of implementing the new procedures. It's rumored that he and Green didn't get along very well. Maybe Thompson wanted Green out of the way."

I had foolishly believed the cats were safe now that Aiden Green was dead, as if someone had cut off the head of the snake. But the Hydra had another head, perhaps more lethal than before. Different person in charge, same deadly policies. "What about the other employees? Was Green well-liked?"

"I'll know more on Monday." Jill made a move for the door. "Let's talk then."

I stopped her. "Jill… are you guys getting ready to head out?"

"Yes, why?"

"Would you mind giving me a ride home?"

Chapter Thirty-Six

In the back seat of Scott's car, I composed a text to Barry. "Saw you were busy, so I caught a ride home with Jill."

I stopped and deleted "with Jill." Let him wonder how I got home.

My finger hovered over the Send arrow. Shaking my head, I put my phone away without sending the text. Barry didn't deserve an explanation. Let him wonder what happened to me. How long would it take for him to notice I was gone?

Manny greeted me at the door, weaving his body between my calves as I made my way inside. I picked him up and held him close. It felt good to bury my face in his fur, relishing the unconditional love of my pet.

I checked my phone—nothing from Barry—then plugged it into the charger on my nightstand. My stomach rumbled. I should have asked for a to-go box and taken my Shrimp Fra Diavolo home. But that would have meant walking past Victoria's table again and watching my boyfriend fawn over her.

I headed for the kitchen, opened the refrigerator, and stared at its contents. Nothing appealed to me. And I was out of ice cream.

Manny meowed at me until I filled his bowl with fresh kibble.

Before undressing for bed, I checked my phone again. Still nothing from Barry. I tried not to picture him in Victoria's arms, but that was all I could think about.

I had just curled up against the pillows with a book in my hands and Manny at my feet when the doorbell rang. Manny started making biscuits on my legs through the comforter, his way of urging me to ignore the interruption.

Setting down the book, I extricated myself from the bedding. I pulled on my robe and went to answer, first peering through the peephole to ensure I wasn't about to let in a serial killer.

Barry's face displayed the requisite amount of contriteness. He clutched a Leonardo's bag in his right hand and had just raised his left fist to knock when I opened the door.

He handed me the bag. "Thought you might want your shrimp."

"Thanks." I snatched it from him and started to close the door.

He pushed it open and came inside.

I headed to the kitchen with the bag. "Is there something else you wanted to say?"

"DeeLo…"

"Thanks for bringing me my food, but you didn't have to."

We faced each other awkwardly, shuffling our feet on the kitchen floor. I hadn't put on slippers, and the tile was cold.

"DeeLo, I'm sorry…"

You'd better be. You blew it. "What are you sorry about?"

He gestured toward the kitchen table. "Can we talk?"

I suppressed my instinct to throw him out in a grand, dramatic gesture of the wronged girlfriend, but he was right; we needed to talk like civilized adults.

He took a seat.

I pulled out a chair and sat across from him. "You can't help how you feel. But I can't stick around while you figure it out."

"DeeLo, I… you're the only woman I want to be with."

I shook my head. "That's how you want to feel. But you can't."

"But…" He looked down. He couldn't deny what I'd said.

"The truth is, you've never gotten over Victoria. I've known that since the first time I saw her walk into our office. The way you look at her, the way you talk about her, the way she gets under your skin."

"But that doesn't mean—"

"She hurt you terribly, and I know you *want* to be over her. But you're not. And there's nothing I can do or say to help."

"Really, I am over her. We've both moved on."

I shook my head again. "Maybe she has. But you haven't. She can still press your buttons, and she loves that power. She won't give it up."

He covered my hand with his. It was warm, and I resisted the urge to squeeze it. "DeeLo, I care about you."

"I know you do. But that doesn't mean we should be together."

His mouth sprang open. "What are you saying?"

"You need to sort out your feelings about Victoria first. There may be trouble with Roy Don, which could leave an opportunity for you two to get back together."

"But I don't…" The denial lacked sincerity, and the sentence trailed off as if Barry realized it wasn't convincing anyone. He reached for my shoulder, perhaps attempting to pull me in for a kiss.

I shrugged him away. "Don't make this any harder."

Withdrawing his hand, he rested his elbow on the table. "Does this mean you're quitting the law firm too?"

I hadn't thought that far ahead… that breaking up with my boyfriend would mean unemployment. Was I ready to face the job market? "Are you firing me?"

"No. You do great work. I just thought…"

I straightened my back against the chair. "If the office dynamic gets too uncomfortable, I'll resign."

"Fair enough." He fidgeted with the edge of the table.

"You should get going." I rose and started toward the front door.

As he stepped outside, he turned to me again. "I'm sorry, DeeLo."

I sighed. "I want you to be happy. But I deserve happiness too."

He averted his eyes. "I'll see you at the office on Monday."

After he left, I heated the Shrimp Fra Diavolo and scarfed it all down. Maybe it was the spices in the tomato sauce, but tears ran down my cheeks as I ate.

Chapter Thirty-Seven

Merilee was willing to meet at Catherine's house to teach us how to apply her barn cat relocation technique to move the at-risk cats from the Patel Shopping Center to Oakwood Studios. Although she'd been to Catherine's place several times to pick up food or equipment, Merilee had never been inside. As we entered, I watched her scan the feline-friendly couches draped with sheets, strategically placed scratching posts, and a selection of well-used cat trees.

Catherine had cleared the dining room table and made a pot of coffee. I moved a toy mouse from my chair and tossed it toward a young tabby tripod, who promptly caught and wrestled with it, unhandicapped by the missing limb.

Snowball, the long-haired, aloof white beauty who ruled the household, perched on the top shelf of a carpet-covered cat condo and watched us curiously as we took our seats.

Merilee ran her slender fingers over the head of an ear-tipped tuxedo cat, weaving between our legs under the table. "You're absolutely sure these kitties can't go back to the Patel Shopping Center? Even with the best intentions and following all the protocols, relocating community cats sometimes fails. It's meant to be a last resort."

Catherine shook her head as she poured our coffee. "Animal Control already picked them up, and the bulldozers will start any day now. They wouldn't be safe even if we were allowed to put them back."

I nodded in agreement. "Sandra has given us until Friday to make arrangements." I left unsaid what we all understood.

"Okay." Merilee sipped her black coffee and puckered her thin lips. She set her cup back on the wooden table. "There's an actor's trailer on the lot that we're not using right now, which will provide shelter. The resident cats hang out there a lot. I can set up my big crate inside the trailer. Are all these cats related, or at least on friendly terms?"

Catherine nodded. "They're a family. More or less."

"Good." As Merilee spoke, Catherine finished her thought, and they said in unison, "It's important to keep bonded groups together."

"How large is the crate?" I pictured the tiny cages that housed the cats at the animal shelter and wondered how stressed the poor refugee cats would be if they had to stay in those prisons long-term.

"Big." Catherine waved her arm dismissively. "They'll be fine. Merilee knows what she's doing."

Merilee smiled and passed me some pictures of relocation cages. "Much bigger than the ones we use at adoption events." She seemed more tolerant of my novice ignorance than Catherine.

Catherine glanced at the pictures, too.

"The cats will stay in the crate inside the trailer for two to four weeks, depending on how fast they adjust to the new environment." Merilee started to sip her coffee, then made another pained face. She probably spotted the grounds that had escaped the filter into the strong brew. "We'll keep the windows and doors open so the resident cats can go in and check out the new arrivals. Everyone will be able to sniff each other, get familiar with their scents, but the cage bars will keep them separated in case they get the urge to fight over territory."

I'd read that colonies of cats could be territorial and would chase off new arrivals. That was one of the arguments I used to promote TNVR as a means of keeping the population in check in a specific area.

"Do you think the other cats will accept them?" I shook the empty carton of half and half and squeezed out a couple of drops. Catherine made no move to replenish it.

Merilee shrugged. "The property is large enough that the residents shouldn't feel too threatened. Eddie and I give them all plenty of food and love."

"You and Eddie will be feeding the cats?" I asked.

"And four or five other employees. We have lots of animal lovers working at Oakwood. The cats will get fresh food, water, and treats every day. We'll put several litter boxes in their crate, which we'll keep scooped."

"How will you do that without the cats escaping?" I remembered how quickly Octomom raced past me the first time I tried to service her quarters in Catherine's basement.

"It has an access panel." Catherine gave me her typical *Aren't you stupid* look as if she were suddenly the barn cat expert.

"I'll show you how it works," said Merilee. "Once the cats get acclimated to the space, we'll open up the crate and let them explore; hopefully, they'll recognize the trailer and the surrounding grounds as their new home and won't run off."

"How can I help?" asked Catherine.

Merilee and I exchanged glances. Who was this woman in our midst? What had she done with Curmudgeon Cat?

"Do you want to be on the feeding rotation?" Merilee asked. "We'll try to do it at the same time every day. We talk to the cats to get them used to the sound of our voices and associate them with food." She gestured around the room at our audience of house cats. Two patch tabbies had emerged from hiding and were staring at us from their perch on the back of the couch. "I'm sure you know how to do that."

Catherine nodded. "Okay. Just tell me when. I want to see how this whole barn cat program works."

"I'll show you how we'll set it up." Merilee drew a diagram of the Oakwood Studios property, the location of the trailer, and then another showing the placement of the acclimation crate.

As we pored over her drawings, I repeated, "So, Eddie Fenton helps you feed the cats?"

Merilee smiled. "Yeah, he's a big animal lover. He's the one who supervises all the shots where animals appear in films. Perfect job for him. I think he was the first employee to notice we had a feral cat colony living on the property."

"I know Eddie's an avid animal advocate." I returned my focus to the drawing.

"Tell me about it." Merilee shook her head. "He's always emailing petitions about animal issues around the office for us to sign."

I remembered the plethora of petitions on his social media postings. "How does he feel about Neuroscience Laboratories? Right in our backyard, doing experiments on cats."

Catherine looked up from the drawings. "Those people are still experimenting on cats?"

"They've been in the news a lot lately," I said. "The man who was stabbed the other night was their CEO, Aiden Green."

Catherine frowned. "Oh. I don't watch the news. Someone got stabbed?"

"It's the talk of Oakwood Studios, as you can imagine." Merilee folded up her drawing. "I still look over my shoulder whenever I walk through the parking lot. You won't catch me staying after dark."

"Do you think volunteers will be afraid to go to that wooded part of the lot to care for the cats?" I wondered if the trailer she'd referenced was the one I saw the first night I trapped at Oakwood Studios—when Aiden Green was attacked.

Merilee shrugged. "We feed mostly in the daytime, and no one will have to go alone, so I don't think security will be an issue."

"Did they ever catch the person who stabbed the guy?" Catherine picked up our cups.

I hadn't finished, but the coffee wasn't very good anyway. "Not yet. And they don't even know if the person who stabbed him is the same one who finished him off at the hospital." As I spoke, I recalled again that Eddie and Zach had been in the hospital lobby the evening I came down from Aiden Green's room. Just as they had both been present at Oakwood Studios the night someone attacked him. And who knew where Victoria was…

"What? Someone finished him off at the hospital?" Merilee's eyes widened.

I nodded. "Looks like it. The police suspect foul play."

Catherine sighed. "Well, if this dude tortured cats, his death is no loss to society."

Merilee and I exchanged amused glances. This was more like the Catherine Foster I knew. "Unfortunately, society doesn't see it that way."

Catherine harrumphed.

"And Neuro Labs isn't doing anything illegal." I felt a furry body rub against my legs and reached down to pat Snowball's head. "A bit unethical, perhaps, since they took a grant to fund testing procedures that don't use animals, and yet, rumor has it, they're still using animals."

Merilee snorted. "I don't think anyone is surprised. They didn't change a thing after the protests. Our efforts fell on deaf ears."

Our efforts? I eyed Merilee. "I heard that Eddie participated in those protests. Were you there too?"

She nodded. "That's where Eddie and I met. It was before Oakwood Studios. I left the site before the protest got violent, though. Too bad some people tried to push too far, and it hurt our message."

"Violence doesn't work," I agreed.

Catherine came back from setting the mugs in the kitchen sink. "It's a shame you guys couldn't get that place shut down."

I turned back to Merilee. "Did you know about Eddie's meeting with Aiden Green the other night?"

She averted her eyes. "I told him it was a bad idea."

"What's this?" Catherine furrowed her brow.

"Eddie Fenton tried to get Aiden Green to admit he still uses cats for his lab tests," I explained. "After Sandra Larson took over the shelter, she refused to give Neuro Labs any animals. Mr. Green was looking for another source, and Eddie offered him cats we were planning to TNR."

Horror, turning to rage, crossed Catherine's face. "What?"

I touched her shoulder. "It was a trap. Eddie was never going to give the lab any cats. He just wanted to record Green taking the deal and expose the company's deception."

"Yeah." With a glance at her watch, Merilee picked up her papers and rose. "Oh, look at the time. Gotta go. Thanks for the coffee, Cat. I'll get the crate set up next week and let you know when we're ready."

She was out the door before we had time to finish our discussion. Just when it was getting interesting. I wondered what else Merilee knew about the night Aiden Green was stabbed. She didn't seem in any hurry to talk about it.

Chapter Thirty-Eight

Getting ready for work, I wondered how awkward crossing paths with Barry at the office would be after our breakup. I took extra time with my makeup, striving to look my best, and even wore the blue jacket he liked. He would regret losing me.

It was mid-morning, and I was trying to project a "business-as-usual" demeanor. I still hadn't seen Barry despite having had dozens of imaginary conversations with him. My cellphone rang. The caller ID read: Sandra Larson.

Had she changed her mind about sparing the cats? Moved up the deadline? "Good morning, Sandra." I tried to keep the anxiety out of my voice.

"DeeLo, I'm so sorry. I had a doctor's appointment this morning, and when I came in…" Her voice trailed off. "This wasn't supposed to happen."

"What, Sandra?" Alarm bells sounded inside my head. It had to be about the cats, and I braced myself for her answer.

Her voice was breathless. "One of the new officers. He didn't know…" It sounded like she'd covered the receiver, but not very well, because I heard her sharp words to someone in the room. "Those people tricked you. You should have called me."

"Sandra, what happened? Where are my cats?" Mittens, Octomom, Big Mack, the others… were they all dead? Executed simply because they didn't have traditional homes?

She came back on the line. "That pompous horse's behind from that crooked animal abusing laboratory…" Again, she put a hand over the mouthpiece. "No, there's nothing we can do now. Go walk the dogs."

"Sandra, where are my cats?" I repeated. I knew they weren't really *my* cats, but I felt invested in their welfare now.

"DeeLo, I'm sorry. But someone from Neuro Labs picked them up this morning before I got here. He told my officer I'd approved the transfer, and no one bothered to check with me."

"How could that happen?" But of course, she'd just told me. I gripped the phone. "We have to get them back. Can't you tell them it was a mistake?"

I was still firing off angry words after Sandra hung up.

* * *

I recalled that Jill was going to Neuro Labs today to interview some of the employees, to gather insights into Aiden Green's work life—and to read between the lines to determine if one of them might have wanted him dead. I phoned to brief her on the situation with the cats. Maybe she could intervene.

I caught her as she was heading out the door. "DeeLo, I have an interview with Greg Thompson at Neuro Labs in half an hour."

"Good. Tell him to give back the cats."

She snickered. "Like he's going to listen to me."

"I think you should do a story about how Neuro Labs deceived the director of Animal Control to kidnap those cats. People should be outraged."

Footsteps clattered across the pavement, and a car door opened. "I'm upset about the cats, too, but my editor won't care. The story I have to focus on now is the murder of Aiden Green." The car door slammed, and the engine started. "Talk to you later, DeeLo."

I stared at the phone wallpapered with Manny's adorable face. If no one else would fight for those cats—one of whom might be Manny's father—I'd have to.

* * *

Neuroscience Laboratories was housed in a gray stucco building on a remote stretch of Loop Road, set far back from the street. The boxy structure, which I'd probably passed many times without noticing, reminded me of a small warehouse. As I turned into the parking lot, I fought the urge to run inside, open all the cages, and free the animals. Just like Eddie, Merilee, and the other protesters had tried to do two years ago.

I expected to see Lisa Ross at the reception desk and hoped she'd be sympathetic to the plight of the Patel Shopping Center cats. After all, she'd fed them when she worked at the insurance company and probably knew many of them by name. Reminding her about the feral cats living on her own property—that I had helped fix and vaccinate—usually won her support for whatever cat-related cause I championed.

But instead of Lisa, a twenty-something woman with neck tattoos, Goth make-up, and lime-green streaks in her short, dark hair manned the desk. She was on the phone when I entered and didn't look up despite the loud whoosh of air from the glass front door as it closed.

I fake-coughed but still failed to get her attention.

Jill was nowhere to be seen; perhaps she'd already gone into Greg Thompson's office for their interview.

Scanning my surroundings while I waited, I was drawn to a series of photographs covering the plaster walls. Testimonials under large black-and-white snapshots of smiling patients surrounded by adoring, grateful family members described the people who had recovered from debilitating diseases—Bell's palsy, multiple sclerosis, brain tumors—thanks to the research done at Neuro Labs. Nowhere were pictures of any animals whose lives had been sacrificed for these miraculous outcomes.

"May I help you?" The receptionist had hung up the phone.

"Uh…isn't Lisa Ross here? I thought she'd be working today."

The woman twisted a strand of green-tinted hair. "Oh… poor Lisa. No. She's still at Children's Hospital in Atlanta. Her son isn't any better."

"What? Her son's in the hospital?" Detective Ross hadn't mentioned it, but then, we weren't really friends.

The receptionist nodded. "Lisa's been at his bedside almost nonstop for the past two weeks."

"What happened to her son?" I was glad I hadn't left a detailed message about relocating feral cats when I called Lisa over the weekend.

The receptionist winced. "Something went terribly wrong with his treatments." She bit her lip, perhaps wondering how much she should share with a stranger, but then must have decided that telling a salacious story outweighed privacy concerns. "Lisa's son has epilepsy, and the seizures were becoming more frequent. He's been in a trial for a new drug, but just got worse. And now he's in a coma."

"Oh, my God! Poor Lisa." *And poor Detective Ross.* "What—?"

The phone rang, and, with a shrug, the receptionist excused herself to answer.

Before I could digest the horrible news about Lisa's and Paul's little boy, Jill emerged from a hallway behind the reception desk. Escorting her was a tall, bald man in a shiny polyester business suit. *Do people still wear those?* His close-set eyes and overbite reminded me of a rodent, and his booming voice reverberated into the lobby. "Thank you for coming in, Ms. Hernandez. As I mentioned, we're all distraught over Aiden's untimely death, but we're determined to carry on our mission to save people from debilitating diseases."

I glanced at the "Successes" wall, marveling at how he used the same phraseology as in the testimonials.

Jill's dark eyes flashed, which told me she wasn't satisfied with the information she'd gathered from their interview. "I appreciate your time, Mr. Thompson. But I'd still like to speak to some of your other employees who knew Mr. Green so I can present a more rounded profile of the murder victim in my story."

Greg's closed-mouth smile did not reach his eyes. "I'm afraid that won't be possible, Ms. Hernandez. Everyone has already been interviewed by the police, and no one wishes to speak with the press."

The woman at the reception desk waved her hand. "I haven't been interviewed yet."

Greg pursed his lips. "Roxie, you don't have time for this nonsense. Have you finished with those files yet?"

Jill and I exchanged glances. I jumped up and rushed over to Greg, eclipsing Jill while she slipped her business card to Roxie.

"Mr. Thompson." I held out my hand. "I'm DeeLo Myer from the Pecan Point Humane Society, and I think there was a little mix-up this morning."

He narrowed his eyes at me, making his face appear even more rat-like.

"Someone from your lab picked up five cats at the Pecan Point Animal Shelter today. But the cats had already been promised to PPHS. I'm here to get them back."

His nostrils flared. "I don't know what you're talking about."

"The cats from the animal shelter. For your research." I shot a glance at Roxie.

She started to open her mouth, but quickly shut it after a warning glare from her boss.

He turned to me with a smile faker than one of Victoria's. "I'm sorry, Miss..." He waved his hand as if he couldn't remember my name, but it wasn't important to him. "We have no cats here."

I stood my ground. "If I could just see your holding cages, I could identify—"

His face reddened. "I'm afraid that area is off-limits. Besides, there's nothing to see. We've upgraded our testing procedures and no longer use cats. Ms. Hernandez can verify, as I told her the same thing. We toured the lab to allow her to observe our procedures."

Alarms were sounding in my head. "But why—"

The acting CEO took a step forward and pointed toward the door. "And now, ladies, I must ask you to leave. This establishment isn't open to the public, and we all have to get back to work." He shot another pointed look at Roxie.

Jill nodded at me, and together, we exited the premises.

We stood between our cars to compare notes. "He's lying," I declared.

"No kidding. He didn't give me anything useful. Our interview was one big PR spiel." Jill shoved her tablet back into her bag.

"Did you at least get an idea about the layout of the building? Any idea where they might be keeping the cats?"

Jill tapped her chin as she thought. "When we toured the lab, I noticed a locked door off to the side, and I thought I heard a meow. Greg said it was a closet, but if I had to guess, I'd say that's where they keep the cats."

I nodded toward the building. "Let's go around back and see if we can figure out which room it is. And if they have any windows."

"DeeLo, are you crazy? We can't do that. I'm not even—" Jill shook her head.

She was probably right; trespassing was a bad idea. "Okay. But I'll find a way to rescue those cats."

Chapter Thirty-Nine

After Neuroscience Laboratories, my next stop was the police station. The tiny lobby was empty, and the desk officer behind the plexiglass screen raised her gray head from her paperwork as I walked in. "May I help you?"

"Is Detective Ross in?"

"No, I'm sorry. He's taking a leave of absence."

"Leave of absence?" As soon as the words left my lips, I knew why. "Because of his son?"

The officer nodded, her lips sealing into a grim expression. "Just terrible. How can we help you today?"

"I'd like to report a theft."

She pointed to a clipboard on the counter containing a stack of "incident report" forms. "Fill this out, and I'll have an officer take your complaint."

I picked up the clipboard and retreated to one of the hard, plastic chairs in the lobby. I scribbled my name and contact information, and then wrote a summary of how the Patel cats were taken unlawfully from Animal Control by a Neuro Labs employee. Frowning at the question "value of the stolen property," I decided on "undetermined." Feral cats weren't anyone's property. And how do you value a life?

After rereading my form, I took it back to the desk officer and watched while she examined it.

Brow furrowed, she peered over her reading glasses. "Feral cats?"

I nodded. Not exactly expensive show cats, but surely, they deserved consideration.

"You own them?"

"Well, no. No one owns them."

Still looking perplexed, she slid her finger down the paper and stopped at a spot in my narrative. "They were 'stolen' from Animal Control?"

"Yes. The Pecan Point Humane Society entered into a binding oral agreement with the director of Animal Control to take possession of the cats, but someone from Neuro Labs picked them up this morning without authorization."

She sighed. "Are you with Animal Control?"

"No, but I represent the Pecan Point Humane Society. We've already arranged a new place for these cats."

She squeezed her eyes shut and shook her head. "If anyone files this complaint, it should be Animal Control. But really…aren't there plenty of cats to go around?"

"That's not the point."

"I've read that feral cats are an invasive species, and they're doomed to short, miserable lives out in the wild."

"But—"

"Why not let their lives come to some good? Isn't Neuroscience Laboratories that company that finds cures for people with terrible brain diseases? Those cats might help save someone's life." She slipped my paper off the clipboard and folded it in half.

"In other words, you're not going to take my complaint."

She gave me a smile that was trying hard not to be condescending. "I'm sorry, but I see this as a civil dispute between Animal Control, the humane society, and Neuroscience Laboratories. It's not a matter for the police."

I twisted my mouth into a frown that tried not to be a pout. "But you don't understand—"

"Have a good day, ma'am." She went back to her paperwork.

It wasn't shaping up to be a good day.

Defeated, I headed back to the office. I placed calls to Merilee and Eddie, but landed in voicemail for both.

* * *

Merilee was the first to return my call. "Hey, DeeLo," she greeted me. "I have the cats' space all prepared inside the trailer. Catherine has been great. Did you know she used to build shelters for the feral cats in the reserve before Nick Norton made her stop?"

"Yes, but…" Merilee's reference to Catherine made me dread giving her the news about the cats. Catherine would make it my fault.

Merilee rushed on to describe the cage set-up: how they'd made little sleeping hammocks for each cat, how the enclosure contained dark hiding places where the kitties could feel safe, how access panels would allow volunteers to clean the litter boxes and supply food and water without risking the cats' escape or harm to themselves.

I waited for her to take a breath. "Merilee…"

She continued talking. I used to think of her as a woman of few words, but I could hear the enthusiasm in her voice as she outlined the plans for enrichment, monitoring, and introduction to the resident cats.

"Merilee…." I cleared my throat.

"Depending on the weather, we'll probably open up the trailer after their second week and let the other cats wander in. They'll be curious about the new arrivals, and we can gauge how well they'll accept them. The new cats will still be inside their crate, so we shouldn't have any bloodshed."

I raised my voice. "Merilee, we have a problem."

"The trailer—" She stopped mid-sentence, and I imagined her brain rewinding and running through worst-case scenarios. "Did something happen to the cats? Sandra changed her mind?"

"Worse." I winced. "Someone from Neuro Labs picked them up from the shelter early this morning."

"What? I thought Sandra wouldn't do business with those people."

"She doesn't, and she's furious. This happened before she arrived at work.'

"Oh, no," Merilee moaned. "Those poor cats."

"I tried to file a complaint with the police, but they said it's a civil matter. I don't think Sandra will push it; she has too much going on. She's mad about what Neuro Labs did, but in the end, those cats are out of her hair."

"That's cold." Merilee seethed.

"It's reality."

Out of the corner of my eye, I spied two of the newer interns nudging each other as they walked past my cubicle. The tall one with a long, red ponytail whispered my name, which caused the short, dark-haired one to stare at me with something like pity in her eyes.

I turned my attention back to Merilee. "I went to Neuro Labs this morning, and they claimed they don't have any cats. The acting CEO is sticking to the story that they no longer use animals for their tests."

"Liar."

"It was obvious he was lying," I agreed. "He wouldn't let us see the empty cages. But I'm at a loss now about what to do next."

Merilee was silent for a moment, and I sensed she was stewing. A faint drumming filtered through the phone like fingernails striking her desk.

"I'm trying to persuade Jill Hernandez to write an exposé for the *Pecan County News*," I suggested.

"Meh. People won't care."

Merilee was right. And Jill was focused on gathering information about Aiden Green, the murder mystery the public *did* care about.

Merilee's tone took on a brightness that hadn't been there before. "Let me talk to Eddie."

"Yes," I agreed. "And maybe Zach can help. He hasn't been elected yet, but—"

"Not Zach. Just Eddie."

Chapter Forty

After work, I headed to Oakwood Studios to meet with Merilee and Eddie. As soon as I arrived, Eddie shut the door to the breakroom. Everyone gathered at the end of a long, white table surrounded by metal folding chairs. Catherine was there too, all fired up about the cats and ready for battle. At least she wasn't targeting her anger at me. By the companionable way they were chatting—laughing, heads together as if they shared an inside joke—I concluded that she and Merilee had bonded over preparing the cats' temporary quarters.

En route to my seat, I passed a large, stainless-steel refrigerator and laminated shelves containing various snack foods. Two coffee makers, an espresso machine, a microwave, and a toaster sat on the Formica counter next to the sink, full of Oakwood Studios mugs, some food-caked flatware, and a few small, partially rinsed plates. A comfy-looking couch faced a flat-screen television mounted on the wall. The room setup suggested that Zach cared about making the employees' downtime as pleasant as possible.

Eddie sat back down, and Merilee craned her neck toward the door. "Is Zach gone?"

"God, I hope so." Eddie rolled his eyes. "I tried to hustle him out earlier, but that man wanted to quibble over our grocery list."

"Why don't you want Zach to join us?" I searched their faces.

Merilee twirled her pencil over her yellow legal pad. "He's running for public office. We don't want to do anything to jeopardize his campaign."

"But..." I gulped. "We're not going to do anything illegal... are we?"

They all exchanged glances.

"Depends on what you consider illegal." Eddie made air quotes around "illegal."

"Trespassing? Breaking and entering?" I could already hear Barry's scolding voice when he came to bail me out of jail. *DeeLo...* If he'd even show up.

Again, they all exchanged glances as if daring each other to speak first.

"Neuro Labs stole the cats." Catherine held her nose in the air; in profile, her flat face resembled a Persian cat. "We need to get them back before they're tortured. Have you seen pictures of what they do to those poor animals in the name of science?"

I shuddered. I had seen too many pictures.

"My contact in the lab told me which window leads to the animal holding area." Eddie held up his phone, displaying a Google Earth image of the building. "If I remember correctly, those windows are tiny and high, so we'll need a ladder. Merilee would probably fit through best, but maybe DeeLo—"

"Guys!" My eyes darted to Merilee and Catherine, whose heads were nodding in perfect harmony.

Merilee leaned forward. "Someone would have to drive my truck. I think I have the only vehicle big enough to transport all those cages."

"How will we get the cats out once we're inside the building? The cages won't fit through those tiny windows." Catherine furrowed her brow. "Can someone go around to the front door? Does anyone know how to shut off the alarm system?"

"Guys!" I held up crossed arms like a referee signaling a personal foul. "We can't break into Neuro Labs and take the cats. We'll go to jail. And even if Zach's not involved, we're his campaign staff. Victoria Barton will jump on that story in a heartbeat."

They all looked at each other and frowned.

"What else ya got?" I scanned their long faces.

Merilee pursed her lips. "A protest?"

"Peaceful?" I rested my chin in my hand.

Catherine shook her head. "Your protest wasn't successful last time."

"Can PETA help?" asked Merilee. "They'd get us national attention. Don't you know some of the higher-ups, Ed?"

Eddie scrolled through his phone. "Still haven't heard back from my contact."

Catherine straightened in her chair. "We have to get that lab shut down."

"And how can we get it shut down?" I asked.

"There must be some law they're breaking." Merilee turned to Eddie. "Haven't your insiders found anything? Health department violations? O.S.H.A. rules?"

"Working on it."

"In the meantime, how will we get the cats back?" Catherine pursed her lips. "Who knows how long it will be before those sadists start experimenting on them? If they haven't already."

I thought about Roxie, the receptionist who had seemed willing to talk to Jill. "I have an idea—"

The door to the breakroom opened, and in walked Zach. Eddie paled.

"What's going on?" Zach's eyes swept our faces and lingered on mine. "Oh, hello, DeeLo."

I swallowed. "Hi, Zach."

"Looks like I walked in on something," Zach tried again. "Anything I can help with?"

We all clammed up like the See-No-Evil, Hear-No-Evil, Speak-No-Evil monkeys.

I cleared my throat. *We should tell him about the cats. Maybe Zach will come up with a solution. A legal one.* "We—"

"Just working out the details of the Meet-and-Greet on Friday, Babe," Eddie said smoothly, his color returning.

Catherine's eyes popped. Planning a political event was probably the last thing she thought she'd be doing tonight.

Merilee flipped to a new sheet of her legal pad and looked around expectantly, ready to take notes. "I think we've nailed down a restaurant that will donate the appetizers. DeeLo's going to take pictures of the food and post them with a shout-out on social media."

Zach smiled. "That's great. Thank you all so much for organizing this, especially on such short notice. By the way, did you think about having any music? I ran into Peter in Costumes, and he has a cover band that would be willing to play if we need someone. They won't even charge us; they just want the exposure."

"Great idea, Babe. I'll get right on it." Eddie had snapped fully into event planning mode. "And I already spoke with Dad. He's coming with a big check."

Good. At least part of my scheme was falling into place.

Zach lingered in the doorway. "Sure I can't help with anything?"

Eddie waved his arm. "Go on to the grocery store so we're not eating dinner at ten o'clock again. I'll see you at home in an hour or so."

We breathed a collective sigh of relief when Zach took the hint and left.

Eddie shook his head. "Now, where were we? Operation Save the Cats."

* * *

Fortunately, I eventually convinced my cohorts that it would be foolhardy to break into Neuro Labs and take the cats without the cooperation of some insiders. We tossed around several other scenarios but couldn't devise a viable rescue plan for the cats. When we adjourned our meeting, Eddie agreed to contact his spies at the company and enlist their help. He also promised to keep trying to contact PETA in the hope of getting them involved.

At home, I heated leftover pasta and ate it at the dining room table by myself. Then I spent a quiet evening reading a new mystery and cuddling with Manny. Barry didn't call, not that I expected him to.

While I got ready for bed, I turned on the evening news. A reporter from Atlanta's CBS affiliate stood in front of the Neuroscience Laboratories building, interviewing a tearful Lisa Ross.

I squinted at the screen. *What was going on with her?*

Chapter Forty-One

I turned up the television's volume. The camera zoomed in on Lisa's face, her eyes red and dripping tears. If she could see herself, she'd be mortified, but the media was playing up the drama. "Those murderers… They killed my son." Lisa gasped and sputtered a big, ugly sob. "My precious baby was a guinea pig!"

Paul Ross, Jr. is dead? My stomach dropped, and I let out an expletive that startled Manny. *What happened?* I couldn't imagine the pain Lisa and Paul must be suffering. Losing their son? It must be a parent's worst nightmare.

Mercifully, the camera cut back to the reporter. With the Neuro Labs building looming behind her, dark and threatening like a haunted gothic castle, she put on her most solemn face. "Lisa and Paul Ross, residents of Pecan County, are heartbroken over the death of their six-year-old son, Paul Jr. But did it have to happen?" Her voice rose an octave. "Young Paul suffered from epilepsy, and for months, his seizures were becoming more severe. Doctors had tried various medications at different doses, but nothing helped."

"Then his mother, Lisa, who works at Neuroscience Laboratories, confided in the company's CEO, the late Aiden Green, about her son's medical dilemma. The research lab specializes in finding cures and treatments for neurological diseases such as epilepsy. Mr. Green recommended Epifelus, a new drug the company had just developed and was about to put on the market pending FDA approval. He assured Lisa it had been thoroughly tested and was perfectly safe." The reporter took a deep breath, enhancing her on-air performance. "But instead of getting better, the child slipped into a coma and never recovered. His shocking death this afternoon is being investigated as we speak."

The screen switched to a close-up of the Neuro Labs building, and the reporter's words came through as a voiceover. "Neuroscience Laboratories was in the news two years ago when a radical animal rights group staged a violent protest over their experiments on cats."

I thought about Eddie and Merilee. *Radical animal rights group?*

"Last year, the company obtained a grant to fund an innovative research method that didn't involve testing their products on animals. But naysayers claim the scientists never implemented the new procedures. And now, according to Lisa Ross, Neuroscience Laboratories has gone straight to human trials—with devastating results for Paul Ross, Jr."

The camera panned to Roxie, the woman I'd seen manning the reception desk that morning, as she exited the building. It was still daylight, so the interview must have been taped earlier; I was watching a rerun.

"Ma'am, a moment, please." The reporter stuck a microphone in Roxie's face. "Are you an employee of Neuroscience Laboratories?" Her eyes flitted to Roxie's ID badge. "What can you tell us about the tragic death of a child after he ingested one of your company's drugs?"

"It's just awful. Criminal even." Roxie shook her head with exaggerated sadness, clearly relishing being on TV. She pushed a strand of lime-green hair away from her heavily lined eyes. "I heard that Epifelus had never been tested before Aiden gave it to that sweet little boy."

The screen returned to the reporter. "Gregory Thompson, the acting CEO, refused to speak with us on camera, but he claims Neuroscience Laboratories has done nothing wrong. He insists all of their drugs are thoroughly tested before being administered to humans. Nevertheless, the lab has been shut down pending an investigation." She signed off with her name and the local station's call letters.

The program went to commercials, but I kept staring at the screen, stunned. Manny rubbed against me, demanding attention.

I pulled him onto my lap as I picked up my phone. My hands were still trembling.

It was too late to call the Rosses, but I composed a text to the detective. "Just heard about your son, and I'm so sorry. Please let me know if there's anything I can do." I hovered over the Send arrow. My words sounded trite and wimpy, but what else could I say? I went ahead and pressed Send. And then instantly regretted it. Should I have sent it to Lisa instead? Should I have at least mentioned her? Should I send her a text, too? I decided one text to the family was enough to express my condolences, however awkward it sounded; the Rosses had plenty to deal with right now.

Next, I texted Jill. "Just watched the eleven o'clock news. Did you see the interview with Lisa Ross? Can you believe it?"

Her reply came right away. "We're on it. Lots to uncover with this story."

And with the lab shut down, what had become of the cats?

Chapter Forty-Two

Sandra called me the next morning shortly after I arrived at the office. "Your cats are back at the shelter. Come pick them up any time; the sooner, the better." After a pause, she added, "They don't appear to be harmed. That big tom with the wild eyes—the one you call Big Mack—is feisty as ever."

I sighed. One mystery solved; at least the cats were safe. For now.

"There were others in the lab, though." Sandra shuddered. "I saw their condition when the officers brought them in, and I wish I hadn't. Unfortunately, some of the animals were too far gone; we couldn't save them. But three of the younger cats might be adoptable. They're with the veterinarian for assessment."

When I was at Neuro Labs, I'd been focused on saving the Patel ferals and hadn't let myself think about any other cats at risk. Cats I'd never met. Part of me had wanted to believe Greg Thompson's claim that they no longer used animals in their research. "The devil has a place for those people," I muttered. "Let's hope the survivors will be okay."

"Fingers crossed." Sandra made a clucking sound. "Terrible what that CEO did."

She was referring to the treatment of Paul Ross, Jr., of course. What happened to the research cats was perfectly legal. Their lives were only spared because a child had died under suspicious circumstances, forcing the closure of the lab.

"Anyway," Sandra continued. "Your kitties lucked out. I hope you have a solid plan for them because they can't go back to that shopping center."

"We do," I assured her, and we said our goodbyes.

My next call was to Merilee to give her the news and make arrangements to move the cats to their new enclosure.

"So, we don't have to break into Neuro Labs after all?" She sounded more disappointed than relieved.

"No, thank goodness. Will you call Catherine? I know she wants to be involved."

"Sure thing. I'll tell Eddie, too. He'll be ecstatic."

As we hung up, my phone dinged with an incoming text. "Thanks," was Detective Ross's response to my sympathy message from last night. Our exchange sparked a pang of guilt for rejoicing over the cats' freedom at the expense of his tragedy.

I should call Lisa. She shouldn't have to receive my condolences secondhand, via a text to her husband's phone. Although we weren't good friends, we were more than casual acquaintances.

I was about to call her when Barry walked up.

"Good morning, DeeLo." Something in his tone said there was more behind "good morning."

"Good morning." I ignored any hidden meaning, refusing to imagine the worst. "What can I do for you, boss?"

"Can we talk?"

Uh, oh. I'm about to get the ax. My heart raced as I followed him into his office.

* * *

Barry closed the door behind us, and I took the chair facing his desk. I put on a pleasant, unsuspecting expression like an eager intern waiting to hear about a new assignment.

"I've missed you," he said as he sank into his swivel chair.

Not what I'd expected him to say. Lately, I hadn't had much time to think about him. But being in the office forced me back to the reality of our breakup and to wonder if my days here were numbered. How much did I really want this job and the emotional turmoil that came with it? Would it be better to rip off the Band-Aid now? Make a clean break—all the cliches for parting ways.

He pulled a thin folder out of his stack and opened it. "You know Detective Paul Ross and his wife, Lisa?" Even though he inflected the end of the statement as if it were a question, he already knew the answer.

I nodded. "I suppose you heard what happened to their son."

Barry grimaced. "Such a tragedy." He turned back to the folder. "Mr. and Mrs. Ross came in a few weeks ago to prepare a financial plan, create their wills and health directives, start a college fund for their son…" He must have noticed the surprised look on my face. "One of the interns has been working with them. That's why you don't have anything in your database yet."

I sighed. It still should have been logged into the database, but the interns didn't always remember to do it. "I guess everything has changed now."

"Exactly. When things calm down, the Rosses will need to come in and figure out their next steps. Unfortunately, the life insurance benefit from their son's policy was small—barely enough to cover funeral expenses." He stared at the wall. "No one expects to have to file a life insurance claim for their child."

"Do you want me to contact the Rosses and set up a meeting?" After I spoke, I wondered if I'd assumed prematurely that Barry was assigning me the Ross file.

He brightened. "Could you?"

"Of course. But shouldn't we wait for them to call us when they're ready? Now is probably not a good time."

"Lisa left me a long, rambling message this morning, asking us to file a wrongful death suit against Neuroscience Laboratories." Barry closed the folder and handed it across the desk to me. "It sounds like she might have a case, but our firm doesn't handle situations like that. Maybe refer her to that personal injury lawyer Catherine Foster used." I was impressed to hear Barry call the attorney who handled Catherine's suit against the trucking company that killed her husband and daughter a "personal injury lawyer" instead of an "ambulance chaser," which was how he usually described that class of legal professional.

"And you want me to break the news to Lisa?" I must not be fired after all.

"Please. You built a rapport with her while you were trapping cats on their property."

"Sure." I'd planned to call Lisa anyway; now it was business. I rose. "Anything else?"

Barry shook his head. "Thank you, DeeLo. I don't know what I'd do without you." With a tentative smile, he bowed his head back into his paperwork.

* * *

As soon as I returned to my desk, I dialed Lisa's number. After four rings, the call went to voicemail, and Lisa's terse greeting instructed me to leave a message.

"Lisa, this is DeeLo Myer from Barton & Barton. I want to let you know how truly sorry I am about what happened to your son." I took a breath. "No parent should have to go through that. Uh… if there's anything I can do, please say the word. Also…" I paused again, searching for an appropriate segue into business. "Now is probably a bad time, but when you're ready, please give us a call at the firm to go over—"

Before I could finish leaving the message, my cellphone rang, and Lisa's name flashed on the screen. I hung up the office phone and answered my cell. "Hello."

"DeeLo?"

"Lisa, I was just leaving you a message about how sorry—"

"Barry needs to make those people pay." Venom seeped from her voice.

"Barry doesn't handle…"

"I know we have a strong case."

"You probably do, but…" I paused. Lisa wasn't going to listen to my excuses. "Why don't you tell me everything that happened so I can point you in the right direction? All I know is what I heard on the news last night."

188

"Well, you know the whole story, then."

Not exactly. "Walk me through the timeline. Do you feel okay to talk about it now?"

"I guess."

"All right. Start when your son got sick. How did Aiden Green happen to suggest the treatment? What's the name of that drug again?"

"Epifelus." With a sniffle, she spelled it out, and I sensed she was fighting back tears. "About six months ago, Paul's seizures got rougher and more frequent. So bad, he was injuring himself, and we had to take him out of school. The doctors tried dozens of different medications, changed the dosage, experimented with his diet, but nothing helped." Another sniffle. "One day, Mr. Green found me crying at my desk and asked what was wrong."

That glimpse of humanity conflicted with my negative impression of Aiden Green, the animal abuser. "He didn't know about your son's medical condition before?"

"No. We never spoke much. I was like another piece of office furniture that could take messages. But after I told him about my son, he seemed sympathetic and anxious to help." She punctuated her statement with a sob. "He told me about Epifelus, the new drug the company was getting ready to launch. It was supposed to manage epilepsy better than anything else on the market, and he claimed it had been thoroughly tested. They were just waiting for FDA approval, which he expected any day." She spat the word "tested" as if her tongue had touched broken glass.

I didn't want to think about the tests and how they were conducted. "Did he suggest you try this drug—Epifelus—on your son?"

Lisa sobbed.

I struggled to fit the pieces of the puzzle together; it seemed like some were missing. "When Aiden proposed using Epifelus, what did your son's doctor say?"

She let out a loud snort. "Dr. Smythe had given up."

Dr. Smythe was Paul's doctor? Dr. Smythe, the bumbling candidate for county commissioner? I shouldn't have been surprised. The bio on his campaign postcard said he'd been practicing family medicine in the community for over twenty years. In a small town like Pecan Point, I was bound to know some of his patients. "But if there was something new, something promising, perhaps—"

"The doctor didn't care. He said…" Lisa's voice trailed off as if she didn't want to repeat what the doctor had said. "We were done."

"But what about getting a second opinion? Seeing a specialist?"

"No. Dr. Smythe wouldn't recommend anyone. Said it wouldn't do any good."

I tried to re-enact her conversation with Dr. Smythe and how she'd arrived at the decision to proceed with an experimental drug without a physician's supervision. Did Detective Ross approve? "So, Aiden Green suggested you give your son Epifelus without his doctor's supervision?"

Lisa sputtered something unintelligible.

A mother's desperation. "But how—?" I was stepping into sleuth mode without realizing how crass I must sound. Was the Neuro Labs CEO practicing medicine without a license?

Lisa regained control of her voice. "He told me Epifelus was safe. But my son is dead because of Aiden Green."

"I still don't understand how…" So many questions swam in my brain, but I couldn't ask a woman who'd just lost her son to answer them.

"DeeLo, you have to help me."

"I'm trying. We'll find someone." Lisa was in no state to hear that Barry wouldn't sue Neuro Labs on her behalf. Now was not the time to talk about the needed revisions to their wills and estate plan—what Barton & Barton *could* handle for them. I'd have to make a few phone calls and screen some reputable personal injury lawyers for her. "When you feel up to it, why don't you write down everything you remember, in chronological order, starting with the time Aiden Green first approached you about the treatment for your son? If you'll email it to me, we'll go from there, and I'll put you in contact with someone who will help."

She agreed, and we hung up. I hoped the exercise would focus her on the crucial details the attorney would need when deciding whether to take her case. If Neuro Labs was responsible for her son's death, they deserved to pay.

Chapter Forty-Three

My next call was to Jill. She'd been reporting the story as it unfolded and should be able to provide more answers about Neuro Labs than Lisa.

"I suppose you want to know what happened to the cats," Jill guessed when she answered.

"Animal Control picked them up. Sandra Larson called me."

"Sounds like the cats lucked out. You must be relieved."

"The Patel ferals lucked out. Others that were in the lab longer… not so much. But what do you know about Paul Ross, Jr.? Did you talk to the TV reporter who interviewed Lisa?" I fingered the file folder Barry had given me, which contained none of the answers I sought.

Jill was quiet for a moment. "What's your interest in Paul Ross, Jr.?"

"The Rosses are Barry's clients. Lisa wants to file a lawsuit against Neuro Labs, and I'm gathering information to refer her to a personal injury lawyer, since Barry doesn't handle cases like that."

"Why does she need a referral from you? Can't she just call one of those attorneys who advertise on TV?"

"Lisa's an emotional wreck right now. I'm helping her organize the facts for whoever takes her case."

"In other words, that's your excuse for being nosy." Jill sighed. "It's creepy. From what I can determine, Aiden Green gave her that drug against the advice of her son's doctor."

"That's crazy." I shuddered. "Green was practicing medicine without a license?"

"According to his bio, Green majored in chemistry and went to medical school for a while, but, you're right, he wasn't a licensed physician."

"How did they decide to test that drug on a child?"

"According to Greg Thompson, Epifelus was ready for market, just awaiting FDA approval."

"What kind of testing did they do?" On cats? Could that really predict how the drug would affect a human child?

"No one has shared that information. Lisa starts crying whenever anyone asks her for details. Aiden Green can't tell us his side of the story, and the company hasn't provided any documents about the testing."

I considered Lisa's tearful exchange with the TV reporter last night and my telephone conversation with her this morning. It sounded like Jill had similar results. And who had the heart to probe further with a woman grieving her child? "What have you found out from the other employees at Neuro Labs? Did that Roxie woman ever get in touch?"

Jill made an affirmative sound. "Roxie is quite chatty. You saw her on the news?"

"It sounds like she has plenty of opinions, but she's not an official spokesperson, is she?"

Jill grunted. "Not hardly. But I think we can forget about talking to an official spokesperson. Everyone else at the company has gone mum. The feds are swarming the place. All Greg Thompson will say is, 'No comment,' and 'Neuro Labs has done nothing wrong.' This morning, he called my editor and threatened legal action if we dare imply that Epifelus caused that little boy's death."

"What are you going to say in your story?"

"Of course, we won't accuse them of anything. But people are smart enough to read between the lines."

"What does Roxie think?" My eyes strayed to one of the interns who had stopped outside my cubicle. The short one with the oversized glasses, whose name I could never remember. She looked like she wanted to ask me a question, but was afraid to interrupt. I smiled and held up a finger.

"You saw how Roxie overdramatizes everything, so I'm not sure how much to believe." A voice grew louder in the background, followed by Jill's muffled words, "Be right there." In a lower volume than before, she continued, "But DeeLo, Roxie thinks Lisa was the one who pushed Green into giving her the Epifelus."

My mouth hung open. "What? How did she—?"

A desperate mother, game to try anything, proven or not. Before I could complete my question, Jill murmured, "Sorry, I have to go."

"Me too. Talk to you later." I hung up and turned to the intern, who was pretending to study the contract in her hand so I wouldn't know she was eavesdropping. "How can I help you?"

***

After work, I headed to Oakwood Studios to see how the cats had settled into their enclosure. The tall wire assimilation crate took up most of the trailer's living room. It was furnished with cat trees and perches, plush beds, hammocks, cardboard litter boxes, and carpet-covered tunnels where the animals could hide. A large access door opened to the trailer's entryway. Merilee had just fed the new arrivals.

"Nothing wrong with their appetites," I mused, watching the felines chow down, eyeing each other suspiciously as they ate to ensure no one was getting better food. "Wait. I only see three cats. I thought there were five?"

Merilee smiled. "Catherine took Octomom and Mittens home with her."

I wasn't surprised about Octomom. "Mittens too?"

"Octomom and Mittens are mother and daughter, you know, and they're bonded."

I chuckled. Octomom and Mittens had hit the jackpot—a welcome reward after their recent ordeal. "Two fewer cats subject to this relocation experiment."

Someone pounded on the trailer door, and in a moment, Eddie pushed his way inside.

"The cops are back asking questions." He sounded breathless. "Zach's called our lawyers, and they're on the way. There's a new detective assigned—" Eddie stopped. "Oh, hello, DeeLo."

Merilee's eyes widened, then darted from me to Eddie.

"Cops?" I asked. "What are they asking questions about?" Surely, they wouldn't care about our cat relocation project. And our plot to break into Neuro Labs had never come to fruition.

Eddie looked away. "Just… something that happened here. You know about it—that guy who got stabbed. Green." He turned back to Merilee. "I thought Detective Ross was done with us, but now some *woman* has taken over the case, and she wants to start the questioning all over again. She says Ross is taking a leave or something—"

"His son died," I supplied.

"What?" Mouths dropping, Merilee and Eddie stared at me.

"Didn't you hear the news story? About the child who died after taking an experimental drug from—"

Merilee clasped a hand over her mouth. "That was Detective Ross's son? Oh, my gosh." She glanced at Eddie. "I see why Ross is off the case. Talk about a conflict of interest. I bet he thought Green deserved whatever he got."

"The detective's wife worked at Neuro Labs when Aiden Green suggested the treatment that ended up killing her son," I explained.

"Unbelievable." Merilee shook her head as she checked the security of the cage door. "I guess we have to talk to this new detective now?"

Eddie shrugged. "Looks like it."

I followed Eddie down the steps and waited while Merilee closed up the trailer. "Let's get it over with," she said.

Should I accompany them? Could I help? Might I learn something notable? But the detective hadn't asked for me, and moreover, I didn't have a lawyer like the others apparently did. "Guess I'll take off. Good luck with your police interview." I took a step in the opposite direction then stopped. "Lisa's having a memorial service for her son on Thursday at the Pine Street Funeral Home. I'm going to pay my respects to the family."

Eddie tightened his lips. "We should go too. I believe in supporting anyone who's been a victim of those awful cat torturers."

Merilee nodded. "I agree. So glad they shut that place down."

The two headed back to their office, and I started for the parking lot.

When I reached my car, I composed a quick warning text to Kwintone. "There's a new detective assigned to the Aiden Green case, and she's asking questions at Oakwood Studios. You might want to alert your lawyer in case she contacts you."

I had just pressed Send when someone rapped on my window.

* * *

The new detective appeared to be in her forties, compact, with distinct Asian features. Her blunt-cut, straight black hair framed her golden face; long, straight bangs almost touched her thin eyebrows. "Delores Diane Myer?" She held a badge against my window. "Detective Olivia Chen. May I have a word with you?"

How had she known I was here? Had she run my plates?

I rolled down my window. "What's this about?"

She lowered her badge. "I understand you were here last Monday night when a man named Aiden Green was stabbed."

"I'm the one who found him and called 9-1-1." I shuddered at the memory of all that blood. "The police have my statement on file."

"I understand, Ms. Myer, and I've read your statement, but I have a few more questions."

Everyone else was smart enough to hire a lawyer, and I had a habit of putting my foot in my mouth whenever I talked to the police on my own. "I need to call my lawyer."

Olivia harrumphed. "You think you need a lawyer? You're not under arrest. I just have a few questions for the report."

My fingers gripped the steering wheel. "It's my right. And I'd feel more comfortable with him there."

A new Cadillac CT5 pulled into the parking lot, and two men in dark suits, carrying briefcases, got out and walked toward the Oakwood Studios offices.

Olivia gestured toward them. "Everybody thinks they need a lawyer today. Makes me wonder why. What are they hiding?" She turned back to my window and handed me a business card. "Okay, Delores Myer. Call your lawyer and come to the police station tomorrow morning at nine o'clock sharp."

Chapter Forty-Four

When I arrived home, out of habit, I phoned Barry, almost forgetting we had broken up. He answered on the first ring. "DeeLo. Nice to hear from you."

"I need a favor." Not detecting resistance in his voice, I forged ahead, explaining that another detective had taken over Aiden Green's case and wanted to interview me. "She's expecting me at the police station at nine o'clock tomorrow morning. Is there any way you can come with me?"

He was silent for a moment, probably stunned by my chutzpah and searching for an excuse to let me down as diplomatically as possible. "I would, but I have a client coming in at nine tomorrow, and it will be hard to reschedule this late."

Of course. What did I expect? "Okay…thanks anyway."

"But let me check with Dad. He can probably go with you."

"Your father?" I wondered if Barry had told his parents about our breakup.

"Sure. The doctor gave him a clean bill of health after his surgery, and he'll be glad to get out of the house."

"Well…" The old man had always been nice to me, but we'd never worked together much. I had no idea if Barry had told him anything about my recent legal troubles. Would he be sympathetic to my situation?

But wait…this could be an opportunity. If Barry's father agreed to accompany me to the police station, I could ask him about the Car King setting up Kwintone's trust fund. "That sounds wonderful. Tell him I'd be very grateful."

"I'll give you a call back as soon as I talk to him," Barry said.

* * *

Barry Barton Sr. met me at the office the next morning. He looked fitter and more rested than he'd been in a while, and the rosy color had returned to his cheeks. Like Barry, he still had a full head of hair, although his was thinner on top and mostly gray, now that he'd reached his mid-sixties.

He asked me to drive us to the police station.

"Are you sure you trust me?" I teased. "How will you get home if they lock me up?"

"In your car, of course. With you driving." He nudged my shoulder. "You're in good hands, DeeLo. They're not going to lock you up."

I'd already briefed him about my connection to Aiden Green's case, from finding him injured on the Oakwood Studios lot, to my stop at his hospital room, to my Neuro Labs visit on Monday—just in case Detective Chen thought it was relevant. During the drive, we steered clear of any mention of my relationship status with Barry.

At a traffic light, there was a lull in the conversation about my impending interview. I seized the opportunity. "Do you remember setting up a trust fund for the Car King? It must have been about twenty-five years ago, so…"

Mr. Barton chuckled. "The Car King. I still get a kick out of that nickname."

The light changed, and I returned my attention to the road.

"Of course, he wasn't the Car King yet back then." Mr. Barton stroked his chin. "I remember him as Edward Fenton, the baseball star. He'd just left the Los Angeles Dodgers and moved to Atlanta to play for the Braves. I was curious about how he found our firm, but he said his wife's parents lived in Pecan County and had recommended us."

"So, you set up a trust fund for his son?"

Mr. Barton eyed me. "This is confidential information, you know."

"Of course. It doesn't leave the firm."

He nodded. "Good. But yes, for Little Eddie. Must be a young man in his twenties by now."

"Eddie?" But of course. The legitimate son would have a trust fund, too.

"Didn't Mr. Fenton also create one for Kwintone Johnson?"

Mr. Barton's brow furrowed. "Oh, yeah. About a year earlier. For the child of Elaine Johnson. The boy had an unusual name; it could have been Kwintone."

"Edward Fenton's son?"

Mr. Barton shrugged. "I assumed so, but Fenton never said. Their relationship wasn't my business. I just handled the paperwork."

We'd reached the police station, and I pulled into a parking space. Show time.

* * *

Detective Olivia Chen was waiting for us. As we all shook hands with phony goodwill, her dark eyes bored into me, perhaps sizing me up as a lying, knife-wielding attacker.

"Thank you for coming in," she said as we sat down. "Mr. Barton, as I told Ms. Myer yesterday, there's no need for you to be here, but of course, she's within her rights to have you stay."

Mr. Barton nodded. "Ms. Myer is happy to answer your legitimate questions, and I'm staying."

"Very well, Mr. Barton." Olivia's finger ran over the printed statement on her desk. "Ms. Myer, you stated you were on Oakwood Studios' property last Monday night to trap feral cats for the Pecan Point Humane Society. Is that correct?" The way she uttered "trap feral cats" oozed skepticism, and I sensed we weren't off to a great start.

"That is correct." I glanced at Mr. Barton for guidance.

"By yourself?"

"Uh, no, not the whole time."

"Who were you with?"

Again, I glanced at Mr. Barton, who gave me a shrug. "A volunteer named Kwintone Johnson."

She turned back to my statement, probably searching for the name. "And was Kwintone Johnson with you when you found Mr. Green?"

"No, he left before that."

"What about Demi Myer?" She squinted at the page. "Your niece? When did she come to help you trap cats?"

I winced. Someone, most likely Detective Ross, had written a big, red question mark on the statement. Although I couldn't read it from my vantage point, I guessed it was the part about Demi chasing after a cat.

"Ms. Myer?"

My eyes darted to Mr. Barton's face, but he gave no signal that I shouldn't answer. I took a breath. "After I finished trapping and drove off, I spotted Kwintone's car on the side of the road. He wasn't inside, but the windows were down, and his phone lay on the passenger seat. I looked around for him, waited for a few minutes, but when he didn't return, I called Demi."

"Why did you call Demi Myer? And not the police?"

I gripped my hands together to keep from fidgeting. "Demi is Kwintone's half-sister. They were supposed to meet up that night. I wanted to find out if she'd heard from him before bothering the police."

"So, Demi came to the scene to help you look for Kwintone? Not to trap cats?" She made a notation. I should alert Demi that she might get a call from the new detective.

Still no warning from Mr. Barton to zip it. "Yes. We pressed the last number in Kwintone's call log and heard ringing from behind a big oak tree. We followed the sound and found Mr. Green lying on the ground. He appeared to be hurt. He was still conscious and begged us to help him, so I called 9-1-1. Demi took off his jacket and tried to stop the bleeding."

"You said Mr. Green was alert when you found him. Did he say what happened?"

"No. And he lost consciousness shortly after we got there."

Detective Chen studied the statement and wrote more notes. "Did you ever find Kwintone Johnson?"

Before I could answer, Mr. Barton cleared his throat. "That question has nothing to do with Ms. Myer's interaction with Aiden Green."

The detective gave him the side-eye and turned back to me. "Ms. Myer, did Kwintone Johnson go to meet Aiden Green after he left you at the trapping site?"

Mr. Barton leaned forward. "Ms. Chen, DeeLo Myer will not speculate about where Kwintone Johnson went. That's a question you'll have to ask him."

Detective Chen clicked her tongue against her teeth and flipped a page. "Ms. Myer, when did you learn about Mr. Green's occupation?"

Mr. Barton gripped the edge of the desk. "My client doesn't need to answer that question. It's irrelevant to this investigation."

The detective raised her eyebrows. "Well… we'll see about that." Had she heard about my visit to Neuro Labs?

I smiled at Mr. Barton, grateful that he'd prevented me from running my mouth into the weeds.

Detective Chen picked up another sheet of paper. "Ms. Myer, why did you go to Mr. Green's hospital room last Wednesday evening?"

"I—"

Mr. Barton's eyes blazed. "Ms. Chen, my client has already answered that question. She was the good Samaritan who found Mr. Green injured and called for paramedics, perhaps saving his life. As a good Samaritan, she was merely checking on his welfare."

Raising an eyebrow, the detective turned to me. "Is that why you sneaked past the security guard to get into the room?"

Mr. Barton jerked his head toward me; perhaps I'd omitted that part when I told him about my hospital visit.

"I didn't *sneak*… the guard was asleep, and I didn't want to disturb him." I sucked my lip.

Detective Chen narrowed her eyes at Mr. Barton. "And what did your client put into Mr. Green's IV while she was in his room?"

I blinked. *What an odd question.* If something in the IV killed Aiden Green, wouldn't toxicity tests show what it was?

Mr. Barton rose and motioned for me to follow. "Detective, I suggest you consult with the hospital staff about any irregularities with the patient's IV. There's no evidence that my client touched anything in that room, and she did not have a motive to poison Mr. Green. Unless you have grounds to arrest her, we're done here."

Detective Chen didn't try to stop us as we left her office and headed for the parking lot.

I turned to Mr. Barton as I started the car. "Thanks for coming with me. Do you think she suspects me of murder?"

"A murderer needs means, motive, and opportunity. Unless there's something else you haven't told me—like sneaking past the security guard— you only have opportunity." He shook his head. "That detective is on a fishing expedition. To boost her career, she has to arrest someone, but right now, she has nothing."

Chapter Forty-Five

As I drove back to the office, one of Zach's campaign brochures slid onto the floorboard from the pile I'd set on the console to make room for Mr. Barton in the passenger seat. He picked it up and perused it for a few minutes. "This must be the other young fellow running for commissioner against Vicky. Have you met him?"

I nodded. "I'm very impressed with his platform, especially his plans for helping animals in this county. In fact, I'm managing the social media for his campaign."

Mr. Barton chortled. "What does Barry have to say about that?"

I wondered again if Barry had told his parents about our breakup. "We've agreed not to talk politics in the office."

Mr. Barton glanced back at the brochure. "You know, Vicky is determined to get elected, but between you and me, I don't think she's running for the right reasons." He winked. "Don't tell Barry I said that."

I smiled. "Barry thinks Victoria got a raw deal the last time she ran for office, and she somehow deserves the job now."

"The sexism was unwarranted, I agree." Mr. Barton tightened his jaw. "But what did her in was the affair."

Victoria's last run for the Board of Commissioners had happened before I moved to Pecan County, before I'd ever met her or Barry, but I'd done a lot of online research about the race. Her very public dalliance with Commissioner Roy Don Whitehead had led to the Bartons' eventual divorce and dissolution of their business partnership. "Barry was her number one supporter. I think he is this time, too."

Mr. Barton stared out the window. "That woman broke my son's heart, and I doubt his mother and I will ever be able to forgive her. He's been so much happier since you came into his life."

No, Barry didn't tell his father about our breakup. *Should I tell him?*

I swallowed. *No, Barry should be the one to break the news when he's ready.* "Well, if you'd like to learn more about Zach Kirkpatrick, we're holding a Meet-and-Greet on Friday evening."

Mr. Barton raised his eyebrows. "Where? What time?"

"At seven p.m. And you won't believe this… Barry and Victoria's old place."

Mr. Barton let out a guffaw. "Priceless! Does Victoria know?"

"Not sure. Zach's assistant made the booking through the Whitehead Realtors online portal."

Mr. Barton examined the brochure again. "I don't know what my wife has planned for Friday, but I'll consider it. This county needs some new people with fresh ideas."

We arrived back at the office, and I thanked Mr. Barton again for accompanying me to the police interview.

"Don't mention it, DeeLo." He grinned as he got out of the car. "You're practically family."

I responded with a smile that looked brighter than it felt. *I should have told him about the breakup.* "Are you coming inside?"

He followed me into the building. "Thought I'd put in an appearance, check on things. I haven't met the new interns yet."

We almost bumped into Barry, who was bidding farewell to his client at the door.

Barry turned to me. "How did it go?"

I cast a sidelong glance at Mr. Barton. "Your dad was a big help. I'm grateful."

"Son, your girl did fine." Mr. Barton winked at me.

One of the interns dashed up, a notepad in her hand. "DeeLo, glad you're back. Lisa Ross is on the line, and she asked to speak to you."

* * *

I excused myself to my cubicle and took Lisa's call there. Simultaneously, I opened my email and searched for the timeline write-up I'd asked her to send. Nothing. Writing down the details of her son's illness and subsequent death must be as hard for her as talking about it.

"Hi, Lisa, what can I do for you today?"

"Have you filed that lawsuit yet?" Her voice sounded anxious, like she'd had too much coffee.

"Lisa—"

"Those people need to pay. Don't let them get away with murder."

I sighed. "Lisa, we're terribly sorry about what happened to your son. I can't imagine what you and your husband are going through. But, as I told you, Barry doesn't handle civil cases like you're talking about. I can help you find some personal injury attorneys who do." I had located the name of the lawyer who handled Catherine's wrongful death suit, but unfortunately, he had retired and closed his firm. I hadn't had a chance to research the matter further.

Lisa was silent, and I pictured the wheels of her brain turning, processing my words.

"I'm trying to put together a timeline of what happened: when Mr. Green first suggested using Epifelus for your son—"

"I already told you everything, DeeLo!"

No, you didn't. Not really. I understood she was distraught. Maybe I was asking too much of her. "If you could just tell me so I could explain it—"

Lisa was sobbing now. "Are you coming to the service tomorrow?"

It was pointless to keep needling her. Did my insensitive questions make her feel guilty? It must be painful to relive the nightmare every time I asked her something. From what I could glean between the lines, she'd administered the drug against her doctor's advice in her desperate attempts to help her son. Would that affect her case? I wanted to help her make it, not judge her. My voice softened. "Of course, we'll be there. See you tomorrow. And again, I am so sorry for all you're going through."

* * *

As soon as I hung up with Lisa, my cellphone vibrated. I glanced at the caller ID: Kwintone.

"Thanks for the warning," he said when I picked up. "That detective just called."

"I spent the morning with her." I glanced over my shoulder. Barry and his father still stood near the entrance, surrounded by several interns. Everyone was laughing and chatting. "Detective Chen asked me about you, but my lawyer advised me not to answer." When Kwintone didn't respond, I continued, "What do you think she's after? What does she think happened?"

"I have no idea. Guess I'll find out when she asks me."

I switched the phone to my other ear, trying to get more comfortable in my chair. "How do you think Aiden Green got stabbed?"

"With a knife, I suppose. Or some other sharp object."

I groaned. "You know what I mean. How did the situation escalate into that kind of violence?"

"I told you I didn't see it happen." His tone was flat, and I wished I could see his face. For Demi's peace of mind—and my own—I wanted to be sure Kwintone was innocent.

"But you must have your suspicions about who did it."

"I don't."

"You told me you saw someone running through the woods and went to check it out. Left your car unlocked and your phone on the seat, so it must have seemed urgent at the time."

He coughed. "I wasn't sure what I saw. And when I got back to the parking lot, Zach and Eddie were heading to their car."

"What about the person in Green's car? You said—"

"I didn't get a good look. Might have only been a shadow."

I drummed my fingers on my desk. "You said you rode with Zach to his and Eddie's place so you could discuss DNA tests. But when you got to their place, and Eddie arrived in your car, what did you talk about?"

"Noth—" There was a beep, and Kwintone excused himself. In a moment, he was back on the line. "That's my lawyer; I have to take this. But to answer your question, we didn't talk about Green anymore that night."

Right. I stared at the phone until the screen went black. *Am I supposed to believe that?*

Chapter Forty-Six

Close to a hundred people crowded into the Pine Street Funeral Home. Even those who didn't know the Rosses were touched by their loss and shocked by their son's death. Some may even have been a little voyeuristic.

The chapel was filled with flowers, stuffed animals, sympathy cards, and family photos showing happier times. A large, color studio portrait of the smiling boy was displayed on a table at the front of the room. Solemn organ music played through speakers as tearful mourners filed past before finding their way to the pews.

Lisa and Paul sat in the front row, hands clasped, faces somber, wet eyes ringed in red. They were surrounded by people who must have been relatives. Uniformed officers representing the Pecan Point Police Department occupied the second row. My pulse quickened when I spotted Detective Olivia Chen among them, even though she didn't look my way.

Barry and I, accompanied by two of our interns who had worked on the Ross documents, found seats midway back. Barry entered the pew first, and I deferred to the two law students before sliding in like a bookend.

I gazed around the room, searching for familiar faces. Roy Don and Victoria strolled down the aisle, her hand lightly touching his forearm, and they slipped into a pew next to two of the sitting commissioners, all wearing conservative dark suits. Even at this time of community mourning, Victoria had orchestrated the optics. In her vintage black Chanel, she fit right in, as if she had already won the election.

I stole a glance at Barry to see if he'd noticed his ex-wife's entrance. Sure enough, he was staring at her.

Dr. Smythe and his wife stumbled into the back row just before the service began. They had to squeeze past the man on the aisle who had no intention of scooting over to make room for them.

I wasn't surprised to see Zach, Eddie, and Merilee seated in the row in front of the Smythes. I chose to think their presence was less about Zach's political ambitions than Eddie's vow of solidarity with someone harmed by Neuro Labs. Across the aisle from them sat Roxie, the receptionist I'd met at the lab, flanked by some people I didn't recognize but assumed were her coworkers. Acting CEO Greg Thompson was not among them.

Jill stood by the door, surveying the crowd. To her, this memorial service must be a newsworthy event.

The music stopped, and a silver-haired, middle-aged minister-type wearing a name badge with the funeral home's logo moved to the lectern at the front of the room. "Ladies and gentlemen, we are gathered here today to remember the life of young Paul Ross, Jr. Only God knows why he was taken from us so soon. On behalf of his adoring parents, Paul and Lisa, we thank you for your love and support."

Lisa laid her head on her husband's shoulder, and he stroked her curly hair as she sobbed. I swallowed. My heart ached for them.

The speaker droned on with generic funeral platitudes that made me wonder if he'd ever met the child we were mourning. I caught phrases like "God's will" and "the Lord's plan" that I doubted were comforting to the Rosses.

After a brief prayer for the youngster's soul, the officiant asked for members of the audience to come forward and share their memories.

Lisa let out a plaintive moan; obviously, neither she nor her husband was in any condition to speak.

A small, fortyish, bald man rose from the front row. He squeezed Lisa's shoulder, and from his coloring, features, and mannerisms, I guessed he might be her brother. When he approached the lectern, the officiant stepped aside.

"Hello everyone, and thanks for your support during this time of sorrow for our family." The man's voice shook, but he took a deep breath and smiled, making eye contact with the other relatives in the front row. "For those of you who don't know me, I'm Lionel, Lisa's older brother. Or as Paul used to say, 'Uncle Lion.'"

Soft chuckles emanated from the front pew, and even Lisa's lips turned up a little.

Lionel went on to talk about what a sweet boy Paul Jr. had been and recounted several funny stories that lightened the mood. "Paul loved those kitties his mama fed and wanted to bring them inside. Lisa explained over and over that he couldn't because he was allergic. Paul told her, 'When I grow up, I'm going to make allergies go away.'" Lionel sniffled and continued, "We used to joke that he'd grow up to become a doctor. I even bought him a toy stethoscope, which he loved."

When Lionel sat down, several other relatives took their turns sharing memories.

A chubby, middle-aged woman dressed in a black pinstripe pantsuit identified herself as Paul Jr.'s kindergarten teacher. "Paul wanted to be a police detective, like his father. I remember when some art supplies went missing, he organized a search party with his classmates and solved the case."

I smiled. *Doctor, police detective, maybe President of the United States.* At six years old, the child should have had plenty of time to choose a career path.

A small, dark-skinned girl about Paul's age, hair in two long braids, got up after encouraging gestures from several adults and other children seated near her. She walked timidly to the lectern, which was taller than the top of her head. The officiant lowered the microphone to her level. She turned and faced the audience. "Paul Ross was my friend." With a glance at her cheering section, she raised her voice and steadied its trembling. "Everyone's going to miss him." Her eyes darted around the room, and she scurried back to her seat.

Tentative claps were followed by louder applause as mourners looked at each other, wondering whether clapping was appropriate. I felt myself joining in. I'd never really bonded with Paul Jr., but hearing all the stories from people who loved him brought tears to my eyes.

After the schoolgirl sat down, there was a lull. Just when it seemed no one else wanted to speak, Dr. Smythe rose and lumbered down the aisle.

"Ladies and gentlemen." He turned to face the audience. "It's a sad day for us here on earth, but rest assured, the Kingdom of Heaven is rejoicing as God welcomes little Paul Ross, Jr." He cleared his throat. "I've known Paul since he was two, and he was a good boy. The Lord works in mysterious ways, and we mortals should not question why He would take someone so young and let others of us keep living and sinning." He clucked his tongue. "But the boy's mother chose to play God with an experimental drug that had disastrous consequences—"

A collective gasp rippled through the crowd, and someone let out an anguished cry.

Lionel and another male relative jumped up as Lisa burst into a fresh round of sobs. Face flushed, Lionel grabbed Dr. Smythe's arm and dragged him off the stage.

"May God forgive her." Dr. Smythe stared directly at Lisa.

I winced. My theory about Lisa administering the drug to her son without medical supervision might be true, and I wondered how that would affect her lawsuit against Neuroscience Laboratories.

Still gripping Dr. Smythe's arm, Lionel addressed the audience. "Please join the family in the next room for a reception where you can share your condolences with Lisa and Paul." He muttered something harsh to Dr. Smythe before shoving him away.

The doctor shook himself off, held his head in the air, and joined his wife at the exit. Was he hoping to further his political ambitions with his bombast? In my mind, he hadn't done his career—political or medical—any favors.

Barry rose, so the rest of our group did as well. Being on the aisle, I led the party out of the pew. "Do we have time to stop at the reception before we head back to the office? I'd like to console Lisa after that debacle."

"Sure," Barry replied, and we headed en masse to the adjoining room.

* * *

As I approached Lisa, Victoria barreled ahead of me and threw her arms around the grieving mother, rubbing her back and smoothing her curls. "That man had no business… You were trying to help your child. If he'd only supported you, done his job as Paul's doctor, maybe this wouldn't have happened… And to think he's running for the Board of Commissioners."

Of course, Victoria would make this about the election. Plug her candidacy.

Detective Ross stood awkwardly nearby. He shook hands with several men, accepted a comforting back pat from a uniformed police officer, and then was alone again. Our eyes met.

I took a step toward him. "Detective, I'm so sorry. I don't know what to say."

He held out his arms and pulled me into a hug. "Thank you for coming, DeeLo. This whole situation has been a nightmare."

"I can only imagine." His fragrant aftershave tickled my olfactory nerves as I touched his muscular shoulder to keep my hands from hanging limply at my side.

"What she did…" he murmured against my hair.

"DeeLo!" Lisa's voice interrupted our embrace before I could decipher his words, and we jerked ourselves apart.

Victoria had left to talk to Barry. I spun to face the detective's wife. "Lisa, I'm so sorry." My words sounded like a CD in a loop. *Why can't I be as articulate as Victoria?*

Lisa moved to embrace me. "Thank you, DeeLo. We're going to make those people pay."

The two Barton & Barton interns had made a beeline for the buffet table, where Zach, Eddie, and Merilee also lingered. When I left the bereaved couple, I headed that way.

Merilee and Eddie acknowledged me grimly. "Tragic what Neuro Labs did." Eddie shook his head. "I hope the family sues them into bankruptcy."

Exactly what Lisa wants. "She asked me to file a wrongful death lawsuit, but our firm doesn't handle personal injury cases. I'm trying to find someone who'll help her. The attorney I thought she could use has retired."

"We know a trial lawyer who specializes in personal injury cases," said Zach. "I'll give you his number." He gazed at Lisa, sharing hugs with a thin, disheveled woman.

I followed his eyes. Was that Evangeline, Aiden Green's ex-wife? Did she and Lisa know each other? Maybe because of their connection to Neuro Labs?

"That woman looks so familiar." Zach nudged Eddie. "Hon, where have we seen her?"

Eddie squinted. "Beats me."

Zach's eyes switched back to Lisa and Evangeline. He clasped his hand to his mouth. "I remember now. She was there that night."

Chapter Forty-Seven

Puzzled, I switched my gaze from Lisa and Evangeline to Zach. "What night are you talking about?"

Zach paled and shot a glance at Eddie, whose face looked like the cat who'd been caught on the kitchen counter.

"The night Aiden Green got stabbed?" I guessed. "You met with him at Oakwood Studios."

Eddie massaged his shiny forehead. "Yes, but we don't know how the stabbing happened. The police keep asking, but we can't help them."

Zach nodded as he set down the small plate he'd been holding. "We invited Green to a meeting in our office, and uh…" He looked up at the ceiling. "Things got out of hand. Green grabbed Eddie's phone and wouldn't give it back. The guy was like an enraged bull. Eddie knew it wasn't worth fighting over the device, and I told Green to leave, or I'd call the cops. He stormed out, and that was the last we saw of him."

"DeeLo, how did you know Zach and Eddie were at the studio that night?" asked Merilee. "How did you know Eddie recorded their conversation with Green?"

"Kwintone told me. To be honest, he felt like Eddie used him, setting that trap for Green."

"Does Kwintone think one of *us* stabbed Green?" Bitterness tinged Eddie's voice.

"I don't think so. He said he saw someone running through the woods, but when he went to check it out, he didn't find anyone. When he returned to the parking lot, you two were on your way to your car." As I spoke, I tried to reconcile their timeline with my own movements: finding Kwintone's abandoned vehicle, searching for him, calling Demi, and following the ringing phone to Green's wounded body. We hadn't seen anyone in the soundstage parking lot, but Zach's office was located on the other side of the building from where we'd trapped, so maybe their account of events made sense.

"Kwintone saw someone running through the woods?" Eddie furrowed his brow. "He didn't tell us that. He said he came back because his car was making a strange noise, and he wanted me to check it out."

"After I heard Green got stabbed, I thought maybe that Kwintone character had done it," said Merilee.

The thought had crossed my mind, too, but I didn't want to admit those suspicions to them. I got the feeling Kwintone was not their favorite person. "But why would he do it? He'd just met the man."

No one had an answer.

I searched their faces. "What did you guys talk about when Kwintone came to your house afterward?"

Zach frowned. "He didn't come to our house."

"Well," Eddie corrected him. "Kwintone bought his Mustang from my father's dealership, and it's still under warranty. He said the engine was making a weird noise, so I told him I'd check it out. I fetched Kwintone's car and drove it to our house, and Kwintone rode with Zach."

Zach nodded. "He didn't come inside."

Kwintone had told me that, while Eddie drove his car, he rode with Zach to their house so he could persuade him to talk Eddie into taking a DNA test. Had Zach shared that conversation with his partner?

"The car didn't make the noise for me," said Eddie. "So, I told him it seemed okay for him to drive home, but he should bring it into the dealership in the morning for a thorough check-up."

"We were done talking about Green," Zach added.

"Besides," said Eddie. "When we left the studio, none of us knew Green had been stabbed. Unless Kwintone knew—because he did it."

I raised an eyebrow. "Why do you think Kwintone could have done it?

Did he have blood on his clothes? Did he look like he'd been in a fight?"

"No," Zach admitted.

Eddie pursed his lips. "I guess not."

"Anyway." I glanced back in Lisa's direction; she was embracing one of the women who had spoken at the memorial service. "You said you saw that woman with Green the night he got stabbed? The one talking to Lisa a minute ago. Her name is Evangeline Powers, and she's Aiden's ex-wife." Had Evangeline been at Oakwood Studios the night her ex-husband was stabbed? Maybe she was the person Kwintone had seen in Green's car. Remembering the rancor in her voice when I brought him up the other day, I wondered if she'd been the one to attack him.

Zach shook his head. "Not her. The woman whose son died. Lisa."

"Lisa?" I spun around to face Zach. "*Lisa Ross* was at Oakwood Studios that night?"

"I'm almost positive." Zach stared at Lisa. "Unless she has a twin sister."

"But…how…? Was she in your meeting?"

"No, she was waiting in the parking lot for him. When Green walked outside, she'd gotten out of the car. She looked mad." Zach placed his hands on his hips, pantomiming an angry woman.

"Did you tell the detective you saw her?" Would Detective Ross have recognized his wife from Zach's description?

"I didn't know who she was." Zach kept watching Lisa. "I just told the police a woman was with Green, and I didn't get a good look at her."

"I wonder what she was doing there," I murmured, mostly to myself. Lisa's son was still alive then, but maybe the harmful side effects from the treatment had started. No doubt she would blame Aiden Green. But why tag along to a clandestine night meeting about procuring cats for research?

"Maybe she's the one who stabbed Green," mused Merilee. "If Kwintone didn't do it."

Eddie snorted, making a *You've got to be kidding* face. "A tiny chick like that? I'd like to see her try."

Grinning, Merilee nudged Eddie in the ribs. "You were afraid to fight him for your phone."

Eddie scowled.

I flashed back to last year when I ran into Lisa and her friend Natalie, headed for their self-defense class on their lunch hour; they both still worked in the Patel Shopping Center then. "Lisa might be tiny, but she studied martial arts. Maybe Green threatened her, and she fought back with something sharp. Her husband's a cop, so there's a good chance he bought her a weapon for protection."

Eddie patted my shoulder. "Sorry, DeeLo. I'm not buying it." He eyed Zach. "Babe, you're seeing things. On the other hand, it sure would be nice to find another witness or a suspect to take the heat off us. That Detective Chen is getting on my last nerve. She called me today, asking again why my phone was found next to Green's body. She keeps trying to poke holes in my statement. I don't think she believes he took it away from me."

"We need to ask Lisa what she observed," I agreed. "Not now, obviously. But if she was there that night, maybe she knows who attacked Green. She worked at his company; she might know who had it in for him. You guys should tell the cops you can now identify the woman you saw in the parking lot."

Spotting Jill headed toward the entrance, I excused myself and left to catch up with her.

"Hey, DeeLo," she greeted me. "I didn't notice you earlier."

I gestured at the large crowd. "Big turnout."

She lowered her voice. "Got to speak with some more Neuro Labs employees. Greg Thompson's not here, so they were more willing to answer questions."

I held my breath. "Did you learn anything more about Green's death?"

Jill's eyes scanned the room. "My contact at the police department told me off the record that the cause of death was poisoning, which most likely happened at the hospital, but the tests couldn't confirm what the substance was. That new detective, Olivia Chen, has been sniffing around Neuro Labs with the feds. Several of the employees think the poison that killed Green might have come from the lab. Something new that doesn't match anything in the standard toxicity panels."

"Wow." *An inside job would make the most sense.* "But how did it get into his IV?"

Jill shrugged. "A lot of employees went to visit him in the hospital. There was a security guard at the door, and he kept a list."

When he was awake...

"Detective Chen is going through those names and questioning everyone who visited."

"I thought Green was unconscious in the ICU most of the time he was in the hospital. Could he have visitors there?"

"Maybe family. But they moved him to a private room once he was stable, and then more people were able to get to him."

How many visitors had been to his room before and after me? Could someone at the hospital check that list for me? I hoped Detective Chen had plenty of suspects to divert her attention. "Was Green well-liked? Did anyone have a motive to want him gone?"

Jill shook her head. "He wasn't popular, but no one was out to get him. Most people I talked to preferred Aiden Green to Greg Thompson."

I gestured toward the thinning crowd. "Why do you think Thompson didn't show up here?"

"Probably afraid to face the scrutiny. And the Ross family." Jill eyed her cameraman, who was shuffling his feet and pointing at his watch, then turned back to me. "And the employees tell me there was no love lost between Green and Thompson."

As Jill headed out, I thought about the rat-faced, autocratic Greg Thompson. Was his name on the security guard's list? Or if not, maybe he had an accomplice.

Chapter Forty-Eight

The rain started early Friday afternoon and never let up. My windshield wipers stayed on high, and I slowed the SUV to a crawl to keep from hydroplaning on the winding streets leading to the Peachtree Lane subdivision, in the hilliest part of town. The red taillights of the vehicle in front of me were my only guide to keep from veering off the narrow road.

My tire got caught in a pothole that had filled with water, sending me dangerously close to the almost nonexistent shoulder of a steep embankment. Gripping the steering wheel, I managed to correct my course.

I hoped the inclement weather wouldn't discourage voters from attending Zach's Meet-and-Greet, but I had a sinking feeling turnout would be low. Eddie and Merilee had worked like beavers planning the event, and they were sure to be disappointed.

As I parked in the circular driveway of 113 Peachtree Lane, my cellphone rang. *Lisa Ross.*

"Hi, Lisa." I greeted her. "Are you still thinking about coming tonight?"

"Where's this Meet-and-Greet again?" She spoke in that same breathless, almost hysterical tone she'd used since her son's death.

"It's at 113 Peachtree Lane. But if you do come, be careful on the roads. It's like being inside a car wash out there." Raindrops beat against my windows.

"I'll be careful. My new car has front wheel drive. I want to meet this guy who can help me file my lawsuit against Neuro Labs."

"I can't promise you Zach's attorney friend will be here. But if not, Zach can give you his number." *And hopefully, we can ask you what you saw the night Aiden Green got stabbed.*

We hung up. I opened the driver's side door, put up my umbrella, and dashed to the covered porch. Someone had placed several baskets at the entrance for dripping umbrellas and a large, sturdy doormat for wiping wet feet.

Entering the mansion, I gazed around the spacious great room, which featured polished marble floors, two-story ceilings, and an oversized flagstone fireplace where gas logs glowed. Two massive faux-marble columns formed a border with the dining area. Floor-to-ceiling windows overlooked a small lake now mostly obscured behind relentless sheets of rain. A velvet rope at the foot of the majestic curving staircase blocked access to the upper story.

This was the first time I'd been inside Barry's former residence, and I was struck by its contrast to the tiny, nondescript apartment where he now lived. Imagining his life here with Victoria made me wonder how well I'd ever known him.

Next to the door lay the guest register with a disclaimer stating that photographs were being taken and, by attending, guests permitted us to use their likenesses on social media.

The band was set up, and the musicians were testing the sound. The acoustics should be good in the large, open space. I didn't know what kind of music they played, but I hoped they'd keep the volume low enough so as not to interfere with conversations. Not only between Zach and potential voters, but the ones I'd planned that would hopefully unlock the mystery of Demi's paternity. And maybe, the attack on Aiden Green.

The caterers had arrived, and Merilee directed them toward the buffet table. "What can I do to help?" I asked, relieving her of a stack of plates.

"See if you can find a mop so we can clean up these muddy footprints." She pointed to a growing puddle near the table. "And have the caterers put the extra trays of mini-cheesecakes in the fridge."

I headed into the kitchen, which was even grander than I'd envisioned—a gourmet chef's dream. *Does Victoria even cook?* Water trickling off his rain slicker, one of the caterers juggled two trays of cheesecake bites. I opened the door to the Sub-Zero refrigerator so he could set them inside.

After trying several doors to pantries and storage closets, I located a mop. By the time the caterers finished their delivery and left, I had cleaned up the puddles and all traces of their footprints. I stashed the mop near the front door; we'd need it again as guests arrived and dripped on the marble floor.

Zach and Eddie descended the stairs, slipped past the velvet rope, and reattached it. Eddie straightened Zach's tie. "You look smoking hot, Babe."

Smoking hot might not be the look we're going for. But in my eyes, Zach presented a professional image, a worthy opponent for the entitled Victoria Barton. Someone who would champion my ordinance changes. I had them pose for a photo, which I promptly uploaded to Instagram with the caption: Pecan County Board of Commissioners candidate Zach Kirkpatrick with his campaign manager, Eddie Fenton.

I snapped a photo of the buffet table—Merilee had arranged our selection of snacks to look like a feast—and posted it to Zach's Instagram feed with a caption. "Don't miss tonight's Meet-and-Greet for Pecan County Commissioner candidate Zach Kirkpatrick. 113 Peachtree Lane. Free refreshments!" I acknowledged the restaurant that had donated the food and tagged them in the post.

The front door opened, and in walked Kwintone, flicking water from his mane like a merman emerging from the sea. He carried an armload of campaign brochures encased in a plastic wrapper.

Eddie relieved Kwintone of the brochures. "Thanks, man. We were almost out."

Zach stepped forward and shook Kwintone's hand. "I appreciate you, bro. Thanks for coming out in this weather."

"I wanted to be here." Kwintone stole a glance at me and mouthed, *Is he coming?*

I shrugged and smiled hopefully. Getting my sister and the Car King together tonight was key to solving the mystery of his paternity and Demi's.

Peeling off the plastic from the package, Eddie looked up. "How's the Mustang running now?"

Kwintone gave him a thumbs-up.

At least there was no open hostility between the would-be brothers after all the suspicions that one of them might have stabbed Aiden Green.

The front door opened as a flash of lightning illuminated the sky, accompanied by a roaring peal of thunder. Rain gushed down like a waterfall.

The Car King entered, peeling off his raincoat. It was my first time seeing Eddie's father in person, and I almost didn't recognize him; the graying mustache and sideburns made him look much older than his picture on the billboards.

My eyes flitted from Mr. Fenton to Eddie and then to Kwintone. I was still convinced there was a family resemblance: the same arresting hazel eyes, the dimple in the cheek, the gap between the top front teeth.

Eddie set the brochures on a side table and rushed to embrace his father. "Hey, Dad. Glad you made it. Appreciate you looking out for Zach's campaign. That check covered this whole event."

"My pleasure, Son. Sorry your mom couldn't come with me. Gramps fell again, so she's helping him and Gram."

Eddie's face contorted with concern. "Oh, I'm sorry to hear that. I hope Gramps will be okay."

The Car King sighed. "It's getting harder for them to live on their own."

Eddie nodded grimly. "Wish they could have been here. But the weather's nasty, so it's just as well. Neither of them sees well enough to drive at night." He grinned. "And we already know they're voting for Zach—no need to give them our sales pitch."

The Car King turned to Zach, and the two men shook hands.

"Good to see you, sir," said Zach. "I appreciate your support. And your son has done a fantastic job—on this event, with my whole campaign." He and Eddie shared a fond glance.

"Happy to help however I can." The Car King beamed. "It's great that you're both taking an interest in the community. Pecan County needs fresh leadership."

Kwintone nudged me. "Offer him something to drink. We can snag his DNA from the cup in case your sister doesn't show."

The Car King's eyes strayed to Kwintone, who was trying to pretend he wasn't staring. "Kwintone? Is that right?"

They each took a step toward the other and converged in a handshake.

"Good to see you again. It's been a while." The Car King released the handshake and patted Kwintone on the back. "How are you, buddy?"

Kwintone studied the man who might be his father. Like me, was he searching for the family resemblance? "Same old, same old."

Right. Except for being questioned in a murder investigation.

Zach put a hand on my shoulder. "Mr. Fenton, I don't think you've met DeeLo Myer. She has joined my campaign as our social media manager."

With a warm smile, the Car King shook my hand. His grip was firm and friendly. "Pleased to meet you, DeeLo. I know these guys are happy to have your help." He scrutinized my face. "DeeLo Myer," he repeated, still gazing at me. "You remind me of someone. Are you sure we haven't met before?"

I shrugged. "Not that I remember."

"Her name was Myer, too." He shook his head as if raindrops had clogged his ears. "It was a long time ago, and she'd be much older than you."

I met his gaze. "Maybe you met my sister, Desiree. She's sixteen years older than I am."

Kwintone caught my eye, and we both held our breath, waiting for a reaction.

Mr. Fenton stroked his mustache. "Desiree…"

Kwintone and I shared another surreptitious glance. *Surely he'll remember… but how many women have there been?*

The door opened, and two couples entered, closing their umbrellas and wiping their feet on the mat. Eddie and Zach snapped into campaign mode and welcomed them.

Before the door could close, Demi and Desiree made their entrance.

The Car King turned their way, and Desiree dropped her umbrella, oblivious to the droplets splattering across the marble floor when she missed the basket. "Ed?"

Chapter Forty-Nine

Desiree and Mr. Fenton froze, staring awkwardly at each other like teenagers at a high school dance. Someone closed the door to shut out the wind and rain.

The Car King took a step toward my sister. "Desiree? How long has it been?"

Hesitant at first, the two moved to embrace each other while Demi, Kwintone, and I watched like fans of *The Bachelorette* waiting for the lead to start the rose ceremony. The big reveal.

"How are you?" Mr. Fenton pulled back to get a better view of her. "You look great."

"Thanks; you're sweet. And so do you." Desiree blushed.

Mr. Fenton gestured toward me. "I just met your sister and told her she reminded me of you. But I never dreamed…"

Side-by-side, our family resemblance was apparent. I stood an inch taller and weighed about five pounds less; her blond hair was shorter and the color more vibrant now that she had help from a bottle.

I returned a close-lipped smile, hoping Desiree hadn't realized she'd walked into a set-up.

Mr. Fenton's gaze strayed to Demi, the dark beauty who towered over her mother and me. At five feet eleven, she was almost as tall as the Car King. "And this must be your lovely daughter."

Demi flashed a Pepsodent smile and extended her hand. "Demi Myer." As they shook, she kept her bright hazel eyes trained on Mr. Fenton's face, probably comparing his features with hers.

Mr. Fenton turned back to Desiree. "Demi has your nose."

Desiree chuckled. "Yeah. Otherwise, she looks exactly like her father."

Demi and I exchanged glances. *Will he admit it? Does he know, or is he just now putting it together? Can he see the family resemblance?*

Before anyone could comment, about a dozen people filed in. Mercifully, the rain had let up.

Mr. Fenton took Desiree by the elbow. "Can we talk in private?"

Desiree nodded and shot Demi and me a warning glare. *She's onto us, but too late. We got them both here. Together.*

Mr. Fenton guided her away from the entrance. They crossed the room to a deserted area and stopped behind a column.

Demi, Kwintone, and I tiptoed after them and huddled on the other side of the huge column.

"I saw you at the airport about a year ago and figured out you were a flight attendant, but had no idea you were based in Atlanta. And to see you in Pecan Point blows me away."

"I have a condo in Vinings, but my sister lives here now. Our mother's in the Pecan Point Memory Care home."

The Car King uttered a sympathetic groan.

"I'm just as surprised to see you. I mean, I pass your billboards all the time, so I knew you were in the Atlanta area. But Pecan Point..."

"My in-laws live here, and now my son does too. He works at Oakwood Studios."

There was a pause, and I strained to get a view of the reunited couple.

"How's Fen?" Desiree asked. "Does he keep in touch, or has he disappeared again?"

Fen? Mouths springing open, Kwintone and I exchanged alarmed glances. *The man in his mother's letters? Wasn't Edward Fenton "Fen"?*

Demi's Taylor Swift ringtone blasted, and, muttering an expletive, she fumbled to silence her phone.

The Car King's voice was audible again. "Robert was doing better for a while. Did his time. Went through rehab. But now..." His voice trailed off, and I couldn't tell if he'd paused or if I'd missed part of his sentence. "You know how my brother is. Shows up every two or three years, swears he's clean, asks for money to fund the next fool scheme, then disappears again."

"I made the right decision," agreed Desiree. "Even at sixteen, I knew Robert Fenton would never settle down."

"I'm sorry for what that loser put you through. It seems like every family has its black sheep."

"It wasn't your fault. You were sweet to offer to help me, but my parents were great…"

The band started a song, and the reverberation from a guitar drowned out the rest of Desiree's sentence.

The Car King sighed. I couldn't see his face, but I sensed an eye roll. "Seems like I'm always cleaning up my brother's messes. It never ends."

"Robert Fenton?" I whispered to Kwintone. "Did Eddie ever mention an uncle?"

"Shh…" Demi twirled toward me with a finger on her lips. "I can't hear."

"Demi keeps asking about her father, and I've resisted telling her." Desiree was saying. "I never wanted her to get hurt. And hurting people is Fen's specialty."

"I can't argue with that. But now that she's a grown woman, she deserves to know the truth if she wants to hear it. I'm sure she can handle whatever happens."

There was another pause. Without seeing their body language, I could only imagine how my sister was reacting. Did she agree? "You may be right, Ed. A few weeks ago, she signed up on one of those ancestry sites and found a half-brother. They've been in touch."

I frowned at Demi and mouthed, "I thought she didn't know?" Demi shrugged.

"Kwintone?" Mr. Fenton guessed.

"You know him?"

I nudged Kwintone. His lips curved into a slight smile.

"Yeah, he's made friends with my son, and I doubt it was coincidence. I didn't realize the connection right away. Fen really did a number on Kwintone's mama. She thought Fen was her fiancé. She lent him money that he never repaid, and then he went and married someone else. It didn't last, of course."

"Do you think there are others?"

A resigned groan. "It's possible, but Robert hasn't mentioned anyone. Like I said, Demi deserves to know who her father is. Whether she meets him and builds a relationship is up to them, but I'm not sure where…"

Demi grabbed Kwintone's arm, and I missed the end of the sentence.

"… for the best." Desiree was saying. "But I think she'd like to know her uncle, especially now that we're all living in the same city. If you're willing…" Her voice took on a more somber tone. "My brother cut ties with our family years ago, and my mom might not be with us much longer. The clan has shrunk to Demi, DeeLo, and me."

"I'm not going anywhere. And I know my wife would welcome new family members. Her attitude is, the more the merrier."

Desiree raised her voice. "Kids? You can come out now."

Sheepishly, the three of us emerged from behind the column. *Silly for us to think they didn't know we were listening.*

Desiree turned to her daughter. "Didn't I teach you not to eavesdrop?"

Demi hung her head but with a sorry-not-sorry expression on her face.

"How much did you hear?"

"My father is a man named Robert Fenton?" Demi flashed a Cheshire smile.

Desiree gave her daughter's shoulder a playful shove. "Demi, meet your Uncle Ed."

Kwintone locked eyes with the Car King.

Mr. Fenton embraced Demi. "My son, Eddie, will be excited to find out he has cousins." He put a hand on Kwintone's shoulder. "Eddie and Kwintone are already friends, but my son doesn't know they're related."

The crowd in the room had grown to around twenty, not counting the planning committee and my out-of-county guests—not a bad turnout considering the inclement weather. I slipped away from the cozy little group—the fifth wheel they wouldn't miss. The others settled in the seating area around the fireplace to chat.

My mission had been accomplished. Demi and Kwintone got answers about their father, although not the ones they'd expected.

After a while, Eddie strolled over to the group around the fireplace. His father stood and flung an arm across Eddie's shoulders and introduced his son to the others, presumably revealing the family connection. The rapport seemed cordial, and I hoped Eddie would warm up to Kwintone now that he knew him as a cousin rather than a long-lost brother competing for his father's love and accusing his father of adultery.

I opened my phone's camera and snapped photos and videos of Zach chatting with constituents, voters perusing the brochures, and guests having discussions around the buffet table. I uploaded everything to social media and emailed Jill several shots of Zach looking commissioner-like; perhaps she'd publish them in the paper. Something to offset the weekly full-page ads Victoria ran. I'd thought Jill would have shown up to cover our event, but she'd texted that she was busy reporting about a big accident off Loop Road. She promised to mention Zach's event in the next day's issue.

The band played Top 40 hits, and I was pleased they kept the volume low enough not to override conversations. I took a video of them with sound and posted it to Zach's page with a thank-you to the band leader for his support of Zach's campaign and a plug for their next appearance.

Desiree tapped my arm. "Demi and I are heading out for dinner at Leonardo's with Ed and Kwin. Why don't you and Eddie join us when you're done here? Zach's welcome too if he wants to come."

"We'll see." Part of me longed to hear more about Demi's birth father and help her adjust to the news that he wasn't an African prince after all. And not even a stand-up guy. However, the other part thought it best to give the newfound relatives space to get acquainted. And I still held out hope that Lisa Ross might show up and provide answers about her encounter with Green the night he was stabbed.

I cruised by the buffet table where Merilee had spent most of the evening. "Need any help here?"

She consolidated the remaining hors d'oeuvres from multiple trays onto one. "I don't think we need to put out any more food. We don't have much left anyway, and things are winding down."

I glanced at my phone's clock. "It's a quarter to nine. Let's start cleaning up." Most of the guests had congregated by the front door, shaking hands, asking last-minute questions, and leaving with brochures.

Merilee packed up the buffet while I retrieved the mop to wipe the floors again.

As another couple said their goodbyes, the front door opened to admit Detective Olivia Chen, a determined frown on her face. Her piercing dark eyes scanned the room, and then she marched toward Eddie, who was gathering up leftover brochures.

"Edward Fenton, Jr.," She brandished a pair of handcuffs. "You're under arrest for the attempted murder of Aiden Green. You have the right to remain silent…"

Chapter Fifty

Eddie dropped the brochures and put up his hands while Detective Chen read him the Miranda rights. "Whoa... What are you talking about? I didn't do anything to that man. How many times do I have to tell you? My phone—"

"Tell it to the judge," replied the detective, opening the handcuffs.

The last guests slipped out the front door, although one woman peered over her shoulder, wide-eyed, as her companion handed her an umbrella. The woman held up a cellphone, poised to snap a photo, but quickly put it away after Detective Chen shot her a scathing glare.

Zach took a step toward the detective and Eddie. "You can't do this, Detective. There must be some mistake. We've cooperated fully with the investigation, and there's no evidence that Eddie Fenton has done anything wrong."

Ignoring Zach's protests, Detective Chen fastened the handcuffs around Eddie's wrists. Stiff but compliant, Eddie eyed the detective's pistol that remained holstered.

"Is that necessary? We'll voluntarily go with you to answer any questions." Zach stared open-mouthed at the injustice being inflicted upon his partner. "I'd like to see that arrest warrant."

"Detective Chen," I began, but she shot me the same glare she'd given the gawking bystander.

Remaining stoic, Eddie allowed the detective to lead him to the door, but called over his shoulder, "Get hold of my dad! I think he left already."

I set the mop beside the door and took my phone from my pocket. "They went to dinner at Leonardo's about an hour ago. I'll text Demi, and she'll give him the message."

Zach was already on his cell. "I'm calling the lawyer. We'll get you out. They can't do this!"

The front door closed, and Eddie was gone. Zach looked up from his phone and stared after them.

I finished my text, picked up the brochures Eddie had dropped, and packed them into a box while Zach made another call.

The door opened again, revealing that the driving rain had resumed in full force.

Lisa Ross entered, wet curls plastered against her pale face, closing a dripping umbrella almost as big as her. "Am I late?" Her eyes flitted around the empty room.

I'd about given up on her showing tonight. But at least Zach hadn't left yet.

"Lisa, hi. I'm sorry, but the event's over. It was only scheduled to go until nine o'clock. The attorney didn't make it anyway, but Zach is still here." I gestured toward Zach, who was talking animatedly on the phone.

"He's the lawyer who'll sue those murderers?"

Grief must have muddled her brain so much that she couldn't retain anything I told her. "Not Zach, but he knows someone who can help you."

"Okay." Lisa pushed her wet bangs off her forehead. "How was your event? I would have been here earlier, but I got a late start and took a wrong turn somewhere, and there was a big accident blocking the road..."

Zach ended his call and looked up. His face contorted, and he pointed at Lisa with his phone. "You!"

Lisa took a step backward and touched her palm to her chest. "Me?" Her cowering body language reminded me of an antelope cornered by a lion.

"I saw you with Aiden Green the night he was attacked. Eddie Fenton didn't touch that man, but the police arrested him anyway." Zach's cold stare jarred me; I'd only seen his agreeable, easygoing side.

"Aiden wasn't attacked!" Trembling, Lisa bit her lip and darted her eyes toward me, perhaps realizing she'd said too much.

"He wasn't attacked? Did you see what happened?" I kept my voice calm to contrast with Zach's hysteria. "The man was lying on the ground with a stab wound."

She shook her head rapidly, spreading droplets of water onto my recently mopped floor. "It was his fault."

"What do you mean, Lisa?" I hoped my gentle tone would lower the fear factor. "How was getting stabbed his fault?"

She shut her eyes. "He came after me! I had no choice."

Zach and I exchanged glances. Was Lisa admitting to being Green's attacker?

"What did you stab him with?" I gambled.

Lisa stared at me, and for a moment, I thought she was going to deny stabbing Green and tell me I was crazy to suggest such a scenario. "I carry a comb with a hidden blade in my bag. For self-defense."

Again, I caught Zach's eye; he stared back open-mouthed.

"Why did you have to defend yourself?" I kept my voice soft and even, like I was talking to one of the feral cats I'd trapped. "You said he came after you?"

"Yes, he came after me." Lisa covered her face with her hands. "It was awful."

"Why would he come after you?" When she just shook her head, I continued, "Did you and Green drive to Oakwood Studios together?"

She nodded, hands still covering her face. "He didn't want me there."

I shot another glance at Zach, then turned back to Lisa. "Why did Green let you get in the car with him if he didn't want you there? And why did you want to go?"

Lisa had started crying, and whatever she said next came out as an incomprehensible babble.

Zach grabbed her arm. "If you're the one who stabbed Aiden Green, then you need to come with me to the police station right now and confess. They arrested the wrong person."

Chapter Fifty-One

"I didn't do anything." Lisa shrugged away from Zach and hunched her shoulders like a tortoise retreating into its shell.

"You just admitted you stabbed Aiden Green in self-defense," Zach insisted, his eyes as fiery as his red hair. "Isn't that what I heard?"

"It was an accident! I didn't mean to hurt him—just stop him." She flailed her arms. "He came after me. It was self-defense. I didn't do anything wrong."

"But neither did Eddie Fenton," I stated, keeping my anger in check and speaking to her as I would to a child—or my mother these days. After the loss of her son, Lisa had seemed increasingly unstable, almost childlike. "Not even accidentally. But the police arrested him for something you did."

Lisa stared at me, her blue eyes glassy, her pale face flushed, then bolted for the door.

"Is that fair?" I caught up with her and touched her arm. "Lisa, you can stop an injustice."

Zach opened the entryway closet and retrieved his raincoat. "Let's go, Lisa," he commanded as he stuffed his long arms into the sleeves.

She remained planted, trembling. Zach was normally a big teddy bear, but Lisa didn't know him, and his anger, coupled with his much greater size, must have frightened her.

"I'll go with you." I gave Lisa's shoulder a reassuring pat. "Your husband's a cop, and you must know all the officers. They'll treat you fairly. You acted in self-defense; just tell them what happened." If I went along, maybe we could get her to talk, and I could record her confession in case she tried to retract it later.

She jerked away from me. "Yeah, right. Do you think I'm stupid, DeeLo?"

"No, but you've already admitted to us what you did. The longer you wait to tell your story to the police, the worse it will be for you. You're smart enough to understand that."

Together, Zach and I coaxed Lisa out the front door and onto the porch. Water gushed from a nearby downspout like a raging river and formed puddles in depressions on the lawn.

Zach shielded his eyes from the torrent. I followed his gaze to his car—blocked in by Kwintone's Mustang. Demi's MINI Cooper blocked my SUV.

I threw up my hands. Lisa had the only unencumbered vehicle.

Zach gripped her arm. "We're taking your car. Give me the keys."

"No way." Lisa snorted. "You're not driving my new car."

"Fine," Zach muttered. "Then you drive."

I shivered. Was this wise, given her state of mind? *But she made it over here in one piece.*

Despite my attempt to shield us with my oversized umbrella, we were all drenched by the time we settled inside Lisa's Honda Civic. My hair clung to my head as if I'd just stepped out of the shower.

I found a towel on the back seat, dried my hair, and wiped the upholstery, then passed the towel to Zach.

Lisa stared straight ahead, Zombie-like, not starting the engine. Her top curls barely rose over the headrest. Rain pounded the windshield.

Zach turned to Lisa. "What are you waiting for? You know how to get to the police station, don't you?"

"Get out of my car."

"Not until we get to the police station." Zach fastened his seatbelt.

Lisa tucked a wet curl behind her ear. I glimpsed her face in the rearview mirror; her eyes brimmed with tears.

"Maybe we should wait for a lull in the storm," I suggested. "The rain has to let up sometime. It's hard to see the road when it's pouring like this."

"While we wait, let's go over what you'll say." Zach undid his seatbelt and twisted to face her. "You went to Oakwood Studios with Aiden Green last

Monday night. In the same car?"

I tapped the record button on my phone.

Lisa nodded.

"He drove?" Zach glanced at the back seat. I tipped my phone toward him, and he continued, a bit louder, "Lisa Ross, you said you rode to Oakwood Studios in Aiden Green's car with him on Monday night two weeks ago?"

"Yes."

"Why did you go with him? You didn't come inside and join our meeting."

"He didn't want me there. And I didn't care about his meeting. I don't even know what it was about."

"Then why did you go?"

Lisa started sobbing. "I wanted to talk to him. He'd been ghosting me. He gave me that 'miracle drug,' Epifelus, that was supposed to help my son get better, but instead, he got worse. But Aiden didn't care about what was happening to Paul. He wouldn't help me. He wouldn't help my son. He wouldn't fix it." She leaned her forehead against the steering wheel.

"I'd been trying for a week to talk to him. He was never around. Never answered my emails or returned my calls. I found out he liked to come in after hours and work in his office when no one else was around. So, Monday night, after I visited my son at Children's Hospital, I stopped by Neuro Labs to confront Aiden."

She sputtered, wiped her nose on her sleeve. "He said he didn't have time to talk to me; he had to get to a meeting. So, I followed him out to the parking lot and jumped in his car. I was sick of him ignoring my complaints, refusing to take responsibility for what he did to my child."

"Did Aiden talk to you on the drive to Oakwood Studios?" I asked, speaking into the microphone.

"I did most of the talking. He didn't have any answers." She sniffled. "He was such an arrogant jerk; didn't care what happened to my son. No remorse at all. Tried to make everything my fault."

"How did he try to make it your fault?" I pressed. Our breath had fogged up the windows, and I could barely see outside through the condensation.

"He said I stole the drug from the lab and didn't use it properly. Claimed he had nothing to do with giving it to my son." Lisa buried her face in her hands and expelled a loud sob.

Zach and I looked at each other. This was painful. I felt sorry for what Lisa had gone through, but we had to keep up the pressure on her to free Eddie.

In a moment, Lisa raised her head, sniffled again, and started the car. "Let's go."

***

We barreled down the road, too fast for the weather conditions, rounding curves at a nail-biting clip. I checked the security of my seatbelt.

Letting her drive was a bad idea. We should pull over so one of us can take the wheel.

Zach focused on getting Lisa to tell more of her story. I kept the recorder going.

"When Green came out of the meeting," Zach began. "What did he say to you?"

Lisa squinted at the road and turned her windshield wipers to the highest speed. "He was pissed. He told me to find my own way home."

"He was going to strand you there alone at night?" I imagined the panic she must have felt. Of course, she could have just called her husband to come pick her up. Or a friend, or a rideshare.

"I told him, fine, but I'd speak to the media the next day, tell all his secrets. What he did to my son. And I'd tell them that Neuroscience Laboratories was a fraud; they took grant money for a testing procedure that didn't involve animals, which they never implemented, never even intended to implement. They were still using cats—and not even treating them humanely." Lisa's voice shook with rage as she spoke.

Well, that was asking for trouble. "What did Green say then?" I prompted.

She took a deep breath and rushed on. "I made like I was going to walk home, and he came after me. Called me a sneaky, lying, b—"

I gasped as the car veered over the center line. Lisa regained control of the steering wheel and eased us back into our lane.

"Slow down!" I croaked. "It's hard to see out here, and the pavement's slick. Not many streetlights, all the glare…" I checked my seatbelt again.

Lisa grunted, and I wasn't sure if it was because of my backseat driver's comment or the memory of her encounter with Aiden Green.

Zach steered the conversation back to that fateful night. "What did you do when Green came after you? That had to be scary."

"Super creepy." Lisa stared at the road, and the car slowed, thankfully. "What a jerk! He was killing my kid, and he didn't even care. I told him I was done covering up the deception."

"That must have made him mad." Zach watched her face.

"Furious. I knew I'd pushed him too far, but I didn't care. He lunged at me; I turned around and ran into the woods."

When the silence grew uncomfortable, I asked, "Did he follow?"

Lisa sniffled. She had started crying again, but quietly this time. "He chased me. It didn't take him long to catch up."

We waited, scarcely breathing.

"He grabbed me; I still have bruises where his thumbs pressed into my arms. Yelled that I was fired, and he'd ruin me and my family if I said anything negative to the press about Neuro Labs. He reminded me of the nondisclosure agreement I signed when I got hired; I'd be in violation. Big trouble. I said I didn't care about an NDA; the world was going to know what he did to my son." She covered her face with one hand, and the car jerked to the side.

Zach leaned over and grabbed the steering wheel, giving it a quick correction to keep the vehicle from veering off course.

With a sniff, Lisa wrestled the wheel away from him and slammed her foot on the accelerator.

"What did Mr. Green say then?" I prompted. I wanted her to get to the part about the stabbing—the confession we needed to free Eddie.

"I was afraid for my life," she sobbed. "He put his big, filthy hands on me again, and I thought—" She used her shoulder to wipe away the fresh tears streaming down her cheeks. "I thought he'd kill me. I had no choice."

"No choice?" Zach clarified, raising his voice for the recording. "No choice but to stab him? With your little comb/knife?"

"I had to stop him! I don't even remember getting it out of my purse." Lisa took both hands off the wheel and covered her face. "I wasn't trying to kill him, but I just—"

"Watch out!" shouted Zach.

High beams bounced off the wet pavement, illuminating the interior of Lisa's car. A horn honked. Our vehicle jerked toward the center line and then whipped back, too fast, spinning out of control.

"Lisa! Oh, my God," someone screamed, and I realized it was me.

The crunch of metal pierced the pounding rain and muffled the squeal of brakes. I heard a crash of thunder and felt the car leave the road, tumbling down the embankment. My seatbelt tightened as the world swirled around me: bodies, kids' toys, shattering glass, tree limbs, rain. And then the scene faded to black.

Chapter Fifty-Two

A bath of bright light seeped through my eyelids as I strained to open them. All I could see was white.

"She's waking up!" Demi's voice emanated from somewhere above.

"DeeLo, can you hear us?" Desiree was there, too.

More anxious voices blended with the sound of shoes shuffling across a tile floor.

A light shone in my eyes, and I tried to flick it away. A machine beeped, reminding me of Aiden Green's hospital room.

My throat felt dry. My voice sounded like it came from an old, scratched vinyl record as I croaked, "Where…where am I?"

"You're in the Pecan Point Hospital," Desiree said. "Do you remember coming here?"

What do I remember? I creased my brow, and my head hurt to think. "Where's Manny?" I squinted, and my sister and niece came into focus.

"Back at your house," replied Demi. "He's fine. I fed him this morning. I'm sure he misses you, though."

I turned my head slowly to take in my surroundings. My face hurt. My neck ached. *Oh yeah, they said I'm in the hospital.* "Why…why am I here?"

Demi and Desiree exchanged glances. "You were in a car accident," said Desiree.

"Accident? When?"

My sister nodded grimly. "Friday night, after the Meet-and-Greet."

"Meet-and-Greet?" *Oh, yes, for Zach Kirkpatrick. I was in an accident?*

"Remember? Kwintone and I came, and we met our Uncle Ed. You know, the famous Car King." Demi patted my leg under the white sheet and gave her mother a sideways smile. "Who would have known he's my uncle? I've driven by his billboards for years."

"You don't remember the accident?" Desiree eyed me, brows knitted.

Accident. I squeezed my eyes closed and saw blinding headlights. A crash. Tumbling into the abyss...

"What happened? Was I hurt?" Slowly, I wiggled my fingers and toes, one hand and foot at a time; all my limbs appeared to be intact. But tubes were taped to each of my arms; the needlelike ends jabbed into my veins, producing a dull discomfort.

"You're pretty banged up, and they think you have a concussion." Desiree pushed a strand of hair off my face. "We were worried when you didn't wake up."

"I wouldn't look in a mirror right now," Demi quipped, earning a rebuking look from her mother.

My head still throbbed. "What day is it? How long—?"

"It's Saturday. You've been here since last night." Desiree poured water from a pitcher into a plastic glass. "Can you drink some water?"

I nodded, and she adjusted my bed to raise me to a sitting position. I accepted the glass and gulped the room-temperature liquid. It soothed the scratchiness in my throat.

"Where were you going?" asked Demi.

Where *was* I going? It seemed urgent. *It was raining. Was I driving? What happened to my car?* I scrunched my face. Why couldn't I remember?

A male voice spoke. Had he been there all along, or did he just arrive? "She should rest. It won't be good to overstimulate her."

Squinting, I focused on a man in scrubs ushering my sister and niece toward the door.

I shook my head and winced at the flash of pain. "No, let them stay. I need to remember." I had a feeling there was something significant buried in my memory, and maybe my family could help me draw it out.

He relented but admonished, "You ladies can stay for a few more minutes, but that's it."

When he retreated, I asked, "What happened to my car? Is it totaled?" My Lexus was less than two years old, and I'd never had a fender bender. Hardly even a nick on the paint.

Demi and Desiree exchanged another perplexed glance.

"I found your spare key this morning, so we moved it from the venue," said Demi. "Your car is safe in your garage now. I'm sorry I blocked you in, but I figured I'd leave first."

"DeeLo." Desiree's voice was soft and maternal, almost patronizing. "You weren't driving. You were riding in a car with Lisa Ross."

"That detective's wife," added Demi. "The one whose son—"

"Lisa?" I had a vague memory of her being there. Why was she at Zach's Meet-and-Greet? And why was I in her car?

"Why were you with her? Where were you going?" Desiree asked.

"Lisa was driving." *Too fast.* I could visualize the inside of her car; I was in the back seat. I was wet. The windows were fogged. "It was raining. Hard."

"Yes, the rain was certainly a factor in the accident," said Desiree. "You remember the weather. That's progress."

"How is Lisa?" I looked around. If we'd had an accident and I was hurt, she might be too.

Desiree put her hand on my arm and cast a worried look at the beeping machines; perhaps the revelation had spiked my pulse or blood pressure or whatever it was they were monitoring.

"Lisa's here in the hospital, too," Demi replied. "But we don't know anything about her condition."

"Where were you going?" Desiree repeated.

The sound of pop music escaped from Demi's handbag. "Excuse me. This might be important." Holding up her phone to shield herself from her mother's glare, Demi retreated to a corner of the room.

I looked back at my sister, wanting to answer her question. *Where was I going? With Lisa Ross? Why can't I remember?* "I... I don't know."

Finished with her call, Demi returned to my bedside. She turned to Desiree. "That was Uncle Ed. He got hold of the judge this morning, and

Eddie's out on bond."

"Thank goodness." Desiree sighed. "What a mess."

I scrunched my face, which exacerbated the pain in my head. *Eddie? Bond? What was going on?*

Demi shook her head. "It's crazy, really. Some new detective wants to make a name for herself and solve the case in a hurry, so she arrested Eddie last night." Slipping her phone back into her bag, Demi continued, "He's accused of assaulting that Aiden Green guy."

Aiden Green. Did I know that name?

"The man we saved?" Demi studied my puzzled face. "You know, the CEO of Neuro Labs, who Eddie and Kwintone were trying to trap into admitting he still used cats in his experiments."

"Why—?" This story sounded very familiar.

"That Detective Chen thinks Eddie attacked Green because Eddie's phone was lying next to Green after he'd been stabbed."

I flashed back to the night Demi and I found a man lying on the ground beside a tree on the Oakwood Studios lot. I'd been trapping cats. Kwintone was missing. We'd found his phone and redialed the last number he called— which led us to the injured man.

"Aiden Green had Eddie's phone," I confirmed.

"But Kwintone can vouch for Eddie's story. He saw Green snatch the phone away after he found out Eddie was recording their conversation. Eddie didn't lay a hand on Green."

Recording. *I was recording something. What?* "Eddie didn't do it," I muttered.

"Of course he didn't," said Demi.

"DeeLo." Again, Desiree did the motherly hair smoothing. "You were the one who texted Demi about Eddie's arrest. Do you remember that? You knew we were with Eddie's father."

I squinted as if the answers were written on the inside of my eyelids. *Detective Chen. Handcuffs. She took Eddie away, and he asked us to get hold of his father. The Car King.* "Eddie didn't do it," I said again.

"He has a good lawyer," said Demi. "Uncle Ed thinks he'll get the charges dropped."

My head throbbed. "Eddie didn't do it." Why was I so sure? "Lisa…"

Desiree eyed me. "What about Lisa? I don't think she's awake yet, but I doubt she knows anything."

I straightened up in bed, and the sudden movement made me dizzy. "Lisa Ross did it! She stabbed Aiden Green in self-defense. You have to tell the police!"

"What?" Demi and Desiree said in unison.

Snippets of last night rushed back to me. Zach had seen Lisa at Oakwood Studios the night they were with Green, after they finished their meeting. He recognized her at her son's funeral as the woman who'd been in the car with Green. Lisa had admitted… "We were going to the police station so Lisa could explain to the detective what really happened, and they'd have to let Eddie go." I was sitting behind Lisa in the car, recording the conversation. "I got her whole confession. Where's my phone?"

Desiree shook her head. "They gave us your purse, but your phone wasn't in it."

My phone had been on my lap and must have gone flying when we crashed. No telling where it was now, or if it had survived. But Zach had been in the front seat asking questions. He was another witness. "Zach heard her, too. Where's Zach?"

Desiree and Demi exchanged one of those looks that said they shared a secret and were debating about whether to tell me.

"DeeLo." Desiree lowered her lashes and put a gentle hand on my shoulder. "I'm so sorry, but Zach didn't make it."

Chapter Fifty-Three

When I awoke from my nightmare, the room was dark, and I imagined myself at home in my own comfy bed. But when I reached for Manny, my hand touched cool, metal bars instead of warm, soft fur. And instead of purring, the steady beep of machines and the glow from their screens confirmed that the nightmare was real.

I was in the hospital. Zach was dead. Eddie, although out on bond, was facing charges for a crime he didn't commit. Which paled compared to the loss of his partner.

The election was in three weeks. Victoria would win. She and Barry would celebrate. My goal of changing the county's animal ordinance died with Zach. Not only had I lost my champion, I'd lost a friend. I'd known Zach for only a few weeks, but it seemed like so much longer—long enough for the loss to poke a hole in my life.

I closed my eyes and willed myself to fall back asleep, into the dark abyss where this alternate universe did not exist.

* * *

When I awakened again, I was still in the hospital. So much for wishing the alternate universe would disappear.

A nurse came in, checked my vitals, and made me swallow some pills.

A few minutes later, a man in scrubs stopped his meal cart outside my room and, humming cheerfully, brought in a tray. "Breakfast time," he sang as he set it on my bedside table.

When I lifted the cover from the plate, the odor of reconstituted scrambled eggs made me gag. I quickly put the cover back to mask the smell and drank some orange juice. The acid in the juice stung the cut on my lip, but the liquid soothed my throat. I set down the empty cup, rolled over, and waited for someone to come take everything away.

I must have fallen back asleep. When my eyes opened again, the tray was gone, and someone had removed one of the tubes that had been taped to my wrist. Did that mean I was closer to getting released?

My room had a television, but the thought of turning it on gave me a headache. Whoever was in the room next to mine had theirs turned up loud enough for us both to hear some sitcom with canned laughter that I had no interest in following. I stared at the remote by my side. Maybe I should turn my set on and drown out the drivel. And there might be some news covering the accident or Aiden Green's murder. Surely Demi and Desiree had told the police about Lisa's confession. Maybe they'd even found my phone and listened to the recording.

I was staring at the wall, thinking about turning on the TV, when a faint whiff of a familiar aftershave drew my eyes to the doorway. Detective Ross moved toward my bedside, deep circles under those green eyes that had once sparkled like emeralds.

What's he doing here? Wasn't he taking a leave from the force?

Had he come to take my statement? Or to defend his wife against my accusations? Maybe even silence me…

"How are you feeling, DeeLo?" Fatigue and sadness had replaced the usual cop-like efficiency in his voice.

I shrugged, sending a pain across my shoulders. Right now, my mental anguish overshadowed my physical pain. My body would heal, but the changes in my life were permanent. Zach was gone, Lisa was in a world of trouble, and Barry was no longer around to lean on. All the good I'd hoped to do for the community had backfired.

But the detective was hurting too; the pain was carved on his face.

"How's Lisa?" *Don't tell me about another death, please. I can't take it.*

He inhaled deeply, then let out a breath. "Physically, she'll recover.

Mentally?" He winced. "She's a wreck. DeeLo, I'm so sorry…"

What's he apologizing for? The accident? Or does he know what else his wife did?

"… I'm sorry she mixed you up in all of this…"

All of what? The death of Aiden Green?

"…She shouldn't have…"

"What did she tell you?" My head hurt too much to listen to rambling platitudes.

He blinked as if coming out of a trance. "Well, she doesn't remember the accident very well. I know she was driving, and I'm sorry—"

"Did she tell you where we were going?"

Another deer-in-the-headlights look.

"She stabbed Aiden Green. Your own wife was the culprit in the case you were investigating." I didn't react to his quiet gasp. "She claims it was self-defense. But she should have come forward. Your colleague arrested a friend of mine for what your wife did. We'd convinced her to go with us to the police station to set the record straight when the accident happened."

The detective's face didn't register much shock or surprise. His former colleagues must have briefed him; perhaps someone had already been to the hospital to question Lisa. And him.

I waited for my revelation to sink in.

"I should have put it together." He stared past me at a point on the wall. "I was working that night, and she was supposed to be at the Children's Hospital with our son."

"She was devastated by what was happening to Paul, Jr.," I offered, trying to put myself in Lisa's head, trying to soften the impact on her husband.

"We both were, but…" Detective Ross wrung his hands. "How could she resort to violence?"

"I don't think she meant for the confrontation to get violent. She just wanted Green to take some responsibility for making false claims about the drug—with such awful consequences. Apparently, he'd been ignoring her complaints and even tried to blame *her* for the complications."

The detective gazed up at the ceiling. "She should have come to me.

Instead, she lied and said she'd been at the hospital with our son all night. She's made things so much worse for herself."

Right. Self-defense is one thing. Murder is something else. "What did she tell you happened at the hospital?"

"The hospital?" His brow furrowed. "The Children's Hospital?"

"No, this hospital." I gestured around me. "Where Green was recovering. Until the night your wife…"

He blinked. "What are you saying, DeeLo?"

"Remember when you questioned me about the night Green died? And I told you I saw Lisa on his floor? Visiting 'her grandmother'?" I made air quotes around the words "her grandmother."

His expression remained deadpan.

"I heard they suspect someone put a toxic substance in Green's IV, and that's what killed him. But they haven't figured out what that toxin is yet. Could it have been Epifelus?"

The detective's face paled, and he shook his head vigorously. "It wasn't her."

I couldn't stop myself from pressing the issue. He needed to know what his wife had done. He had practically accused *me* of poisoning Aiden Green. No wonder he was off the case, maybe even off the force. "It's a good thing you're not working the investigation anymore. Did you ask Lisa where she was *that* night? Why she told me she was visiting a grandmother who had been dead for two years?"

"She wouldn't. She couldn't. No way." Backing away from my bed, he argued, "You're wrong, DeeLo. The evidence points to someone from Neuro Labs."

"*Lisa* worked at Neuro Labs. Ask her what she was doing on Green's floor the night he died," I called as Detective Ross left the room, probably tuning out my next words. "Are you going to protect your wife at all costs?"

Chapter Fifty-Four

I must have sunk into another fitful sleep after the visit from Detective Ross. Lisa haunted my dreams—her bouncy Shirley Temple curls, her squeaky Minnie Mouse voice. Thinking about everything she had done made my head pound. What would become of her now? And how much had her husband known—or willfully ignored? I wondered if they'd ever let him return to the police force once all the facts were out.

"Hey, DeeLo." Jill's voice pierced my brain fog.

I blinked toward the sound, and my friend came into focus, her dark hair cascading around her shoulders. *Is it still Sunday?*

"How're you feeling?" Trying to hide a grimace, she patted my shoulder.

"Demi told me not to look in a mirror." It hurt to touch my cheek.

Jill chuckled, her white teeth flashing. "Good advice. Looks like someone punched you." She quickly sobered. "I'm sorry about Zach."

Tears welled in my eyes.

She handed me a tissue. "He was a good guy."

I sniffled and composed my voice. "He would have made a great commissioner."

"Yeah…" We'd both had high hopes that he'd help us update the animal ordinance.

"Have you tried to interview Lisa Ross? Can she have visitors yet?"

Jill sighed. "She's awake but not very coherent. Neither she nor her husband will say much. After everything that went down, he must be in shock, too."

"What's going to happen to her?" I tried to sit up but wasn't very comfortable. "I guess Demi told you—"

"She did. But your guess is as good as mine. Lisa needs serious help."

"Do you believe her self-defense story?"

Jill shrugged. "No one is around to dispute it."

"But what about the poisoning? That wasn't self-defense." I pushed a button on my bed to move myself to a sitting position. "Or accidental."

"She claims she didn't do it, and her husband agrees. There's no proof."

If not Lisa, then who? "Did they ever find out what exactly killed Aiden Green? Was it really something toxic in his IV?"

Jill glanced toward the doorway as Detective Olivia Chen sauntered into the room, her confident posture making up for her diminutive size.

"Well, look at Delores Myer, amateur detective. Thinks she can solve the case. With her reporter friend." Clicking her tongue, the detective edged Jill away from my bedside.

"Detective Chen." Jill gave a tight-lipped smile, staying back but not making a move to leave the room.

The detective narrowed her dark eyes at me. "Looks like you can talk now."

I forced a smile. Even that hurt. "What would you like to know?"

She glanced at Jill. "You can go now, Ms. Hernandez. This is police business."

Jill headed toward the door but stopped short of exiting.

Detective Chen turned back to me. "Start at the beginning. Where were you going when the car accident occurred?"

"I think my niece told you we were on our way to the police station."

"I'm asking you, Ms. Myer, not your niece. Why were you going to the police station?"

"Eddie Fenton is innocent."

Detective Chen pushed her straight, black bangs across her forehead. "Don't be so sure about that. I know he was at the hospital the night someone poisoned Aiden Green. And so were you."

So now she had moved on to the poisoning? Friday night, she had only arrested Eddie for assaulting Green—*attempted* murder, not the actual murder.

She waved her hand to dismiss my blank stare. "Eddie Fenton has a good lawyer. Powerful father. I wouldn't worry about him if I were you."

What's that supposed to mean? Is she warning me that I'm a suspect? Has she moved away from Eddie?

"I…" Despite Eddie's contempt for Aiden Green and Neuro Labs, I still couldn't believe he was capable of murder. He was Demi's cousin, practically family. "Have you interviewed Lisa Ross?"

The detective pressed her thin lips together. "Don't you worry about my conversation with Lisa Ross."

I shrugged, again reeling from the sharp pain in my shoulder. "I just wondered if she told you the same story she told Zach and me."

"Let's see." Detective Chen reached into her pocket and pulled out a device encased in a plastic evidence bag. She slapped it on my tray table. "Does this look familiar?"

I recognized my phone. The screen had a hairline crack, but otherwise, it was intact. Someone must have charged it up.

"You need to open it." She took the device out of the bag and handed it to me. "Your niece said you wanted me to hear something."

* * *

My facial recognition software didn't recognize my battered face. With a flinch, I typed in my password and turned on the recording. There were parts where Lisa's voice faded out, and the rain provided more background interference than I'd realized, but the important statements in her confession were unmistakable.

Jill raised her eyebrows at me. She had inched back to my bedside while the recording played.

Detective Chen whirled on her. "This is off the record, Ms. Hernandez. I told you to leave."

Mercifully, the detective stopped the recording at the crash.

"See?" I threw her a defiant look. "Zach wanted you to hear Lisa's confession so you'd let Eddie go."

The detective shook her head. "This recording might not be admissible in court."

"Maybe it's not enough to convict Lisa, but it casts enough reasonable doubt to free Eddie."

"Eddie Fenton's free. For now." She cut her eyes at me. "You saw Eddie at the hospital the night you 'went to check on Mr. Green's welfare'?" Her tone oozed distrust. Maybe she did still suspect me.

"Eddie and Zach were talking to a campaign donor in the lobby when I came downstairs. I never saw either of them on Green's floor. However, I did see Lisa Ross—"

"I know about Lisa Ross. And you. I have a list of all Green's visitors."

"Did Lisa tell you why she was at the hospital, on that floor? She told me she was visiting her grandmother." I tried to sit up higher. Pain shot through the muscles in my back. "But her husband told me both Lisa's grandmothers have been dead for years."

Detective Chen shook her head. "Delores Myer, Detective Extraordinaire." Making that tsking sound again, she headed out of my room. "Good thing you can't go anywhere right now because you're not in the clear."

I glanced at Jill after the detective left the room. "I don't think she likes me."

Jill laughed. "Ya think?"

"What did I ever do to her? I'm trying to be helpful."

"Maybe that's the problem. She doesn't want your help."

I watched Detective Chen stop and speak with someone outside my room, then continue down the hall. I turned to Jill. "Did Lisa tell you about being on Green's floor the night he died?"

Nodding, Jill scrolled through the notes on her tablet. "I didn't get the 'grandmother' story, though. She told me she was talking with a friend."

"What friend? Aiden Green?"

Jill re-read what she'd written. "Lisa never gave me the friend's name. Got the impression it was a woman, though."

I clicked my tongue in imitation of Detective Chen. "Thought you were a better reporter than that."

Jill waved her tablet at me in a mock swat. "Trying not to alienate my sources. I'd like to see you get that information out of her."

I gazed around at my bindings. Only one tube remained attached, and I could probably figure out how to remove it. "Did Demi and Desiree leave me any clothes?"

Jill peered into a bag on the couch. "Looks like it."

"Great. Help me get out of here."

Chapter Fifty-Five

After lying in bed for almost two days, I felt slightly disoriented as I wobbled toward the door. Jill gripped my arm to steady me. I paused at the entrance to my hospital room and scanned the Lysol-scented hallway. The coast was clear.

"Which way to Lisa's room?"

Jill nudged me to the left. "I still think this is a bad idea."

"Maybe you should wait outside so she won't think she's on the record."

Lisa was alone when we arrived at her room. I was relieved not to have to deal with Detective Ross.

As agreed, Jill hung back in the hallway. Before I could set foot in Lisa's room, Jill's phone rang. She waved me inside and turned her attention to the caller.

Lisa appeared to be sleeping while a machine at her side steadily beeped. Her light brown curls were flattened against the pillow, her forehead sported a huge purplish bruise, and her face had enough nicks to have been put through a meat grinder. "Paul…" she murmured when I tiptoed in.

"Hey, Lisa. It's me, DeeLo." I approached her bed.

Her eyes flew open, and she gasped. I remembered Demi's advice about avoiding mirrors. If my face looked anything like Lisa's, I probably gave her a fright.

I smiled, hoping a cheerful expression would make my appearance less repulsive. "How are you feeling?"

She shrugged, and I imagined she was experiencing the same aches that plagued my body. "Not so good." Eyeing me again, she muttered, "I'm sorry.

I guess I lost control."

I assumed she was referring to the car wreck and not to her encounter with Aiden Green. "It was a terrible accident." I wondered if she knew about Zach yet.

"I'm sorry," she repeated, wincing at my face. "How are *you* feeling?"

"I've been better. But I'll recover."

She buried her forehead in her hands. "I feel awful about Zach. He was your friend?"

I nodded, fighting back fresh tears.

"I screwed up bad. I'm in so much trouble. My husband hates me." Lisa uncovered her face. "I should have died instead. Then I'd be with my son."

I shook my head. "That would have been too much for your husband to bear."

She blinked as if processing that concept. "But it still might have been better. Now..."

It was time to get down to business before someone came in and kicked me out. "Eddie Fenton had to spend the night in jail. Fortunately, he's out on bail now, but once you come forward, they'll have to drop the charges altogether."

"Yeah..." Her eyes stared past me at the bare wall.

"So, will you do that? Even though we didn't make it to the police station Friday night, you still have the power to exonerate an innocent man."

"Yeah..."

"Did you tell your husband? Did you tell Detective Chen what we talked about?" I wondered how much of her detached state was real, a result of her trauma from the accident and losing her child, and how much was a convenient ploy to avoid facing the consequences of her actions.

"Uh... yeah."

"That's good. What did she say?"

"Who?"

"The detective who took over the investigation after Paul went on leave."

"Oh."

Gritting my teeth, I strained to keep my tone patient. Lisa was grieving the loss of her son, but that didn't give her the right to blame others for her actions. "What did Detective Chen say when you told her you were the one who stabbed Aiden Green?"

Lisa shook her head, and her voice grew shrill. "It was an accident. Self-defense."

"Did she ask you about what happened to Aiden Green at the hospital?" I held my breath. We hadn't broached this part before the car crash.

"The hospital?" Lisa's eyes scanned the room and returned to my face as if to say, "What are you talking about? We're in the hospital."

"You know. Did she ask why you were on Green's floor the night he died? She asked me about *my* visit to his room."

"But I didn't go into his room like you did."

How did she know I'd gone into Green's room? Did her husband tell her? Detective Chen? "You weren't visiting your grandmother."

Lisa bit her lip, which must have hurt because it was bruised and swollen. Instinctively, I touched my own bruised mouth. "I don't know why I told you that," she said. "I was nervous running into someone I knew when I wasn't supposed to be there. And talking to Angie felt kind of like talking to my grandmother."

"Angie?" *One of the nurses?*

Lisa sighed. "Okay, I did go to Aiden's room. But I didn't go inside. There was a guard at the door."

"He wouldn't let you in?"

Lisa fumbled with the bed's motor, struggling to rise to a sitting position, then gave up and flopped back down. "I wanted to tell Aiden what his poison had done to my son. Show him before-and-after pictures of my son. My poor baby boy lying in a coma. I wanted to tell him how the doctors at Children's Hospital didn't think Paul would ever wake up. I wanted to say all that while Aiden was trapped in that bed, unable to get away, force him to listen to me like he never would before."

"And did you?"

She shook her head. "I ended up talking to Angie in the hallway. She was there to air her grievances, too, so I had to get in line. The guard made us wait while the nurses were doing something to Aiden."

"Who's Angie? Someone who works at Neuro Labs?"

Lisa stared past me. "He screwed her over, too. The story of his life. What a jerk. I should never have trusted him."

A jaded lover?

"The guy's a CEO. He owns two vacation homes and a boat. And he wouldn't give her a dime in the divorce."

Angie? Evangeline! I flashed back to Paul's memorial service when Lisa and Evangeline had embraced; I'd wondered then how they became acquainted, but figured Neuro Labs was the connection.

"I guess you told Angie about your son's circumstances?"

Lisa nodded. "I'd brought a syringe of that vile poison. Angie said she had connections at a reputable lab, and she'd take it there to be analyzed for me. She suspected Epifelus had something illegal in it that would nail Aiden once he woke up."

I did a double-take. "Wait. You brought a syringe of that medication with you to the hospital? Epifelus? The drug you'd been giving to your son?"

Lisa eyed me like I was a slow learner. "Well, yes. Like I said, I wanted to remind Aiden what he promised me."

"And you gave the drug to Evangeline instead? Angie?"

"Yes. She had a better idea about how to get even with him. Her last act of revenge before she moves to Florida next week."

"*Evangeline* was going to have the drug tested? Where? Didn't they test it at the Children's Hospital after your son was admitted?"

"Well, yeah, but—"

"Ms. Myer, there you are. What are you doing out of bed?" The stern voice of one of the nurses who had been taking care of me interrupted us.

"DeeLo!" Detective Ross chimed in. "What are you doing here?"

I turned to Paul. "Detective, your wife—"

The nurse grasped my arm and steered me toward the door. "Come on, Ms. Myer. Let's get you back to your room."

Chapter Fifty-Six

After enduring a scolding about the dangers of getting overstimulated following a concussion, I settled back into my prison-like bed. Once the medical team left me alone, I reached for the landline on my nightstand and called Demi.

"How are you feeling?" she asked cheerfully. "Kwintone and I were thinking about coming to see you later today if you're up for a visit."

"How soon can you get here?" I ran my fingers along the bars of my bed. "I need a ride to Pecan Point Memory Care."

"What are you talking about? Are they releasing you already?"

I recounted my visit to Lisa's room and recapped our conversation about Aiden Green. And Evangeline. And my theory that she'd placed the Neuro Labs drug, Epifelus, in his IV, perhaps leading to his death. "Will you help me? Time is of the essence, because the perp is leaving town next week."

Demi snorted. "You're out of your mind. It must be the concussion."

I figured she'd say something like that.

"Why don't you just tell the cops what Lisa said? Isn't that Detective Chen still working on the case? She seems very focused and would probably appreciate the information. After all, she believed Mom and me when we told her about your phone."

Who was this woman speaking in my niece's voice? Was Demi now BFFs with the detective? "Chen doesn't like me much. And I don't have any proof."

"And you think you'll get proof by confronting this Evangeline person?"

I sighed.

Demi tsked with her tongue, reminding me of Detective Chen. "You're asking for trouble."

"What's Evangeline going to do to me at the memory care home? With patients and staff all around?"

"She might bolt. Or get you thrown out. Again."

I winced.   The first time I'd taken Manny there, he went berserk after seeing his former owner's murderer. It had required some delicate negotiation with management to allow me to bring him back as a therapy cat.

Demi paused. Maybe she, too, was remembering the incident. Then she murmured, "Do you really think Evangeline put that drug in Green's IV?"

"Well, it wasn't me. And Lisa claims she didn't go into his room."

"If you can believe her."

"There's that. She hasn't been completely truthful. She might even have suggested the deed…"

"Hmm…but the spouse, or the ex, is always a suspect. How come they haven't questioned that Evangeline woman?"

"They probably have."

"Then…"

"But maybe they didn't ask the right questions."

"And *you'll* ask the right ones that will get her to confess?" Demi's tone had a hint of sarcasm.

The meal cart rolled down the hallway and stopped in front of my room. A worker brought in a tray and set it on my table.

"Thank you," I mouthed to him, then turned my attention back to my phone call. "Evangeline and I have a decent rapport. I can get her to talk to me."

Demi let out a puff of air. "I guess you'll never learn. But Kwintone is coming with us."

I wasn't sure how Kwintone could assist us, but if his presence was the price of having Demi help me escape the hospital, so be it.

"And I think you should give Detective Chen a heads-up," she reiterated.

"Yeah, right. Chen will just tell me to stay out of it."

"That's my advice too. As your older, smarter—"

"Save it."

But I knew my niece would come through.

* * *

Kwintone managed to commandeer an unattended wheelchair and pushed it into my room. With a flinch, he averted his eyes from my face and helped Demi load me into the chair as if my departure were official. Staff passing us in the corridors didn't give us a second glance, and we made it out the front door without anyone stopping us.

They had arrived in my SUV, which annoyed me a little—no one else ever drove my car—even though I knew both Kwintone's and Demi's cars had almost non-existent backseats. Kwintone drove. He'd pushed the seat all the way back, moved the mirrors, and changed my radio stations as if he were in his own vehicle. I held my tongue. They were doing my bidding after all.

Demi helped me into my backseat, where I had never ridden. It was roomy and reasonably comfortable. As I settled in, a plaintive cry alerted me to the pet carrier on the seat next to me. I reached through the bars to stroke my cat's soft fur. "What's Manny doing here?" I asked Demi. She must have known how much I missed him.

"Duh. Don't you usually bring Manny when you visit Mom?"

"He's our cover," added Kwintone.

"So they won't think you just came to snoop," said Demi, handing me a tube of concealer. "Put this on your face so you don't scare Grandma."

As I attempted to camouflage my bruises, I wasn't sure how to feel about Manny being with us. On one hand, he had a calming effect, and as they said, he provided a great diversion. But if things got ugly… I didn't want my cat in harm's way. Or my mother.

Maybe this wasn't such a great idea.

* * *

I was relieved to spot Evangeline's ten-year-old Chevy in the parking lot of the Pecan Point Memory Care facility. At least she hadn't gotten spooked and moved up her departure date. She'd said she worked there six days a week, so the odds were in favor of finding her on duty, but Demi had called ahead to make sure. The first time I'd seen Evangeline get into that car, I'd wondered why her personalized license plate read, "Angie.2." Now I understood.

Kwintone picked up Manny's carrier before I could grab it. Demi insisted on helping me out of the car as if I were an invalid. After inspecting my face, she handed me an Atlanta Braves ball cap. "Here, wear this, and pull down the visor."

I shrugged her away. "Do I really look that bad?"

"No." Kwintone bit his cheek, and his voice lacked sincerity.

Manny glanced at me and let out a yowl; I wasn't sure what that was about.

Mom wasn't in her room, so we checked the common areas and found her playing cards with two other elderly women and Mr. Connors, Victoria's father. My eyes made a quick search of the room for Victoria; fortunately, she was nowhere to be found.

"Manny!" my mother squealed when Kwintone set down the cat carrier. Her brow furrowed as she met his hazel eyes.

"Grandma, this is Kwintone, my brother." Demi put a hand on Mom's shoulder. "Remember, I told you about finding him online?"

Of course, Mom didn't remember.

I knelt to let Manny out of his carrier, fastened his harness, and placed him on Mom's lap, giving his soft head a reassuring pat. The other card players had already forgotten about their game and were reaching for the cat.

Mom stroked Manny but kept her eyes fixed on Kwintone. "Are you DeeLo's new boyfriend?"

Demi suppressed a giggle, and my face flushed as I jerked to a standing position. "No! I don't have a boyfriend right now." Uttering those words stung as I digested the reality of my breakup with Barry.

Mom squinted at my face. "What happened to you?" She extended her hand toward my cheek.

"I was in a car accident, but I'm fine now." I put a hand on her shoulder. "Don't worry about me."

"A car accident? Your beautiful new car?"

"My car's fine, Mom. I wasn't driving it."

"Oh… I hope no one was hurt."

Demi and I exchanged glances. I swallowed, willing myself not to think about Zach. "I'll be fine, Mom."

She squinted at me again. "What happened to your face?"

Kwintone knitted his brow and opened his mouth to speak, but Demi stopped him. "What game are you playing, Grandma? Are you winning?"

Mom smiled and stared back at the card table. She fingered the cards in her abandoned hand as the blue-haired woman on her left picked up Manny and moved him to her own lap as if he were part of the game.

I excused myself to search for Evangeline.

She wasn't in the yoga room or the kitchen. I made a quick tour of the hallways to see if she was in a resident's bedroom and ended up in the courtyard.

And there was Evangeline, puffing on a cigarette, ashes hanging over a potted plant.

When I shut the sliding glass door and approached, her eyes widened as if she'd met an attacker in a dark alley.

Chapter Fifty-Seven

Evangeline coughed, waving her cigarette in front of her face. "What happened to you, Honey?" Her lip curled as she studied my face, the smoldering cigarette still hanging from her fingers.

"Oh." I touched my tender cheek, apparently not camouflaged well enough by the makeup. "Car accident."

She stubbed out her cigarette in the soil surrounding the potted plant and moved closer to examine my wounds. "I'm sorry. That looks painful. Was anyone else hurt?"

I nodded, again trying not to think about Zach. I'd start crying and lose focus. "It was bad. I'm the lucky one."

"Poor baby." Her face wrinkled in sympathy, making it hard for me to picture her as a killer and even harder to accuse her.

"I was in the car with Lisa Ross. She was driving. You remember Lisa, don't you?"

Evangeline's brow furrowed. "The woman whose son died. Oh, no! How is she?"

"Still in the hospital. You think this is bad?" I pointed to my face. "You should see her."

Evangeline shut her eyes and shook her head. "Poor lady. This is the last thing she needs."

"Are you good friends with Lisa? I saw you talking to her at the memorial service." I'd found my opening.

Evangeline sighed. "So sad. So unnecessary."

She hadn't answered my question about their friendship. "How long have you known Lisa?"

"Oh… not long. We just met recently."

"But I guess Lisa told you how her son died."

Evangeline nodded. "That drug was supposed to make him better. Aiden had no business giving it to her, testing it on a child. It wasn't ready for the market."

"How did you know? Did he still talk to you about his work?"

She shrugged. "Some. And I know how he operates. How he cuts corners to make a buck."

"I heard you were going to have that drug analyzed. What did you find out?"

Evangeline's face froze. "Where did you hear that?"

"Lisa…"

"Why would she tell you that? How would I have it analyzed?"

"Are you saying it's not true?"

Evangeline reached into her pocket and pulled out her pack of cigarettes.

Watching her study the cancer sticks as if contemplating whether to smoke another one, I ventured, "Lisa's story sounded a bit odd to me. Why would she ask *you* to test that drug? I thought they would have tested it at the Children's Hospital when she brought Paul in."

"Yeah, probably." Evangeline took a fresh cigarette out of the pack.

"So, did she give you the vial of Epifelus?"

The unlit cigarette hung in Evangeline's hand.

I watched her carefully for telling reactions. "Lisa told me she brought a syringe of that medicine to the hospital with her. She planned to dangle it in Aiden's face and describe what it had done to her son, show him pictures of the poor boy in a coma. But then she ran into you."

Evangeline narrowed her eyes at me. "What are you saying?"

I swallowed. "Aiden died shortly afterwards."

"They don't know how he died. And they won't."

"I heard they've been running toxicity tests."

Evangeline lit the cigarette and took a deep drag. "Yeah. They won't find anything."

"What if they test for Epifelus?"

Evangeline took a few more puffs on her cigarette. "They'll never think to do that. It's not on any of the panels they run."

I watched the rings of smoke morph into a gray cloud, then gazed into the overhead camera aimed at us. "What if they find it? What if they test for all the drugs that Neuro Labs makes?"

"Ha! Our hick-town cops aren't smart enough to think of that. And the coroner is a buffoon. He'd never look for it."

"But what if they do? Make a lucky guess?"

"Ha!" She took a deep drag on her cigarette.

I just stared at her. Was she really confident enough to think she'd gotten away with murder?

Exhaling, she noticed me staring. "Are you accusing *me* of killing Aiden?" Her laugh sounded more like a cackle. "Oh, that's rich! And even if I did, he got what he deserved."

"Really?" I glanced at the camera.

She followed my gaze, then gestured at the ceiling. "Those haven't worked for months, Honey."

My eyes strayed to the sliding glass door. Was anyone on the inside paying attention to us?

Evangeline put out her cigarette and picked up a hand rake someone had left in the flowerbed. Gripping it so tightly her fingers turned white, she glared at me. "Are you trying to trick me into confessing to a murder? Who are you working for? The cops?"

I felt dizzy; my legs had turned to rubber. Demi had warned me that this was a bad idea.

"No…" I waved my hands at her like an animal trainer calling off an attack. "I'm just trying to figure out what happened. You see, I went to visit Aiden that night, too. My niece and I were the ones who found him in the Oakwood Studios parking lot after Lisa…." I stopped. Maybe Evangeline didn't know about Lisa's role in putting her ex-husband in the hospital. "After he was stabbed. I just wanted to check on him and find out how he got hurt. But the cops brought me in for questioning; they thought *I* did something to him."

Evangeline loosened her grip on the hand rake but did not put it down. "Well, then, you know how it feels."

"I do." *Good save.*

"But you know, even though the hospital has cameras in the hallways, there were no cameras in Aiden's room. Lots of people went in and out. Neuro Labs colleagues. Hospital staff. Maybe people dressed up as staff." She winked. "Plenty of suspects. So, I think you're safe if you don't admit to anything."

"You think someone dressed up as hospital staff?"

"Oh, I don't know. Aiden had some pretty vindictive ex-squeezes. Never could stick with one woman and treat her right." Her facial features contracted as if she'd tasted something bitter.

"I guess you supplied the cops with names."

She shrugged. "I did what I could to help the investigation."

"And take the spotlight off you."

"Of course. Like you're trying to do now."

I cocked my head. "But what if they find the empty syringe? There could be a trace of Epifelus inside. What if they lift your fingerprints from it?"

"Fingerprints?" Evangeline laughed. "You think I'm stupid?"

"Of course not. You'd make sure your prints were wiped off. Or you might even have worn gloves."

"And I got rid of that thing as soon as I left his room. They'll never find it in all those tons of contaminated medical waste. They have no proof of anything."

The sliding glass door opened, and Detective Olivia Chen strode into the courtyard. "You're right about no cameras in Aiden Green's room, Evangeline. But there are two out here, and they're working just fine. So is the audio. By the way, we did test for Epifelus, and the sample came back positive."

Evangeline brandished the hand rake. "You can't—"

Detective Chen gave a thin-lipped smile and nodded at me. "Thank you, Delores. Evangeline Powers, put down your weapon. Don't make things worse for yourself than they already are. You're under arrest for the murder of Aiden Green." The detective unbuckled the handcuffs from her belt.

"No way." Still holding the rake, Evangeline pushed past us toward the open door. "You've got nothing."

"Stop!" yelled the detective.

Evangeline kept walking, headed into the common area where the seniors played cards and fawned over Manny. Detective Chen and I followed.

Like a wildcat, Evangeline looked over her shoulder at us and dodged several residents in wheelchairs. She slashed at the air with the rake as they cowered away from her.

"Angie!" cried my mother, her brow furrowed. "Where are you going?"

Demi clasped a hand over her mouth as Evangeline ran past. The seniors halted their card games and stared after her.

Evangeline stumbled, almost knocking over a man pushing a walker.

"Hey, watch it," shouted Mr. Connors. "No running in here."

"Stop," ordered Detective Chen. "You're under arrest, Powers. And this building is surrounded."

Evangeline kept moving toward the exit.

Kwintone jogged after the fleeing woman and quickly overtook her. He blocked Evangeline's egress as if he were a goalie guarding the soccer net. Her eyes darted around the room like a feral cat searching for another escape.

Manny leaped down from the blue-haired woman's lap and dashed toward Evangeline, his leash dragging after him. He wove around her legs, slowing her movements. The rake dropped from her hand, barely missing the cat.

Evangeline teetered and reached for the feline as he looped the leash around her legs again. "Manny, no!" she cried, trying to pick him up and move him out of her way. "Ow! He bit me!" She jerked back her hand and lost her balance, tripped over the leash, and tumbled to the floor.

Detective Chen and I rushed over. The detective and Kwintone helped Evangeline up, and Chen fastened the handcuffs around her wrists.

"You can't do this," screeched Evangeline. "I'm hurt! I need a doctor. And I did the world a favor. No one will be sorry that Aiden's gone."

"Evangeline Powers, you have the right to remain silent. Anything you say can be used against you…" Detective Chen grabbed Evangeline's arm and shoved her toward the exit.

I picked up Manny, smoothed his puffed fur, and cuddled him against my face. "My little hero cat," I cooed. "Did that bad lady hurt you?"

Manny purred and butted his head against my cheek.

Demi and Kwintone joined us, and each gave Manny a pat.

"Good thing I called Detective Chen," said Demi. "Since I knew you wouldn't. And Kwintone helped the director fix those cameras before we picked you up."

"Really?" I met his hazel eyes. The man had hidden talents.

He gave me an "aw shucks" grin.

"I think we make a pretty good crime-solving team," said Demi. She took a bow. "You can thank me now."

I sniffed and kissed my cat on the head. "All right, thank you. But it was still Manny who clinched it."

Epilogue

Victoria won the election, and Barry was ecstatic. Soon afterward, they moved back into their mansion together.

Zach received over thirty percent of the vote—not bad for a dead guy. He got mine.

Demi and Kwintone helped Eddie plan a beautiful memorial service for Zach, and the turnout was even bigger than expected. Zach had gained a lot of friends and admirers during his short time in Pecan County.

Detective Chen got promoted, and Detective Ross resigned from the police force, probably to deal with his wife's legal and mental problems. I heard through the grapevine that their marriage was crumbling. Losing a child must be tough enough without all the other drama. They haven't moved out of their house, though, so someone still looks after the cats on their property.

One December day, I helped Merilee and Catherine build shelters for the feral cats living on the Oakwood Studios lot. The trailer where we'd set up their assimilation crate had been thoroughly cleaned and was again used for actors starring in the latest movie being filmed there. Fortunately, the Patel Shopping Center cats had bonded with the resident cats and stayed on the grounds.

Catherine touched my shoulder as I carried an armful of straw to one of the new shelters. "Shh… there's Big Mack."

I stopped. The massive tabby, whom we believed to be Manny's father, had crept to the feeding station. His wild, golden eyes scanned the surroundings, and then he bent his huge head to eat.

"Nice, thick winter coat," I remarked. The cat looked even bigger and furrier than I'd remembered.

Catherine grunted. "What's going to happen with that animal ordinance now? I thought Zach Kirkpatrick was going to help us get those revisions passed."

I closed my eyes and pictured Zach's smiling, freckled face, so eager to please a constituent, the earnestness in his eyes as I explained the problems with Pecan County's animal ordinance. A tear slid down my cheek, and I wiped it away with my sleeve. "He wanted to. I truly believe that."

"Well, what's your plan now?" Catherine put her hands on her hips. "Are you giving up?"

"No." Obviously, I couldn't go to Victoria, but there were four other commissioners I could approach. Roy Don had been supportive in the past, and maybe, especially now that he and Victoria had broken up, he'd be willing to work with me again. Narrow the focus to just the TNVR provisions and not get bogged down with more controversial changes. If not, I'd charm the others with my statistics and projections. After all, how could those bureaucrats say no to saving the county money? I was full of fresh ideas about how to present my case. I turned to Catherine. "I'll never give up."

THE END

Acknowledgments

It's hard to write a novel in a vacuum—at least for me. Fortunately, I have the support of my critique groups to keep me on track: the Peachtree City Writers Circle, the Hometown Novel Writers Association, and my morning Sisters in Crime Zoom write-in buddies: Angela Costa, Linda Sands, and Liz Tully.

Donna Black and Lily Zhang did a terrific job as beta readers. I would also like to thank Shawn Reilly Simmons for the thoughtful developmental edit, which greatly improved the story, and the team at Level Best Books for bringing this series to the world.

And of course, thank you to Michael, my loving husband, for everything.

About the Author

Sharon Marchisello is the author of the DeeLo Myer cat rescue mystery series, which began with *Trap, Neuter, Die*. She is a long-time volunteer and cat foster for the Fayette Humane Society (FHS) with a Master's in Professional Writing from the University of Southern California. She also published three mysteries with Sunbury Press—*Going Home* (2014), *Secrets of the Galapagos* (2019), and *Murder at Leisure Dreams - Galapagos* (2025). Sharon has written short stories, a nonfiction book about personal finance, training manuals, screenplays, a blog, and book reviews. She is an active member of Sisters in Crime, the Atlanta Writers Club, and the Hometown Novel Writers Association. Retired from a 27-year career with Delta Air Lines, she now lives in Peachtree City, Georgia, and serves on the board of directors for the Friends of the Peachtree City Library.

AUTHOR WEBSITE:

sharonmarchisello.com

(https://smarchisello.wordpress.com/)

SOCIAL MEDIA HANDLES:

https://www.facebook.com/SLMarchisello

https://twitter.com/slmarchisello

https://www.goodreads.com/author/show/4297807.Sharon_Marchisello

https://www.linkedin.com/in/sharonmarchisello

https://www.instagram.com/slmarchisello/

https://www.bookbub.com/profile/sharon-marchisello

Also by Sharon Marchisello

Trap, Neuter, Die (Level Best Books, 2024)

Going Home (Sunbury Press, 2014)

Secrets of the Galapagos (Milford House, fiction imprint of Sunbury Press, 2019)

Murder at Leisure Dreams – Galapagos (Milford House, fiction imprint of Sunbury Press, 2025)

Live Well, Grow Wealth (2018-nonfiction)